BRIAR & THE DREAMERS OF MIDNIGHT

SUSAN EE

WWW.SUSANEE.COM

<u>Midnight Tales novels</u>

Cinder & the Prince of Midnight

Ruby & the Huntsman of Midnight

Briar & the Dreamers of Midnight

Hansel & the Witch of Midnight

Don't miss a new story from Susan EE!

Sign up to hear about them at:

www. S u s a n E E .com

*Aim your phone camera at this image to see the Midnight Tales
novels*

All rights reserved. For information, contact the publisher at:

www.feraldream.com

ISBN-13: 978-0-9835970-8-7

ISBN-10: 0-9835970-8-1

CHAPTER 1

I was eating a bowl of strawberries and cream, like I used to. I had no idea what was in my future and was happily licking the spoon.

The sweet taste of the berries reminded me of summer. It tasted even better knowing that the cook had made it just for me. Life was good then, and even at seven years old, I felt it in my heart.

The dining hall was full of banners of every color and sigil. They wafted in the breeze coming in through the open arched windows. The castle was full of knights in shining armor and ladies with pointy hennins perched jauntily on top of their heads. That kind of hat went out of fashion so long ago that I'm not sure anyone remembers it anymore, but it was the height of fashion back then.

The dresses were of every color and texture, and I was having a grand time comparing my new dress with those worn by the grownup ladies. The ones that caught my eye the most were the dresses worn by the fairies. They were quite exotic, and I'd never seen anything like it.

These fairies were special diplomatic guests. Graceful and

fierce at the same time, they flowed through the crowd like sharp ribbons in the wind. Even as a little girl, I knew that these were important guests. I did my best not to drip berry juice on my dress so as not to shame myself in front of them.

My father was negotiating a truce in the Wild Wars, and it was deemed a good gesture of peace and trust to invite the fairies to my birthday celebration. He was a good king, my father. Everyone said so.

The trumpets blared. Father looked up from the turkey leg he'd been chewing to see what new lord or lady was coming to celebrate my birthday. He looked handsome and splendid with his crown circling his curls and a majestic white robe draped over his shoulders.

Those were the days. Sunshine. Laughter. People who'd not only see me but pay lots of attention to me. I was not just little Princess Briar to my doting parents. I was a princess in real life.

Gads, I miss those days.

Then the usual thing happens, as it almost always does in my dreams. The sky begins to grow dark with roiling clouds. Lightning strikes and thunder booms. All the fine ladies, lords and handsome knights look out through the windows with dread in their eyes.

While they're all looking at the sky and grabbing their hats and scarves to keep them from flying in the wind, I stare at the hall entrance.

My stomach clenches into a knot. I've had this dream before. I know what's coming.

The doors open as the trumpets blare.

All the other times, beautiful people had strolled in with sparkling clothing and elaborate hairstyles. Each dress outshone the previous. Until now, I was eager to see if the next guest would be an exotic fairy.

The guests had all been regal and holding a birthday present for me in their arms. Several of the gifts had been so large that they had to be pulled by servants. Even though nothing they brought delighted me more than my bowl of strawberries, it was great fun to see what the next gift would be.

But when the trumpets blare this time, I know that the person who is about to enter will bear a gift that strikes terror up my spine. A gift that makes my stomach cramp and my feet itch to run behind my father.

I drop my spoon, and it plops into my bowl. A bright red berry splashes onto my dress, staining it.

At first, there seems to be no one waiting behind the doors. When it opens, it only frames a gaping darkness.

Then black mist oozes along the walkway, too heavy to flow in the wind.

Then *she* saunters in.

But I can never see her. I just catch wisps of black mist curling around the hems of her dress and the reactions of the nobles around her.

She has many names, and in the dream, I don't know a single one of them. I wouldn't be able to pronounce them even if I did. Fairies like their names complicated.

Ordinary people often give them simpler names that they can pronounce, like Jane or Joe, or Bringer of Death. But the names of each fairy are never consistent because the people who name them usually don't live long enough to tell others about them.

I don't know what name this fairy went by at the time, and of course, no one bothered to ask her. The Wild Wars were still new enough for people to believe that there could be peace with the fairies, so people tried to be polite when they met one at an event like this.

What no one realized until that day was that fairy

intrigue was deadly. Inviting some fairies to a royal event, but not others, could be a fatal insult.

My dream always ends there. The lightning, the thunder, the tendrils of black mist coming through the open doors. Then *she* saunters in.

Some people say that this happened on the day I was born. But this isn't just a dream. This is a memory. A memory I can never quite see to the end.

I keep dreaming about it. My mind keeps going through it over and over, and I keep thinking that this will be the time when I see her face. But I never do.

Sometimes, I get glimpses of the color of her dress or an inkling of her voice. But I never actually see her. I just get that stupid red stain on my dress and the heavy sense of dread.

I know she's coming for me. I know she'll curse me in the next few moments. I might even know what the curse will be. But right then, I'm mesmerized by the anticipation of being able to see this newcomer.

And then I wake.

I wake to the reality of being trapped in a body that sleeps in a tower for countless years.

I wake knowing that even though my mind is still fully alert, I'm unable to twitch even a single finger.

CHAPTER 2

*M*y mother and father did their best to make me comfortable. Soft sheets and plump pillows. Lace drapes around the four-poster bed. A hidden tower of my very own in a secret location.

But none of that makes being helpless feel any better. I'm supposed to just lie here until someone comes to rescue me.

It's been a long time since anyone came to visit me. I know that my parents would visit if they could. But since that horrible butcher murdered them and declared himself the Dark King, there's no one to miss me anymore. I don't know what happened to the other people I grew up with, but I know enough to know that they're no longer alive.

I roll, tearing myself a little from my body, and begin the arduous process of pulling myself out. It's like trying to pull away from sticky tar. It seems to be getting harder and harder to get out of my body these days.

I struggle and push, trying to keep the worry at bay. What if I can't get out?

It took me forever and a day to learn to get out in the first place. It took me half of forever to even wake up. It was a little like becoming awake while your body was still cozy asleep, except that I couldn't curl up or shift or roll onto my side. I simply became aware while my body slept.

I was trapped there for a long, long time. It felt like hundreds of years, but I learned later that it was decades.

For every second of my time trapped in my immovable body, I was desperate to get out. Desperate in a way I had never experienced before. I wanted to cry, scream, plead. But I couldn't do any of that.

It must have been insane desperation that eventually got me to escape. When I finally did, I swear it was almost worse than being trapped in my frozen body.

It was a complete nightmare for a long time. I didn't understand what was happening. There I was, standing over me. Was I a ghost? Was I dying?

No. My chest continued to move up and down steadily. I could hear my soft breathing, so I was still alive. I was still the maiden princess who fell asleep when she pricked her finger.

Aside from not understanding what was happening to me, I had another problem. I kept seeing the room as I assumed it would be in real life.

A lot of people these days don't know that the original purpose of bed canopies was to catch the bugs that drop from thatched roofs. It was designed to keep bugs out of your sleeping space. Disgusting, no?

Well, my bedroom tower has a stone roof. But when I first "woke up," and then eventually managed to get out of my still-sleeping body, there was a rotting pile of bugs on top of the canopy.

It stank. The weight of the decomposing bugs had soaked through the canopy for years. While I watched, the canopy slowly ripped, dripping squirming bugs and a brown mush of decomposing bugs onto my face and chest.

I screamed and tried to pull my limp body out of the bed. I couldn't, of course.

I couldn't even get a grip on my arm. My hand just went right through it. I was insubstantial—a ghost of a sleeping body, even though my mind was fully alert.

All I could do was to watch the canopy slowly rip and dump all that disgusting, squirmy goo onto my chest, my legs and, worst of all, my face.

I screamed and cried a lot in those early days. I probably went crazy for a while. Heck, for all I know, I could be crazy still.

Whenever I let myself think about it too much, I become convinced that I have gone mad. And who could blame me?

But if I spiral like that, I'm letting that fairy bitch who cursed me win. It was bad enough that she started the cascade that brought my parents to be murdered and dethroned. Everyone said they were good people and good rulers. They were certainly good parents.

It's bad enough that I'm still suffering through this wicked curse. If I let myself spiral, I'd be letting that evil fairy win over my mind, over my entire being.

I can't do that. I won't do that.

She stole everything from me. Killed everyone I loved and took away everything I ever cared about. I will never give her the satisfaction of taking away my sanity.

So even in those early days, when things looked as bleak as could be, I survived. I held on to my fury and clawed my way back to sanity.

I discovered and created a new life. I made myself accept and think through whatever it was I was experiencing, no matter how bizarre, no matter how disorienting.

I learned to navigate the Dreaming.

CHAPTER 3

I wear a peasant dress with colorful ribbons in my hair. The roar of the tavern washes over me as I weave my way through the throng. I serve a tankard of ale to a man who is a hunter in his waking life.

The hunter is a brute of a man. He looks like he hasn't bathed in months, and I'm sure that if it wasn't his dream, he'd reek to high heaven. It's interesting that most dreamers see themselves as the way they are in the Waking.

I tilt my head to get a better look at him. He's missing a few teeth. I suppose he could be worse in real life, but I doubt it.

I smile brightly at him. Sure enough, he smiles back. Men are so easy to distract.

All around us, sounds from the outside begin to penetrate through the windows of the tavern. The door begins to shake from the noise. It's the sound of howling, not just from a single animal, but a whole pack of them.

It's enough to wake the dead.

But I'm determined to not let it wake this dreamer. He

looks up at the ceiling with a curiosity and alertness that I don't like.

I brighten my smile and whistle to get his attention. He looks back at me. I wink suggestively at him, and I know that my tavern wench's body is hard to resist.

The men at the table laugh and clap him on the shoulder. They're specters—people conjured by the dreamer to populate their dreams. They're often people the dreamer knows in their waking life, but they're just as likely to be strangers like me.

When I first fumbled my way into the Dreaming, I tried to talk to the specters. If I was a conscious, living being, wouldn't it be possible that they were too?

No matter how much I tried, though, none of them ever responded to me in any meaningful way. If the specters have a life, it isn't in any way that I understand. The dreamers who create them, on the other hand, are easy to interact with.

I turn from my target dreamer and swish my way back toward the bar.

The howling outside grows louder. I look back at the dreamer with an arched brow. The filthy hunter looks over his shoulder again, but looks back at me with longing.

"That's right, big boy," I say. "You know you'd rather stay." I glance up the stairs suggestively.

If my father the king ever knew what I did in my spare time, he'd roll over in his grave.

I mentally kick myself. I hate that saying. Do you know what I'd give to be able to roll over in my bed?

I crook my finger at the dreamer in a come-hither gesture. No one ever said I had to be subtle.

I'm not wearing *my* face, and it's all too easy to behave however you want when you're wearing someone else's. I'm pretty sure I'm in the body of someone the dreamer knows in his waking life, but that's the kind of thing I never know for sure.

The dreamer looks at the front door one last time before getting up to follow me. I give him my best smile and swish my way up the stairs with a giggle.

I'm doing my best to get him to ignore the howling outside. What are they doing out there, singing a chorus to wake up the entire castle?

Halfway up the stairs, I step out of my dream body and stand aside. The serving woman that I just stepped out of and the dreamer continue up the stairs without me. That's the great thing about specters—they don't ask questions and they don't get confused.

The dreamer and his pretty specter disappear into one of the upstairs rooms.

I don't like to brag, but I have a good sense of when a dreamer can take over his dream on his own. I just have to nudge the dream in the direction I need it to go. In this case, that's any direction that will keep him asleep and ignoring the holy racket that's going on in the Waking.

I admit that I hungrily listen, even though it's just noise. It's noise coming from the Waking. I listen carefully to refresh my memory of what a real howl sounds like.

Every chance I get, I like to listen to whatever sounds a dreamer might hear. It's one of the few tenuous connections I have to the Waking. Usually, it's hard to tell if it's a sound from the Dreaming or the real thing. This time, though, I'm working a rescue mission for my friends and howling was expected. So I know it's coming from outside.

I enjoy being on a mission, but this one is pretty tough. I'm supposed to be in several dreams at the same time and keep the dreamers asleep for as long as I can. The way I do that is to keep them completely engaged in their dreams.

Learning how to do that took some practice. But when the alternative is to lie around in a body that can't move, counting sheep in your head, you get pretty good at nudging dreamers.

I let out a long breath before leaving the tavern.

CHAPTER 4

*O*utside the tavern, there's nothing but darkness.

This is my least favorite part. I can hop directly from dream to dream, but that's usually when two dream islands drift close enough to overlap. I still haven't mastered a good way to jump from one person's dream to another.

To reach another dream, I have to walk through the sea of darkness between dream islands. It's creepy every single time.

I look back at the tavern. Warm light glows from the windows. Shadows of people move behind the curtains, and I wish I was among them. It's an island of color, light and sound in the sea of darkness.

The sound of the tavern fades quickly as I walk away from it. Walking in the dark between islands is like walking on black water. One of these days, I might fall through and drown. Until then, this is my kingdom.

It took me a long time—years, maybe—to figure out that the distance between the dream islands is determined by me. If I was unsure, I'd have to walk a long time in the dark before I saw the next island. Eventually, though, I figured out that when I know where I want to go—when I *believe* and am confident about my direction—then the next dream island appears.

I don't remember anymore if life used to be like that in the Waking. But if it was, I wonder if I would have ever figured it out. Life is so full of—well, *life*—that it's hard to see past the distractions.

I think about the hunters that I'm supposed to keep asleep while my friends are on a rescue mission. My friends are stranger than I am. At least, I like to tell them that they are.

They are the kin of wolves. They are either people who turn into monstrous wolves, or wolves who turn into people. I'm not sure which they were originally.

If I was a normal person in the Waking, I'd be afraid of them. Everyone else is. They're sort of…monsters. But I kind of like them. They accept my strangeness, and I accept theirs.

I'm not sure the wolfkin would call me a friend. I'm not sure they'd call anyone a personal friend. You're either a part of their pack or you're not. But they do have friends of the pack, and I'm probably one of them. Maybe.

Either way, as far as I'm concerned, anyone who talks to me like a real living person is a friend of mine. Hell, anyone who talks to me at all is a friend.

There's no one here other than me. Everyone else is asleep.

This mission is very dangerous for the wolfkin. They're rescuing their alpha who was captured by the Dark King's hunters. My job is to keep the hunters asleep so they don't notice that something nefarious is afoot.

But there are too many hunters, and the wolfkin are making far too much noise. How am I supposed to do my job when they're causing such a racket?

In front of me are three dream islands. The dreamer is brighter than the rest of the people on their island. It's not that the specters are dim. It's just that dreamers glow a little. They're just a little more emphasized than the specters.

I'm in luck. Two of the islands have the same girl.

Perfect. What could occupy manly hunters more than a little friendly competition?

I concentrate to bring the islands closer. They're all in different locations in their dreams.

This is the biggest mission I've ever done. I've never tried to influence so many dreamers or tried to merge three dream islands before. So it's a little sloppy when the islands come together, but it'll have to do.

In the end, it's a mash-up of barnyard, tavern, outside, inside, night and day. It's not pretty, but I've seen worse.

I walk into the mess of a giant island, wearing the body of the girl that two of the men are dreaming of. So now there's three of us. Two of the girls are paying attention to their own dreamers, while I go around flirting with the others and bringing them all together.

Flirting is gross.

I don't know what any of them see in each other. They're all ugly, as far as I can tell. Even when they dream themselves into something better than what they are in the Waking, I know that deep inside, there's still a part of them that's basically an ogre.

It takes some work to bring all the hunters together in one part of the island. But once that's done, I don't have to do a lot to spark their competitive streak.

For all I know, the dreamers could be best friends in the Waking. But here, in *my* world, they're free to push and shove and yell at each other all they want without any Waking consequences.

Before long, most of them do all of that with enthusiasm. They don't even seem to hear the howling wafting through the island.

Two dreamers drift off and sit at a table, talking and drinking together while the other hunters begin their brawl in earnest. No one seems to remember the girls they were fighting over. In fact, the girls are nowhere in sight.

So long as they're occupied, my job is done. I count the hunters. These plus the previous ones I took care of earlier don't add up to the dozen I was assigned to distract. But I could swear I got them all.

I step out of the merged island. It's now much smaller, since all the dreamers are concentrated in one location. I walk into the darkness. I do my little trick where I pull in all the islands. I concentrate on *believing*.

Still, no new island appears. I shrug. There isn't much I can do if a hunter is staying up late. Once he falls asleep, he's mine. But until then, he's out of my reach.

The wolfkin will have to deal with the one hunter who is probably on his way to investigate the noise. I won't lose any sleep over it. They're big boys. They can handle it.

As for me, I materialize a comfy chair and a mug of honey cider. That's a new trick I learned recently, and I can't wait to show it off.

I relax in the dark just outside the dream isles, drinking my hot cider and keeping an eye on the dreamers as they go about their nightly lives.

CHAPTER 5

*D*id I say that the darkness in between islands was the worst? Well, being stuck in my tower is really the worst.

I stand like a ghost over my body.

The girl in the bed is no longer covered in the squirmy bugs, as she was the first time I saw her. There are enchantments all over this keep, so I should have known that my body wouldn't be eaten by worms.

Why? Because the evil fairy needs me.

After the spell was cast and the fairy drama over, one of the invited fairies explained what the curse really did.

"This curse is known to us," said one of the invited fairies.

She introduced herself as Leafla, even though everyone knew that wasn't her true name. She wore a gown of autumn leaves, accented with strings of tiny green acorns.

I can't remember that part of the day, but I've heard the story enough times to be able to see it.

"This is a Morpheus spell," said Leafla. "Very powerful. Very dangerous."

"Can you break it?" asked my father.

My nannies told me that he looked intimidatingly royal standing protectively beside me. His anger was so hot that everyone in the hall could sense it boiling.

The guards had been uselessly frozen during the curse. No one, not even the other fairies, could stop her. She simply sauntered in, cast the curse that destroyed my life, then sauntered out.

"It cannot be broken with a spell," said Leafla. "But I can partially change it."

"To what?" asked Father.

"To a curse that can be broken with a kiss from a prince," said Leafla.

"We can invite princes from our neighboring kingdoms," said Mother.

"It won't be that easy," said Leafla. "The fairy who cast the spell will know when her curse is being altered. She'll make sure the sleeping princess is guarded somehow. The prince must get past that guard before he can kiss Princess Briar awake."

"What kind of guard?" asked Father.

"Something dangerous. Lethal to anyone but the most determined prince."

"This is the best you can do for her?" asked Father.

Leafla nodded.

"Then do it. Please," said Mother.

"One more thing you should know," said Leafla. "You must hide Princess Briar. She who cast the spell will try to find Briar before a prince does."

"Why would she care?" asked Mother. My nannies told me that they had never seen such a deep frown marring her face. "She will have already punished us by putting our daughter to sleep."

"Punishment is a convenient excuse," said Leafla. "If it was only punishment she was after, your daughter would fall under the curse right now rather than waiting until her sixteenth birthday."

"Then what is she after?" asked Father.

"Righteous anger is an ingredient of the Morpheus spell," said Leafla. "The caster of the spell must have a wrong committed against her. This is why we fairies are ever so careful to avoid insult. If one must insult another, it's best to kill them soon after."

"Tell us what the spell does," said Mother in a near whisper.

"So long as Princess Briar sleeps, the fairy who cast the spell won't have to. She'll never tire. She'll never need sleep. It works better with a grown person rather than a child. By delaying the curse until Briar's sixteenth birthday, the spell will have full effect."

The castle hall became silent as people thought about what that meant. That was when it truly dawned on everyone that I would not live beyond sixteen.

"Fairies do age, although very slowly," said Leafla. "The fairy who cast the spell will enjoy years of her waking youth while all her enemies sleep."

"That sounds like a powerful advantage," said Father. "Why don't all of you do it?"

Leafla straightened her shoulders and arched her brow. "Each of you in this great hall has the power to enslave or murder the person sitting beside you and take everything from that person. Yet most of you don't. For the same reasons, most of us fairies don't cast the Morpheus spell. Being able to do it and actually choosing to do it are very different things."

"Is this a crime among your people?" asked Father. "Can you bring me justice?"

Leafla frowned, looking like she was trying to figure out how to translate her thoughts. "It is...frowned upon. It takes a fairy of great power to withstand the...disapproval...of the others. Possibly, she is mad. Sometimes that happens. Usually, the Morpheus spell is done in secret with the victim being someone no one would miss. When the sleepers are found, they're often found in basements, caves or other such places that are hidden away."

"Briar will not fall victim to this evil spell," said Father. "I'll make sure of it."

"What will happen to our daughter if the evil fairy finds her before the prince does?" asked Mother, her lips ashen.

"She'll be doomed to sleep forever," said Leafla. "And the fairy who cast the spell will never have to sleep again."

My nannies argued over whether Leafla sounded apologetic when she said this. I've long suspected that none of my nannies were in the hall that night, but of course, the castle was abuzz with stories of what happened for months. If everyone who claimed to be in the hall that night really had been there, there would have been no room for anyone to sit or to see anything.

They all agreed on one thing, though. My father slumped at Leafla's answer, looking old and defeated for the first time.

CHAPTER 6

I pace among the flowers in front of Silver's cottage. She's the village flower peddler. She was a soldier back in my time when I was still awake.

Silver still remembers when the kingdom used to be called the Kingdom of Midnight Roses. When the Dark King murdered my father and took over, they say that people lost heart and began to call it the Kingdom of Midnight.

I wonder sometimes if that's why Silver grows flowers. Maybe it reminds her of those olden times when a good king still ruled.

"Do you ever sit still, Briar?"

I spin to see Silver walking toward me. I smile when I see her trim body and purposeful gait. Her thick hair flows over her shoulder like a silver braid decorating a captain's uniform.

"I can sit still when I'm dead," I say. "Until then, I need to move."

Silver comes over and hugs me. She hugs me for so long that I have no choice but to stand still. After a while, I feel calmer. Just because my body is in a permanent state of stillness doesn't mean that I have to be jittery all the time.

Funny, Silver is one of the toughest people I've ever met. She served my father during the war, then continued to fight even after the Dark King took over.

I never would have guessed she was the hugging type. I sometimes wonder if she does it just for me rather than it being a habit for her. If it wasn't for Silver, I would have forgotten what it felt like to be touched. I almost had by the time I met her.

When she hugs me, I remember what it was like. It's squishier than I remember a hug being in the Waking. Not quite as warm, either.

But hardly anything is just like the Waking here, so it's good enough. It's real enough. I close my eyes and settle into Silver's warmth. This is what it feels like to be hugged by a living, breathing, moving person.

Silver has a granddaughter. It's very strange, considering how Silver looks my age whenever I see her. But that's just how she sees herself and not what she truly looks like in the Waking.

I've always wondered why everyone doesn't look young and beautiful in their dreams. But if there's one thing I've learned in peering into people's true selves through their dreams, it's that people are complicated.

I think Silver thinks of her granddaughter when she hugs me. It must be the case, because her hugs are so genuinely caring. Don't get me wrong. Silver will just as easily smack me upside the head if I give her cause. But I swear that I can feel love when she hugs me.

Or maybe that's simply the feeling of being touched rather than the feeling of love. I'm not sure anymore. It's been a long, long time since I've felt either.

I tear up a little if I think about it too much. If I think

about anything in my life too much, I tear up, so it's best to just stay busy and enjoy life whenever I can.

Silver always hugs me as if she's glad that I'm still alive. As if she knows that I might turn into a ghost and fade away forever without her embrace.

"So what are you going to teach me today?" I ask as we step back from each other.

I feel energized from her touch and ready for a brisk training session. I begin to bounce on my toes, warming up my nonexistent body.

"Training is over for now," she says.

I stop bouncing. "What do you mean? We're just getting started on how to handle multiple assailants."

"You don't need physical fighting lessons, Briar. If anything, it's more likely to hamper you to be tied to real-world tactics."

"But I like my lessons."

I start to get nervous. Without the lessons, I might not see Silver anymore.

Life was pretty dull before her, and I only had a jumbled, vague idea of what was happening in the Waking. Once Silver came into my life, she told me what was really happening out there. So now, I know that both waking and dreaming, we're all trapped in a nightmare.

To get rid of my nervous energy, I race at the wall of her cottage and run up it, doing a triple somersault in the air before I land.

Silver watches me with a raised eyebrow. As usual, she doesn't seem impressed. Despite the warm hug she always gives me, Silver isn't the type to coo over kittens or to coddle anyone. That makes her hugs all the more special.

"Someday, when you rejoin us in the Waking, you'll likely break your neck on the first day trying something like that."

Silver always talks like it's guaranteed that I'll wake in that dusty tower someday. I wish I could be so sure.

"You just said I shouldn't hamper myself with real-world tactics. Which do you want me to do?"

"I want you to come into your own style, in your own environment."

"But I don't know my own style. That's what you're here for—to teach me."

"Is that what I'm good for?" She arches a brow at me.

I shrug. "That and a host of other things, like saving the kingdom from evil and providing the good nobles of the land with flowers."

"My life sounds rather silly when you put it like that."

"I wish mine was that silly."

"Your life can be as magnificent or as miserable as you make it," says Silver. "You, above anyone else, can make that happen."

I nod, trying to believe it. Silver's always telling me stuff like that. But she can see that I don't truly believe it.

"You are more capable and have greater strength and power than any of us realize," she says. "Don't waste it by doubting yourself."

"I've been pushing myself, just as you told me to do. You should see all the things I can do now, Silver. You'd be amazed at what I've learned."

I certainly was. Who knew that I would be able to manipulate dreamers and reshape the Dreaming?

"And you'll learn more. Keep experimenting. Keep trying different things. You need to believe that you can do things no one else can. *You* define reality here. I'm glad you're waking up to that fact."

I swell with her words. I may not be able to wake up my body, but I can wake up to my own reality. There's a delicious freedom to that, even if it's dampened by the fact that it's a reality only in my head.

"Show me what you've learned to do since I last saw you," says Silver.

I smile and begin to demonstrate some new tricks that I learned while distracting the hunters.

CHAPTER 7

*B*efore Silver's granddaughter was taken from her, I hardly ever saw Silver. She came to me one day and asked me to help find her granddaughter, Ruby. That's when we really became friends. She'd seen me floating in and out of her dreams before, but I doubt if she trusted me before that.

There aren't many people who still dream of me. Those dreamers are either old enough to remember the sleeping Princess Briar, or they are noblemen dreaming about rescuing the legendary Sleeping Beauty, as they like to call me. Luckily, I haven't met a dreamer who is both.

Silver was one of the former. I was drifting around in the Dreaming and saw myself. I was a little girl, laughing at a dragonfly that was buzzing around me. To either side of me were my parents, looking young and regal—laughing at *me* as I buzzed around them.

I couldn't help but come back to Silver's dreams after that. That little snippet from Silver kept me lurking in her dreams, night after night.

It turns out that golden snippet was one of her rare happy

dreams. Like everyone else in Midnight, she mostly has nightmares. Dark and anxious, often looking for someone she lost, fighting a battle that never ends.

Then one night, she came looking for me. I hadn't even known she'd noticed me watching at the edge of her dreams. Silver's like that, though. She notices a lot of things.

Silver's granddaughter disappeared during a hunt. Lots of girls did. I try to stay away from those nightmares. There's nothing I can do to help, and it's too difficult to stand by and watch.

But Silver convinced me otherwise. She sent me off searching from dream to dream to find Ruby.

Once we figured out that Ruby was being held in Midnight Castle, we knew we wouldn't be able to get her out. So Silver asked me to help train and advise Ruby through her dreams. It was our way of keeping her alive until we figured out a way to rescue her.

After that, Silver and I met regularly. At first, I showed up as Ruby, but Silver didn't like that. I kind of liked it, though. I liked the way she looked at me. As though I belonged with her. As though I was family.

Anyway, she didn't like me pretending to be Ruby, so I went back to myself. She'd teach me fighting techniques and survival strategies so that I could go into Ruby's dreams and pass on the lessons.

If I was doing it now, I'd probably get them to meet in a joint dream, but that's a new skill that I didn't know how to do until recently. I'm glad I didn't know, because otherwise, I would have missed Silver's full attention. I would just have been a lurker in her granddaughter's lessons.

In Ruby's dreams, I showed up as Silver. But Ruby's version of Silver is much older, so that was a little strange to get used to. Anyway, strange should be my middle name, so I got used to it.

"So, is this a social visit?" I ask.

"Not quite. Can you bring together a meeting?" asks Silver.

I frown. "I thought Ruby is safe now."

"This doesn't involve her. It's a different matter."

I don't like meetings so much. It's a lot of work, but that's not what bothers me. In order to time the meeting correctly, I have to wait in my tower so that I'll know what time it is in the Waking.

Usually, the last thing I want to do is sit and wait in my tower.

Time is funny in the Dreaming, and I don't have much need of it. But time is everything to those in the Waking. The only place I can be sure of knowing the time in the Waking is by the clock tower outside my window. Anywhere else, it's simply dream time.

"How many dreamers?" I ask.

"Me, two wolfkin and two agents from the castle. Can you bring it together?"

I nod. "All right. When?"

"Tomorrow night, the usual time, usual place."

Even in dreams, Silver is careful. She doesn't like to identify the time and location, even when the meeting takes place in a dream. Habits run deep, and she never jeopardizes anything unnecessarily, asleep or awake.

I can tell she wishes I could pull together the meeting tonight, but it isn't easy getting everybody to the same place at the same time. There's no way to tell if everyone is asleep at the same time unless you schedule it, especially now that night is getting longer.

"I'll let the wolfkin know," she says. "Can you contact the agents?"

I nod.

I'll do anything to help the cause. I'm not an official

member of the Order of the Midnight Rose, the way Silver is, but I might as well be. I've helped the fight against the Dark King ever since I met Silver.

The Midnight Rose and the wolfkin stand against the Dark King and the fairies. They want the kingdom free of their tyranny as much as I do, which is saying a lot. Like me, every member of the Order and every wolfkin have someone they loved who's been killed or enslaved. I have the honor of being the only one who's been cursed, though.

"I'll see you tomorrow," says Silver. Then she disappears.

CHAPTER 8

I don't know how much time I have, so I don't dawdle. The wolfkin get grouchy if my people are late to meetings, even though I've explained a million times that it's not my fault. They're not exactly the warm and fuzzy kind of canine.

So I always make an effort to get everyone to the meeting on time as best I can. That means preparing my dreamers ahead of time.

Luckily, this isn't the first time I've met with castle agents. That makes it a whole lot easier to enter their dreams. It also cuts down on the time I need to convince them that this is a real message and not just some throwaway dream.

But first, I step out of the Dreaming and into my tower. As much as I dread being stuck here, I need to check the time.

If I tell the agents about the meeting while they're in the middle of their sleep, they'll likely forget. It's best to catch them right before they wake. They're much more likely to remember that way.

I wish I could tell time in places other than my tower, but

it's the only place I know where time ticks regularly and predictably. It took me a long time before I figured out that my tower is at a juncture of Dreaming and Waking. Like me, my tower is suspended in a twilight place that overlaps the two realms without belonging to either.

Eventually, I learned how to step into the Dreaming without being a dreamer. The Waking held nothing good for me, and so I abandoned it. Same with lying in my body and entering the Dreaming as a dreamer. I abandoned that as well, except for the few times when I get really, really bored.

Being an ordinary dreamer is like riding in a carriage that someone else is driving. Being alert and walking into the Dreaming is like being able to turn that carriage into a sled and flying with it. It's pretty amazing. It's hard to go back to being an ordinary dreamer once you've experienced the Dreaming while you're internally "awake."

Once I get back to the tower, I do what I always do when I'm here—I do my best to avoid looking at my sleeping body. Instead, I peer out through the arched window.

I swear the thorns have grown since the last time I looked. The courtyard has been covered in them for years, but now, it's creeping up my tower to my window.

Leafla warned us that there would be something dangerous that kept the prince away from me. People assumed it would be a dragon or some such beast.

It turned out to be deadly thorns. Hundreds of thousands of them. That's what my parents got for naming me Briar. The evil fairy must have thought it was funny. I suppose I should be glad my name isn't Fang-Claws.

To hide me from the evil fairy, my parents built this tower in a secret location for me and surrounded it with a high wall that protected the courtyard. Despite all his reassurances about how the spell will never get me, my father had the tower built anyway. He finished it before my sixteenth birthday when the curse was supposed to trigger, just in case.

I miss him, even after all this time.

As I look out my tower window, I see movement.

At first, I think it's a couple of red birds. But they couldn't be shifting and jerking the thorn bush beneath them.

A head appears between the two birds. It's only then that I realize that the birds are really bloodied hands.

It's an ogre. A giant one. It must be for it to climb over the courtyard wall like that.

The walls have crumbled a little here and there over the years, but it's still high. The thorns cover it. I'm sure it's as thick on the other side as it is on this side.

When the ogre drags himself up, he is streaked in blood. I can't see the details from this high up, but I can see that his clothes are torn to dirty rags and every part of him is bleeding.

He roars as he climbs to the top of the wall. He tears at the thorn branches that are stuck to him. They cling to his skin and tear at his hands. As the branches tear away from his body, they rip his flesh along the way.

These aren't ordinary thorns. They're meant to pierce, slice and kill with a thousand little wounds.

They covered the walls and half the courtyard by the time I figured out how to escape my body. The first time I looked out my window, I saw the dead body of an ogre who had climbed to the top of the wall.

The thorns were meant to keep out my prince until the evil fairy could find me. But so far, there have been no princes. So far, the only ones who've tried to reach me have been ogres. Big. Ugly. Terrifying.

My nannies used to tell me stories of ogres when I was bad. They'd tell me that I couldn't ever leave their sight, otherwise, an ogre might get me. And everyone knew that ogres ate children and dragged off maidens to some night-mare place.

Ogres are crazy strong, and this one looks especially muscular. The other ogres who tried to reach me all ended up dead, so I shouldn't be nervous. I really shouldn't.

Why they keep coming or how they even know where to find me, I'll never know. Perhaps my parents hid me too well for a prince to find me. Perhaps they accidentally hid me in the middle of ogre territory.

This one makes me more nervous than I care to admit.

I quickly check the time. It's four in the morning.

In my previous life of being a princess, four o'clock would have seemed too early even for castle servants. But I know better now. Nobles and royalty don't want their fires stoked and breakfast served until midmorning, but there's an endless amount of preparation and cleaning that needs to be done before that.

Perfect time for me to catch some dreamers before they wake. I rush out of my tower, trying not to think about the monstrous ogre outside my window.

CHAPTER 9

*V*isiting Midnight Castle is always tricky. The dreamers who live there have the worst nightmares.

Once, I accidentally stumbled into a nightmare of one of the prisoners in the deepest levels of the dungeon. I don't know what they do to the prisoners here, but it must be something fiercely bad. I barely made it out of that nightmare alive.

That was the first time I wondered what happens if I die or get eaten in a nightmare. For most people, it's an academic question. For me, it's something I intend to do my best to never find out.

I walk through the torchlit hallways of the castle. It's bustling with life. There are both dreamers and specters here.

Since most of the dreamers agree on what the castle actually looks like in the Waking, I can be reasonably sure that this many people would ensure that the castle in the Dreaming is pretty close to the real thing. Sure, a dreamer can create a fantastical variation, but that lasts only one night, and the other dreamers will make sure the main portions of the castle remain intact.

"Who goes there?" asks a nobleman in purple finery.

He has a guard's helmet on his head and points the tip of his spear at me. I can't tell if he's a nobleman dreaming of being a guard or a guard dreaming of being a nobleman.

"The queen," I say with utter confidence.

The noble guard's eyes grow wide and he bows deeply. "Your Majesty."

By the time I walk by, he has another intruder to stop. I don't know if I look like a queen to him, but to me, I'm still just me. I'm not sure what he envisions as the queen, but he certainly had an image of someone.

The Kingdom of Midnight doesn't have a queen at the moment. From what I can gather, the last one was executed years ago, and the king hasn't remarried. The closest thing we have is Princess Malyn, the crown prince's bride.

There's been a lot of talk about her lately. Some say she used to be a commoner. Some say she's a princess from a faraway land. Some even say she's a spy from another kingdom.

She doesn't follow the Dark King's habit of insisting that commoners call the royal family by their titles rather than by name. The people have forgotten the name of their prince, but they know the name of his bride.

Mostly what people say is how beautiful she is. There were so many dreams of being the royal bride during the days leading up to the wedding that just the thought of a woman in a wedding dress made me sick.

Speak of the devil. There she is.

Princess Malyn is lording over a dreamer who is trembling on her knees. The dreamer is cringing while the princess stands over her. She's monstrously tall and her face is glowingly beautiful. Cold but beautiful.

I walk by, knowing that it's not a proper representation of her. Then I see her again. Malyn seems relaxed and smiling this time, but she holds a knife in her hand.

She's surrounded by nobles who are dressed for a grand ball. Every time she puts her hand out to be kissed by the fawning nobles, she cuts their face a little. The dreamer stands beside her, her face covered in cuts.

I'm getting the distinct impression that Malyn is not well loved here. On the other hand, I would be surprised if any of the royalty were loved by anybody.

I make my way through the castle to find the Midnight Rose agents. Along the way, a third of the dreams I see are of the princess. Another third involve the Dark King himself.

The rest are the usual stress dreams where someone forgets to put on clothes and walks around official functions in their undergarments. There's a sprinkling of the mundane as well as trysts here and there.

It's all fairly normal in the Dreaming, except that I get the distinct impression that the Dark King's control by fear seems to be challenged by his new daughter-in-law.

Finally, I see the agent. I've seen him before. He is known as Black Rose. Silver showed me what he looked like by dreaming of him. He was just a specter in her dream, but it was enough to show me what he looked like.

He doesn't look the same in his own dream as he did in Silver's, but that's fairly common. The strange thing is that he looks older in his own dream than in Silver's. Life must be difficult in the castle.

"Hello Black Rose," I say.

He looks around, obviously afraid that someone will hear.

I sweep my hands in a clearing gesture. The castle and all the inhabitants push away, and we're left alone in the darkness. My dramatic flair isn't necessary, but what's the point in learning skills if you can't show it off?

As soon as we're alone, Black Rose stands taller and becomes younger. The gray in his hair darkens and the lines on his face clear.

He's an unremarkable man of average height, build and looks. His hair and eyes are brown and his skin color is not too light and not too dark. Black Rose is an easy to forget sort of man.

He blinks a few times, realizing what is happening. Then he looks around again, making sure it's just the two of us.

"The king is going to murder Princess Malyn," he whispers.

I frown. "There's a meeting tomorrow night. Same place, same time."

"I think the princess suspects."

"Who cares? Did you hear me? There's a meeting tomorrow—"

"Tell them the princess suspects, and I fear she will retaliate." He looks genuinely scared.

"Tell them yourself. The king is always trying to kill somebody. Better Malyn than us."

"That woman is powerful," he whispers.

Black Rose must know that no one can hear us in his dreams, yet he looks worried about it.

"You're acting strange, Black Rose. Is everything all right?"

"*Listen*," he hisses. "Princess Malyn is not...normal. The king thinks that the prince has been fooled. That they've all been fooled. The king has had spies in Malyn's chambers ever since the day she arrived. Every morning, when the servants go to her chambers, she's as fresh and beautiful as ever. No one needs to dress her hair, and her face is always perfect. It must be a glamour, yet no fairy has ever been summoned to refresh it."

"All right." I shrug. "She's naturally beautiful, and the king is paranoid. So what? Why do we care?"

He jerks, looks up, then disappears.

"Hey!" I try to grab him, but he's gone before I can reach him.

Someone woke him.

I can often keep a dreamer with me if it's noise or motion that's waking him. But if it's a person shaking a sleeper, keeping him dreaming is impossible.

I'm left there alone in the dark with his last words echoing in my head. *No fairy has ever been summoned...*

Everybody knows that glamours need to be refreshed regularly. But that's only if a person is under a glamour. The Dark King went out of his way to make sure that his son's bride was not under a glamour, so it's not surprising that she's natural.

And of course Malyn's beautiful. The prince would never choose someone who's anything less than stunning.

But despite my determination not to care, there's something about the newest member of the royal family that nags at me.

I shake my head and leave the empty dreamscape.

CHAPTER 10

*T*he second agent is easier to convince, thank goodness. She's known as Dahlia. Like Black Rose, no one knows her real name. Her job at the castle is to serve the ladies-in-waiting who attend to the princess.

Dahlia is wiry and looks like she could use a good meal. Her hair is pulled back with a strip of cloth and, although she's well dressed by servant standards, she has a meek look to her that makes others easily dismiss her.

Little do they know that Silver personally trained her. Dahlia could probably kill half a dozen royal guards before anyone had time to scream.

"There's a meeting tomorrow night," I say. "Same time, same place."

Dahlia nods. Then she goes back to polishing her knife. It's a wicked blade and larger than it should be. All around her are specters of ladies who rush about, assisting Princess Malyn with her dress.

I suppose Dahlia heard me, but I don't like it when I give a quick message in the middle of a busy dream. There's too good of a chance that the dreamer might not remember it when she wakes up.

"Don't forget," I say, waving my hand in front of Dahlia's face.

She looks up at me and says, "Go. Before you attract her attention."

At first, I don't know who Dahlia's talking about. Then the back of my neck prickles.

Princess Malyn stands in front of her vanity with her back to us. The vanity is missing its mirror but she holds a hand mirror. There's something wrong with it.

I have to look closer to see what is wrong, and I see that the reflection is shattered within its silver frame. Malyn is looking at me through her broken mirror.

Her reflection is cut by the shards, but I can see her eyes clearly. She's watching me. *Seeing* me.

I frown, confused. She's a specter, I'm sure of it.

But now, both the mirror and Malyn are glowing a little. It's not as obvious of a glow as a dreamer. It's just a little glow, as if they're only a little here, but the glow is getting brighter.

I've never seen that before. Either it's a dreamer and she glows, or she's a specter and she doesn't. This is more of a specter becoming aware—like she's stepping into the Dreaming.

Whatever it is, it freezes my insides to see it.

Without thinking, I run out of Dahlia's dream. I'm in such a rush that I don't pay attention to what I'm running into.

And boy, is that a mistake.

The pain is excruciating.

Every joint feels like it's tearing; every muscle feels like it's burning. I can't open my mouth wide enough to let out the size of the scream that rips through me.

My vision is weirdly small and warped. I have a magnified view of a nose with a pair of dark witch's eyes that seem a mile away.

I'm in a binding dream.

I've been through this before. It's the worst nightmare there is in Midnight, and that's saying a lot.

If I don't get out of here, I'll be bound to a dead horse. It'd be just my luck to be bound to a badly decaying one too. Usually, smells are not a problem in dreams, but both times when I've been in a binding dream, it has reeked enough to make my eyes water.

Binding dreams are the only ones where I merge with the dreamer. It's doubly disturbing because the dreamer is a fairy. Somewhere in the castle, a captured fairy is dreaming of the time she was bound to a wraith horse.

I get out of there as fast as I can.

It's not like the other dreams, where I can step out cleanly. Binding dreams are sticky and cling to you like glue as you pull yourself out.

Nasty. My face is sour as I step out onto the streets of the village below the castle.

Like the castle, the village is a common creation of all the dreamers. So it's fairly consistent every night. It's always twilight or dark here, as it is in most Midnight dreams.

I'm sure it wasn't always like that. But by the time I became aware and learned to walk the Dreaming, the darkness had taken root in the kingdom. Hardly anyone has good dreams filled with daylight and flowers anymore.

It begins to snow. The air is bitterly cold, but I like the misty frost of my breath. It reminds me that I'm still alive.

I let the fluffy flakes dissolve the remnants of the stickiness of the binding.

No one has greater reason to hate fairies than I do. But I have to admit, the binding of the captured fairies to decaying horses is particularly cruel. I wish I didn't know what it felt like to be bound, but those fairies have a lot of nightmares about it. It's a maze of traps around the castle.

I walk through the empty streets of the village, clearing my mind of the stickiness. Through the windows, I can see all kinds of dreams being played out. But surprisingly few are played out on the streets.

If I'm being honest, I'm not just clearing my mind. I'm wandering around in case the princess and her creepy mirror are following me. I know that sounds crazy paranoid. But when your helpless body is sleeping in a secret hideaway, and an evil fairy is out to hunt you so she can enslave you for eternity—being crazy paranoid is the only way to be.

I walk for a long time before I finally get tired of the cold and empty night. I look around to make sure I'm not being followed. The cobblestoned lanes are dark and empty as they gather snow under the moonlight.

I step out of the village roads and into my tower.

Home sweet home.

I try not to look at the body in the four-poster bed as I settle into a corner to rest.

CHAPTER 11

*I*t's hard to rest with an ogre grunting and swearing outside my window.

He managed to clear a little place for himself on top of the wall. He sits there, looking down at the thorn-covered courtyard as he rips thorn branch after thorn branch off himself.

It must be pretty intimidating to see the courtyard for the first time. For one thing, it's covered in layers of deadly brambles. There's not an inch of space that's open for someone to walk through without getting covered in thorns. For another, there are dead bodies in various stages of decay stuck among the branches.

"Be smart," I call out to him. "Go away while you still can."

He can't hear me. I'm nothing but a ghost to those in the Waking. My tower is in the twilight border between the Dreaming and the Waking. But I don't think it's a straight border. It might be more like waves on a shore. It shifts. There might even be tides.

I swear some of the other ogres saw me sometimes. But only sometimes. Like everything about the Dreaming, there

42

are no hard rules, and it's difficult to predict any given moment in it. Yet, like the tides and waves lapping the shore, there must be a pattern to its shifting.

Not that I would know what that pattern is. It's hard to tell a pattern when there's no one from the Waking who can tell me if they see me.

This ogre doesn't see or hear me right now. He just stares morosely into the courtyard. Whatever ogres have in place of a mind must be grinding away slowly in that thick head.

Just as I'm about to turn away out of boredom, he begins climbing down into the courtyard. Doesn't he have any self-preservation instincts? Or do ogres just think that their strength is infallible?

They probably don't think at all. He does his best to avoid the majority of the thorns, but there's no way to avoid it.

This monster is too big for his own good. The brittle branches cannot hold his weight. They sag, lowering him halfway down the wall. But then one snaps.

He falls off the wall.

He lands with a scream into the thicket of thorns in the courtyard. It greedily swallows him up, and all I can see is the bloodied thorns.

I wince. The thought of this ogre or any other monster reaching my helpless body terrifies me. But I can't help but feel bad for him.

I know from experience that if he survives the fall, he'll be screaming for days. First, it'll be loud and frantic. Then, over time, it'll get weaker and weaker until it turns into hoarse groans and moans.

It's horrible to hear. But my window has no covering to shut. I swear the screams and moans call the other ogres to come and try this deadly obstacle themselves. They must see it as the ultimate challenge for their strength and stubbornness.

The screaming stops.

I'm both relieved and disturbed by the silence. If I didn't see him fall, I wouldn't even know that there was anyone there. It makes me wonder how many dead bodies are truly littering the courtyard.

I assume there must have been a few humans trying to rescue me, but if so, there hasn't been one in a very long time. My parents must have tried to send princes to rescue me. They were the only ones who knew where I was hidden.

When I first saw the courtyard, I could see glimpses of skeletons shining white in the light. One made it as far as the middle of the courtyard. The other was draped over the castle wall. I imagined that they'd been valiant princes and that more would come. But they never did.

The brambles cover both of them now, and I can't see any sign of them anymore. I sigh, wishing I had something to block the window. But even if I did, I couldn't move. I'm just a spirit here.

Maybe if I was an actual ghost, I could meet some other ghosts to keep me company. We could have a ghost gathering or something.

But I'm not a ghost. And I can't see ghosts. So I'll just have to settle for a gathering of one.

Maybe I'll call it the Briar Council. All lonely outsiders could join, and we'd have meetings on the shore of a sunny lagoon. I could place it beside a waterfall.

I've been trying to expand my mind to what I can do ever since Silver started encouraging me. She says I can shape my reality in the Dreaming. She says I shouldn't be stuck in my mindset of the Waking and go beyond what ordinary people can do.

I look across the thorny courtyard to the clock tower. There's still enough light in the twilight that I can see the clock face. It's almost seven o'clock.

Telling whether it's day or night in the Waking is not trivial. It's usually some degree of twilight here, and when it's not, it's dark. That's an aspect of my tower that seems to be fixed in the Dreaming. The clock tower, though, seems to be fixed in the Waking.

I can tell whether it's day or night in the Waking by the number of dreamers in the Dreaming. It's an all-night party, but then it's mostly quiet in the daytime.

I resist glancing at my body sleeping on the four-poster bed. It's been a long time since I learned how to step out into the Dreaming without being a dreamer. Ever since, I haven't seen the squirming bugs crawling all over the bed. Still, a part of me always expects to see that.

The girl lying on the bed has her hands over her chest. She has brown hair, and even though her eyes are closed, I know they're golden brown. Her lips are still full and red and her cheeks are still smooth and full of color.

My body looks oddly healthy. I suppose that's part of being suspended in sleep—never aging, never decaying.

People used to tell me I was pretty. But then again, I was a princess, so what else would they say?

To me, my body just looks sad. Like a statue that never lived. Like a painting that was never finished.

Even though I have all day to wait for the meeting, I step out of the tower and back into the Dreaming.

CHAPTER 12

I'm way early to the meeting. It's not just that I'm eager for the company of people who know I'm not some specter, it's that there aren't many places for me to go during daylight hours.

Everybody is awake and hardly anyone takes naps anymore. Sure, I could visit the old and sick, but honestly, they don't have the best dreams. Their dreams tend to be hijacked by their ailments and are often as disturbed as those of prisoners.

So here I am, pacing around the council table. I can see the lakeshore outside as well as the keyhole-shaped penin-sula upon which our council room stands.

Our first council room was in a manor in the forest. I happened to stumble on it once while I was exploring the Dreaming. It must have been dreamt by an elder, because the woods streamed with beams of sunlight and exuded peace and tranquility, just as I remembered it from when I was little.

But it made the others nervous. They told me that the forest is not what it used to be.

Everyone is afraid of the forest now. Even the wolfkin who live there are careful in the woods. It makes me sad, because I still remember it as being magical. I used to go there alone to walk my cares away.

Silver says I should never go into the forest unless I have to, even in my dreams. So now, we meet in the ruins of a keep by a lakeshore. The walls are only partially standing, so we have a spectacular view. And there's a stone table with solid wooden chairs that are perfectly intact in what was probably a council chamber.

I see movement in the shrubs nearby. I tense until I see Ketter and Lanson walking out of the shadows. They are the kin of wolves. If I ever feel like a freak, all I have to do is think of them and I'll feel perfectly normal.

A simple but beautiful boat floats into sight on the lake. That's Silver. She always comes here by boat, even though I don't think she has a boat in the Waking. This one has a single mast with a beautiful design on it. I know she'd put a Midnight Rose on the sail if she could, but even in dreams, we need to be careful.

I'm not sure why. I suppose it's because it's not a place any of us truly control. I have the most experience with it since I live here, but even I occasionally have mysterious experiences like the one I had with Princess Malyn watching me through her broken mirror.

"You're late," says Ketter. Unlike Lanson, Ketter is a stout man. Like most of his kind, he has more facial hair than is common.

"I was here before you," I say.

"He means we're glad to see you, Briar," says Lanson. "Where are the others?"

"I gave them the message. I can tell them to come, but I can't drag them here."

"Sure you can. I've seen you do it," says Ketter.

"It's not my usual or preferred method." I arch a brow for effect the way I've seen Silver do it.

"If they agreed to come, they'll be here," says Silver as she steps into the chamber.

Silver takes a seat at the head of the table. She usually doesn't hug me when there are others, especially if we're on official business. I'm grateful and miss it at the same time.

Ketter would make fun of me for being the little girl who needs hugs. Lanson wouldn't make fun of me, but I'd feel awkward anyway. Wolfkin are tough, and they expect everyone they deal with to be the same. They probably nip and bite to show their affection. The more blood the better.

"Here's Dahlia." Lanson nods toward the lakeshore.

Dahlia walks briskly toward us. She looks back behind her a couple of times as she nears. I get goosebumps wondering if she's looking for Princess Malyn.

We all look around for Black Rose, but he's nowhere to be seen. The moonlight glows on the shimmering water and the breeze gently moves the tree branches by the lakeshore.

"Oh, I almost forgot," I say as I sit at the large table. "Black Rose rambled when I saw him. I know he heard me tell him about the meeting, but it was like we were having two different conversations."

"Rambled about what?" asks Silver.

I try to remember what Black Rose said. "Something about the king planning to poison the new princess?"

Dahlia walks in and hears the last part. "Princess Malyn? What about her?"

I open my mouth to repeat what I said, but then glance at Silver and the wolfkin to make sure it's all right. Dahlia works for the princess while Black Rose works for the Dark King. There are times when it's best for the agents not to know what the enemy camp is planning.

"Are the king and Princess Malyn enemies?" asks Silver.

Dahlia nods. "They hate each other. I'd be surprised if one of them isn't dead by the next full moon."

Ketter snorts. "It's no secret that the king kills for entertainment. It's just a question of when and who. Sounds like the princess stumbled into his view at the wrong time."

"Why did you word it that way?" asks Silver.

"What way?" asks Dahlia as she sits at the table.

"You said you'd be surprised if one of them isn't dead by the full moon," said Silver. "Isn't it obvious that it's the princess's life that's in jeopardy?"

"No," said Dahlia. "Not so obvious. It's deadly to underestimate that woman."

Silver raises her brows. "She's a match for the Dark King?" There's skepticism in her voice, as there should be. No one is a match for the Dark King.

Dahlia nods. "That. And more."

CHAPTER 13

*D*ahlia's face changes. It becomes scratched and lines of blood flow over her cheeks. Long gashes begin streaking down her face and she can't seem to look at us.

"What's happening?" I ask.

"Is this real?" asks Silver.

A dreamer presents herself the way she sees herself. Silver looks young in her dreams because that's how she sees herself. Damaged people sometimes show it in their appearance in their dreams. Since this is a meeting of dreamers who are lucid, these things can be a little confusing.

Dahlia nods.

"What happened?" I ask.

A bloody spot looks like a teardrop on Dahlia's cheek. "I spilled face powder on the princess."

I wait for more, but that's all she says.

"And?" asks Silver.

"And Princess Malyn didn't like it," Dahlia mumbles with her head lowered, as though it was shameful for her to admit.

"So she raked her nails down your face." Silver talks like she's seen this sort of thing before.

"Her real nails, not just a harsh scolding?" I ask. Sometimes, an emotional scar can show on a dreamer's face, but I don't think that's what this is.

Dahlia nods.

Lanson clenches his jaw and Ketter turns red as though he has lava churning inside him.

"She got so angry that she disfigured you?" I ask, still unable to believe it.

Under normal circumstances, Dahlia could have easily defended herself. But she wouldn't be able to raise her hand against the princess, not if she wanted to keep her cover and her life.

"If she was angry, she would have had me boiled alive. This was a casual scolding."

We all stare at the cruel marks on her face.

"She's no better than the king," says Ketter. He turns and spits.

I glare at him, hoping to shame him into wiping the nasty Ketter slime off my floor. He's a guest in my world and should be more polite. He glares right back, letting me know that I'm lucky he didn't pee to mark his territory.

"She thinks she's better than the king," says Dahlia. "Malyn's just toying with him. When she gets tired of the game, she'll kill him."

"Black Rose said something about the king planning to murder the princess," I say. "He seemed to think it was important."

"Where is he, anyway?" asks Lanson. "Shouldn't he be here by now?"

"You told him about the meeting, right?" Ketter asks me.

"Of course I did."

I look at Dahlia's scarred face and wonder if Black Rose

spilled anything on the Dark King. It's a sad state of affairs when scratching a person's face is a mercy compared to what the Dark King might do if he's in a bad mood.

A part of me is convinced that Black Rose is dead. I can't reach the dead.

Well, maybe I can, but I sure as roses don't want to. Who wants to be surrounded by ghosts? Dreams can be creepy, but when you're as close to death as I am, you can wait to find out what happens after you cross that threshold.

There's a lull in the conversation. I can tell by the looks being exchanged that I'm not the only one who wonders if Black Rose is all right.

"One of the ways Princess Malyn toys with the king is to ensure that 'accidents' happen to his servants," says Dahlia.

"Why?" I ask.

"That way, the Dark King worries if the new replacement is a spy or an assassin," says Dahlia. "I hear it keeps him awake at nights and makes him more irritable during the days."

"Why not just try to kill him?" asks Ketter. "Preferably by feeding him to the dogs while he's still alive."

"Don't be surprised if she does," says Dahlia. "Just as soon as she's done toying with him."

"Anyone else on the throne is better than the Dark King," says Ketter. "Right?" For once, his bluster is gone, and he sounds unsure.

"Anyone else but *her*," says Dahlia. Her eyes are swollen from the claw marks that streak right over her lids. I wonder if she'll have stripes down her face in the Waking for the rest of her life.

"She's that bad?" asks Lanson.

Dahlia nods with knowing eyes.

There's a collective sigh in the room. Silver hasn't said much. She sits at the head of the table, contemplating.

Knowing her, she's probably coming up with all kinds of strategic scenarios on how to manage the situation.

"How's your lord?" Silver asks the wolfkin.

I didn't think it was possible for the men to look grimmer than they were looking, but I was wrong.

"Recovering," says Lanson.

"But not fast enough," says Ketter.

The wolfkin's alpha was captured by the royal huntsman for a time. I helped with that rescue with my distraction of the hunters the night of the rescue. I missed one, but I couldn't help that. There's nothing I can do if someone doesn't go to sleep.

"What's wrong with him?" I ask. "Was he injured?"

"You could say that," says Lanson.

"Come on, I worked hard that night to help rescue him," I say. "The least you can do is tell me if your alpha is injured."

"It's pack business," says Ketter. His lips get all thin, as if he's clamping his mouth from saying more.

"He's recovering," says Lanson. "It'll take time. Until then, the pack is unable to do much other than nip along the edges."

"Can't someone else take over until your alpha gets better?" I ask.

Ketter snarls. I swear he was born a wolf and transformed into a man instead of the other way around. Maybe I should call him mankin rather than wolfkin.

"Someone is trying to take over the pack as we speak," says Lanson.

Ketter growls.

"I see you don't approve," says Silver.

"It's fracturing the pack," says Ketter. "And we're already too small." He opens his mouth to say more, but Lanson cuts him off.

"We won't be solving pack politics here," says Lanson. "It's pack business."

He gives Ketter a pointed look. Ketter settles down and looks at the ground. I can almost see his hackles falling. That's a pretty neat trick Lanson has.

"So this princess who wants to be queen," says Silver, "is she dangerous to the kingdom?"

"Yes," says Dahlia without hesitation.

"Is she dangerous to the wild fairies as well?"

This time, Dahlia hesitates. "Perhaps. Perhaps not."

"Explain," says Silver.

"She is beautiful in an almost unnatural way. Cold but perfect in her looks, her movements—some say she is grace herself."

"But?" asks Silver.

"But no one has seen her with a fairy. No one has witnessed her refreshing her glamour."

"I've heard that," I say.

"There is such a thing as a natural beauty," says Lanson. "Are you sure it's a glamour?"

"She has gentle sparkles in her hair first thing in the morning. It's never messed, even under a stiff breeze. Her lashes are long and dark. It's as though her eyes have kohl around them, but she never needs to refresh it. Her lips are blood-red and often change with the light—darker or brighter, depending on the color of her dress. Yet no one has ever seen her put anything on her lips. I should know. I work in her chambers."

"What are you saying?" asks Silver.

"I believe Princess Malyn may be a fairy," says Dahlia in a hushed voice. She touches her face gingerly and runs her fingers down the angry streaks.

CHAPTER 14

I walk through the halls of Midnight Castle, looking for Black Rose. Even though it's daylight in the Waking, the moonlight streams through the arched windows here in the Dreaming. A few torches are lit, and I can see the empty corridors stretching out ahead of me.

A cool breeze blows through the open archways, and I wonder if the same is happening in the Waking. Is there a dreamer taking a nap in the castle who feels the breeze?

My shoes echo down the hall, and I think about silencing it. But there's no need. It's all right if I'm seen and heard. Dreamers will just think that I'm a specter in their dream, just one of many.

Only, right now, I seem to be the only one here, which is weird. That kind of thing usually happens to the dreamer, not to me. Normally, there are dim specters drifting around in the Dreaming even when there are no dreamers about.

I can't ask the specters about Black Rose anyway, so it's all right that they're not here. Still, it's odd. Do specters avoid certain areas?

It would be surprising to find Black Rose in the Dreaming

during the day. But it was either look for clues as to what might have happened to him or sit in my tower all day. Sometimes, a dreamer leaves artifacts and residues of his dreams—a note, a sketch, a bloody knife.

I get an eerie feeling as I walk through the corridor. Now, that's not unusual. I get that same feeling in nightmares, and in Midnight, there are plenty of those. But usually, the nightmares involve things that threaten the *dreamer*. I am not the dreamer. I am a mere observer.

I look behind me to see if there's anything stalking me. The torchlight causes long shadows to flicker and dance, but nothing out of the ordinary.

At the end of the hallway is a set of double doors. It's the old queen's chambers. Midnight hasn't had a queen in years, but apparently, the princess has claimed it as her own.

I still remember it as my mother's chambers.

I shake off the memories and push my way into the room. If Princess Malyn had anything to do with Black Rose not being able to make the meeting last night, maybe I can find a clue in these chambers.

Inside, the room is larger than others, but it's not as big as one might imagine for a queen's antechamber. At first, I think that it's empty because it's not filled with ladies-in-waiting.

All I see is the fireplace with the crackling fire and the arched windows framed by velvet drapes. Then I see her. I don't know how I missed her when I walked in.

Princess Malyn sits with her back to me at her vanity. There's a frame on top of the vanity that should hold a three-paneled looking glass, but it's empty and simply shows the wall behind it.

Malyn holds up a handheld mirror, the one that's broken. I can see myself in the reflection with fractured lines all over me. I look like myself except that I'm faded compared to my sleeping body.

The would-be queen watches me through the cracked mirror. I don't know what her eye color is in the Waking, but here, her eyes are ice-blue and otherworldly.

"So you're awake," she says.

I look around, unsure of who she's talking to. There's no one else here, so she must be talking to me. I wonder if I should pretend to be a specter and act like one of her ladies-in-waiting. But why do that when I can get away with acting the way I want to act? No one expects people to act normally in a dream.

"What are you doing with that broken mirror?" I ask.

Malyn strokes her mirror possessively. "It was once glorious. I can't seem to mend it, so I suppose it'll always be broken."

"Are you trying to kill the king?" I ask.

"Do you wish me to kill the king?" She watches my reflection, but doesn't bother to turn around to look at me directly.

"Yes." The word comes out of my mouth before I can censor it.

I know that Dahlia thinks this princess is worse than the Dark King. But the king murdered my father and usurped his throne. He's been torturing the people of my kingdom ever since.

She narrows her eyes as she assesses me. I wonder how much of what I'm thinking shows on my face.

"What will you bargain in exchange if I kill the king for you?" she asks.

"You wouldn't be killing him for me. You'd be doing it for yourself."

She smiles at me. Her lips and teeth are jagged and broken by the cracks running along her reflection.

"No matter," she says. "You want him dead. I can make that happen. You will gain by my actions regardless of whether I want to do it for my own reasons." She leans in, and her reflection makes it look like she's leaning in toward me. "What will you give me in exchange?"

I think about it. Everyone wants the Dark King dead—his enemies, his subjects, even his so-called allies. He has no friends, and rumor has it that his only surviving son stays as far away from him as possible.

I would give Malyn my kingdom if she killed the Dark King. Seems like a fair trade, since she would do it anyway and I've already lost my kingdom.

"Nothing," I say. I'm almost surprised at my own answer. "You'll try to kill him anyway. But why? That's what I want to know."

She arches a perfectly shaped eyebrow. Then she begins to laugh. "You really are a child. Why does anyone in the royal line kill the king? Isn't it obvious?"

"But you'll have no more power as the queen as you do as the crown prince's wife."

She smirks. "You have no idea how right you are, do you, child? Only, I would put it another way. As the princess, I have as much power as I will when I'm the queen. The only difference is that people will know who truly rules."

It's odd that she calls me a child, since she looks as young as I do. It's also odd that she continues our conversation with her back to me. I know she's beautiful, but the cracks in the mirror make her look distorted and frightening.

"What do you intend to do as queen?" I ask.

Her smile turns mysterious. "You're just as innocent as when I last saw you. You asked a lot of questions then, as well."

"When was that?" I frown.

I can't remember a dream where I asked a lot of questions

in front of her. This is the only time that I've spoken directly to her.

"I'll show you."

She turns the mirror so that I can only see her piercing eye through one of the smaller shards. The rest of the pieces show me standing by the door—fractured and weirdly malformed.

Then the mirror changes. The broken lines fade and the pieces meld together to show one uniform image. The shard with her eye is still there, but otherwise, it's like a window into another place.

I recognize the place. There are sigils on colorful flags on the walls. Below them is a line of knights in shining armor guarding the doors and windows. And in the center of the great hall, there are rows of tables filled with noble guests.

At the far end of the great hall is the king's table, raised above the others. There sits my father, the king. And beside him is a child version of me.

This is my father's dining hall on the day I was cursed.

CHAPTER 15

The banquet plays out in the cracked mirror just as I remember it. There is one crucial difference, though. My memories end with the evil fairy being introduced into my father's hall. I can't remember anything beyond that.

This time, the scene doesn't stop with the trumpeting of the announcement of the fairy. This time, the herald announces her. He trips over her name, making an unintelligible sound and mumbling at the end, clearly embarrassed by his obvious mispronunciation.

I try to memorize the sound of it because this is the first time I have a name that I can attach to the fairy who cursed me. But trying to memorize the unfamiliar and mispronounced name is useless. Fairies change their names when they talk with humans anyway.

I hold my breath, wondering if the vision will go farther.

She walks into the hall.

Her dress is of the lightest blue, except for the icy white that flashes in the highlights every time she moves. Her hair is coifed in the most intricate and beautiful way. If she were human, it would have taken her servants days to set her hair that way.

Of course, it's the face that catches my attention the most. I'm prepared to burn her face into my memory. One day, I'll meet her and give her what she deserves. Knowing what she looks like is step number one on that path.

It turns out that I don't have to memorize the fairy's face. I know her already.

It's Princess Malyn.

Her icy eyes watch me as I try to manage the shock. I will not give her the pleasure of seeing me reel.

I remind myself that this could all be a dream within a dream. But that doesn't make it any less real.

I'm convinced that Malyn's not human. She must be a wild fairy or perhaps a powerful witch. But that doesn't mean that she's *my* evil fairy.

Malyn looks exactly the same in the vision even though the curse happened decades ago. Ice-cold and beautiful.

The fairy in the mirror begins to speak. She's cursing me.

I heard the story over and over again as a child. I must have asked my nannies about it a thousand times. Every time, it was the same—the evil fairy who was not invited to my birthday banquet came and cursed me.

I was cursed to sleep forever when I accidentally pierced myself. But then a good fairy cast a counter-spell, partially deflecting some of it. There would be a long sleep and a prince who would wake me with a kiss.

I suppose there was always a part of me that wondered if maybe the story the nannies told me was too fanciful. Too romantic.

I mean, really? A handsome prince was going to wake me with a kiss? Maybe that sort of thing was possible in another place. Maybe it was even possible in my father's time, when our kingdom was the Kingdom of Midnight Roses.

But did I really think it could be true here and now? In my life?

"Here's my birthday gift," says the fairy. "I curse Princess Briar from now until forever. She will prick her finger and fall into a deep sleep. She'll sleep until the rest of you have turned to dust. Until the rest of you have all been eaten by worms."

The nobles gasp. Malyn seems to be enjoying herself.

"She'll wake by the kiss of a prince. But only after she's given birth to his twins. That's when she'll know that this prince is the Prince of Ogres."

Malyn laughs. She's obviously pleased by her own joke of a curse.

Then she spins in a whirl of silken fabric and leaves.

I blink.

The fairy left. And although the great hall breaks out in shocked chatter, no one stands up to give the counter-curse.

My mother bursts into tears. She shoves her chair back and holds me in her arms. The little me looks around, stunned.

"Is there no one here who can help my daughter?" asks my father.

The dining hall quiets as everyone looks to the fairies who were invited to the banquet. The beautifully dressed fairies sit quietly, letting everyone know that there's nothing they can do, or are willing to do.

My mother sobs louder and holds me tight. I remember her doing that. I remember being held in her arms as she wept.

The mirror clouds over, then clears again. I stare at my cracked reflection. I look stunned and horrified.

Where was the counter-spell?

My prince is an ogre? And I'll have babies by him while I'm still asleep?

I start to shake all over. With her back still to me, Malyn watches me in amusement through one of the shards.

"That was you," I whisper.

Malyn's eye narrows, and I know she's smiling. "I hadn't anticipated that you'd figure a way out of your prison. Impressive."

I get chills as I realize she might take my one route to freedom away from me. I suddenly get paranoid about what she can and can't do. Fairies must have their limitations, don't they? No living creature is all-powerful.

Yet I can't help my reaction. I spin and run out of her chamber.

I can hear her soft laugh echoing after me.

I almost panic at the thought of her taking away my only freedom. I'd be forever trapped in my sleeping body while being wide awake.

I race away as fast as I can.

CHAPTER 16

I hate fairies.

My feelings for them are so strong that I want to rip out flower petals, counting all the ways I want them to suffer. But there are no flowers in my tower, and even if there were, I couldn't tear anything in the Waking anyway.

A breeze stirs my bed curtains. If this was a dream, it would blow the gauzy curtains like flags, making everything look dramatic. Instead, the stirring of the curtains are hardly noticeable, but it's enough to bring my attention to the sleeping girl lying helpless on the bed.

I sit against the wall, wanting to scream at her to wake up.

Until today, I used to think that I hated the Dark King the most for all the horrible things he did to my family and my kingdom. But now, I'm realizing that maybe I hate fairies more.

Is that possible? Could I really be such a shallow person that I could rank the creature who trapped me in a curse lower than the person who murdered my family?

I used to think that the good fairies tried to do something to help when I was cursed. That's what everyone told me. All this time, I believed that there were only a few fairies who ruined things for everybody. That most fairies were good and wanted peace as much as we did.

But I should have known better. I grew up in the palace. I know what palace politics are like.

Even during my father's time, the castle was a place swirling with agendas. It was a place where yes meant no and no meant maybe. A place where alliances were forged and favors won by saying things that people wanted to hear, even if the listener didn't even know that it was what she wanted.

It was a place where enemies of the kingdom were recast as friends in order to try to sustain a truce. A place where nannies told their little princess what she wanted to hear to keep her happy and believing all the things that a little princess should believe.

On the other hand, it could be Malyn who lied. She could have nudged the vision just enough to distort things. The night of the curse could have happened just as my nannies said it did.

But seeing it is so much more convincing than hearing about it secondhand. All the servants claimed to have been there that night, but I knew they hadn't been. I hadn't had nannies accompany me at formal functions since I was five years old. So how could they know what had truly happened?

Seeing the ogres climb over my wall always made me feel sick. It wasn't that I worried that they would kill my true prince. It was that a part of me knew that one of them could *be* my so-called prince.

The Dark King—as horrible as he is and as horrible as his method was—beat down the fairies. He's been the only one. The members of the Order were the best soldiers and agents the kingdom had, and they haven't been able to push back the fairies in the way that the Dark King did.

Of course, the king used black magic to enslave the fairies. The Order of the Midnight Rose didn't deal with black magic. But maybe that's what it takes to deal with fairies.

I push myself away from the stone wall and pace around in my small tower.

What if the ruler who replaces the Dark King is worse? What would happen if the new monarch is an evil fairy who doesn't just torture people but would happily get rid of them altogether?

CHAPTER 17

There's a grunting sound outside my tower.

I walk over to the window, bracing myself to see another ogre climbing over the wall. The dread in the pit of my stomach has a new urgency now that I've seen Malyn's version of the curse.

There's no new ogre, but down in the courtyard, a patch of thorns stirs. Apparently, the ogre who fell into the brambles is still alive. He must have been knocked out by the fall and is regaining consciousness.

I almost step away but stop myself. I've watched several ogres die, and it's not a pretty sight. But I can't help myself. The nervous fluttering and nausea tells me that I need to watch, just in case he makes it to my tower.

There's nothing I can do, of course, should an ogre climb through my window. But I'm transfixed by the sight of the hideous ogre muscling his way up from the thicket of thorns in the courtyard.

He's drooling in long strings that stick to the thorns. His fat tongue lolls out of his mouth as if too big to be contained. And he grunts like a pig.

I'm about to turn away in disgust when he gets pierced by an unusually large thorn. The ogre cries out as the thorn pierces his hand all the way through. I can almost feel the thorn bursting through the skin.

He roars in pain so loudly that I have to clamp my hands over my ears. Amazingly, despite what must have been horrific pain, he manages to pull it out and stand on his feet.

Despite knowing better, I glance over at my sleeping form to see if the noise had any effect. Of course, since I'm still standing by the window, my body obviously isn't waking.

Outside, the ogre grunts and yells, cursing every step as he painfully tries to get steady on his feet.

That fall must have been torture. I marvel that he managed to stay alive.

Worry gnaws at me. The wall is the hardest part. The courtyard is filled with thorns, but it's flat. Someone strong enough and determined enough could walk or crawl over to the tower so long as he could withstand the pain and damage of the thorns.

I've seen others turn back once they made it into the courtyard, realizing that they weren't strong enough to survive the trek to the tower. Their only chance of survival was to climb back over the wall.

This ogre doesn't seem to have those rational thoughts. He doesn't even look back at the wall. This one just keeps on coming toward the tower, one relentless step at a time.

With my heart in my throat, I spin to face my helpless body. I run over and jump onto the bed.

I slap the sleeping girl's face, hoping against hope that I can wake her. But my hand just whooshes right through her head. I try to grab her shoulders and shake her, but she just lies there, completely unresponsive to my hands floating through her shoulders.

Then I do a stupid thing. I'm so desperate that I lie down and go into my body to try to get it to move.

I put all my will into moving. My hand, my head, my eyelids—*anything.*

Nothing.

I try again, feeling like I'm suffocating with the effort. I'm probably not breathing, but I don't care. I will myself to *move.* Anything, anywhere, just move.

Nothing.

What was I thinking? I tried this countless times when I first woke. It never worked. And each time, the fear of not being able to get out of my meat prison grew larger and larger until it became a conviction.

Panic taints me like blood in water.

I pant, unable to get air into my lungs. I'm trapped. I'll never be able to leave my body again.

I don't even bother to try to calm myself. What's the point?

I feel the muscles and bones solidifying around me. It's trapping me, not wanting me to leave again.

I scream in panic, thrashing about inside my body until I can feel my head, hands and feet disconnecting with the flesh. I'm sobbing as I rock side to side, back and forth, terrified that I won't be able to get out.

Then I finally roll out of my body.

I jump off the bed. I never want to lie on a bed again. I hate beds and bedding and pillows and bed curtains. I hate everything to do with beds and never want to be near one again.

I stumble over to the wall and slide my back to it until I'm curled in a ball. There, I sob as I listen to the ogre grunting in the courtyard below.

*a*t the next meeting, I argue until my throat is raw. The wolfkin won't listen to me about the dangers of allowing Malyn to take control of the kingdom. They sense the kill nearby and can't resist their one chance to hunt the Dark King.

Silver listens, but I can't convince her either. She thinks that what I saw in the broken mirror was a dream gone sideways.

But who knows dreams better than me? I know a nudged dream versus the real thing. By real, I mean an unadulterated experience in the Dreaming, because I have no idea what's real anymore. I just know that Malyn is the evil fairy who cursed me.

"Our orders are clear," says Lanson, standing at the head of the table. "We allow Princess Malyn to overthrow the Dark King. If we can help make that happen without risking ourselves, we'll do it."

Lanson leans in toward Silver with his hands propped against the table. Even in human form, he can't help looking as intimidating as a wolf sometimes.

"I spoke with members of the Midnight Rose," says Silver. "We agree with the kin of wolves. If there's something we can do to help Malyn take down the Dark King, we'll do it."

"But what about Black Rose?" I ask. "She killed him."

"We don't know that," says Ketter. "The castle is a dangerous place. Any number of people could have done him harm. Or he could have been exposed and fled."

"My people are still trying to find him," says Silver. "No one's heard from him in days."

"What about Dahlia?" I ask. "Didn't you see what Malyn did to her face?"

"No one is pretending that Princess Malyn is a good person," says Lanson. "But there's plenty of room to hope that she's better than the Dark King."

"What if she's a wild fairy?" I ask.

The room goes quiet. Outside the windows, the crickets chirp under a full moon. Somewhere in the distance, a Dreaming coyote howls.

The wolfkin and Silver all exchange glances. It's not something they want to accept or even consider. I don't blame them. The implications are monstrous.

A wild fairy. In charge of our kingdom.

"If Malyn is a fairy, the Wild Wars would be over without even the satisfaction of a single battle," I say.

"There have been plenty of battles," says Silver.

"Not in a full generation," I say. "The people of the kingdom would be like children, waiting to be slaughtered."

"The fairies would not slaughter them," says Ketter in an unusually quiet voice. "They would enslave them. No need for a binding. It would be as easy as it gets."

More coyotes add to the howl in the distance.

The Dark King has captured and enslaved a lot of fairies during his reign. The tables would be turned if a wild fairy was the ruler of the land. The only difference would be the ease with which a villager could be enslaved, as opposed to a fairy, which requires a magical binding.

"We need to stop Malyn from taking the throne," I say.

"She won't take the throne," says Ketter. "If the king dies, the prince will be crowned."

"She could rule through him," I say.

"It's possible she could rule through the Dark King too, but she doesn't," says Ketter. "Besides, there's no evidence that she's a wild fairy. Humans are perfectly capable of committing evil."

"She's not human," I say. "She showed me herself what she is."

There's an uncomfortable quiet as they exchange looks. I know what they're thinking. I've been in the Dreaming too long. I am not a reliable source of what's true in the Waking.

"Malyn could clout the prince on the head and rule in his stead after the king dies," I say. "Or she could have a child and then murder her husband. That would make her queen regent, and she could rule on behalf of her child."

"Briar, let's not get too far ahead of ourselves," says Silver. "You're assuming that Malyn can kill the Dark King. That's a major assumption."

"If she can do that," says Ketter, "we can worry about what comes next after we celebrate and get so drunk we'll end up pissing in our soup bowls."

"That's your idea of a celebration?" I ask.

Ketter shrugs. "Isn't that everybody's?"

"The Dark King is supremely paranoid," says Lanson. "He's always searching for traitors among his subjects and allies. His entire selection process for determining his son's bride was centered around making sure she wasn't a fairy."

"He's right, Briar," says Silver. "Nobody could have been more diligent about making sure the prince's bride was human. We can't expect to do better."

"I can," I say. "What if Malyn found a chink in his paranoid armor? What if—"

"What if you just leave it alone?" asks Ketter. "Every decision is a risk. That's why I follow orders instead of trying to second-guess the situation. Our orders are clear."

"Because of your biased report to your alpha," I say. "Maybe if you tell him about my visit to the princess's chamber—"

"No," says Ketter. "He's got enough on his plate."

"You mean he's damaged and healing," I say. "Is he even capable of making good decisions right now?"

Ketter wrinkles his nose and growls at me. He partially changes into wolf form, looking intimidating. I don't know if he can do that in the Waking, but in the Dreaming, he does it whenever he gets mad.

"Ketter," growls Lanson.

Ketter turns back into full human, although he keeps his sneer.

"This is about backing the lesser of two evils," says Silver. "The Dark King is the more immediate threat. Once he's gone, we'll see what we see."

"The Dark King is a blight on our kingdom," says Lanson. "He must be taken down at any cost."

"He's right, Briar," says Silver. "If there's a chance that we can get someone else on the throne—anyone else—it's too good of an opportunity for us to pass it up. We must back the king's opposition."

"Even if it's an evil fairy?" I ask, putting all my frustration and conviction behind my words.

"We just have to hope she's not," says Silver.

I can hear the worry in her voice. She knows that this could lead to disaster, yet they're all hanging the fate of the kingdom on the hope that Malyn will be better than the Dark King. Or maybe there's something in the bigger picture that I'm not aware of. When it comes to matters of the Waking, they still think of me as a child.

But doesn't everybody know there isn't much hope left in the Kingdom of Midnight?

In my frustration, I fling my arms out and try to destroy the old walls of our meeting chamber.

A low rumbling begins. Everyone freezes, looking around at the walls. I keep my stance with my arms wide, feeling dramatic.

The walls vibrate, and dust and tiny pieces of stone rattle down to the floor.

I fling my arms out again, this time making fists and throwing my weight into it.

A stone from the top of the wall rattles, then falls in a shower of dust. Then several other stones follow, causing a satisfying ruckus accompanied by dust.

Everyone ducks, a habit from their waking lives. They look at me wide-eyed. They didn't know I could do that.

Neither did I.

But I don't let my surprise show on my face and pretend this is normal for me.

I stalk out of there, feeling some satisfaction from the crunching of broken rocks beneath my feet.

CHAPTER 19

I dab ointment onto Dahlia's face. She flinches, but does her best to stay still.

She shares a tiny room with three other servants, but because all four of them serve ladies-in-waiting who serve Princess Malyn, there's a much larger dressing room attached to their sleeping quarters. We sit on a bench in that room, surrounded by fine silks and wool, shoes and accessories that their various ladies-in-waiting might need.

"Will you be able to keep your position?" I ask, dabbing the slick ointment onto a particularly long gash that runs from her eye to her jaw.

"That depends on whether I heal completely and quickly," says Dahlia bitterly. "No lady wants a scarred servant, particularly in the royal chambers."

"Even if the scars were caused by the princess?"

"Especially if they were caused by the princess. Nothing but beauty surrounds her, and nothing can mar the illusion of her tranquility."

"So how can you still be here?"

"They'll give me a few days to see if I heal. If they got rid of all the girls they hurt, they'd have to spend all their time training new servants." Dahlia sighs. "I wish you'd come in the real world and put magic ointment on me."

Only Silver knows my true story. Even the wolfkin think I'm one of Silver's students who happens to have this tremendous ability to navigate the Dreaming. They think I can walk around in the Waking just as they do.

"Sorry, too dangerous," I say. "Besides, this works as well, if not better, than ointments in the Waking."

"Are you sure? How can a dream ointment help?"

"I don't know how exactly, but I like to think of it as healing from the inside out. Once the gashes heal on your dream body, they'll heal faster in the Waking. I've seen it happen before."

Both Silver and her granddaughter Ruby had injuries that I tended to in their dreams. Both had come back, telling me how quickly they'd healed in the Waking.

I can do wonders with a wolfkin, making them seem even more supernatural than they are. I slathered gobs of ointment onto Lanson recently, and he healed shockingly fast. There's a reason why the wolfkin put up with me.

Dahlia flinches again, even though the ointment shouldn't hurt. It's hard for dreamers to leave their waking life reactions and limitations behind.

"I wish you could come visit during the day, anyway," says Dahlia. "I could use a trusted friend. Or just anyone I could trust at the castle."

I know how she feels. I'm tempted to become her friend, but I don't want to put her in any more danger than she's in already. Being a true friend means having them truly know you. I can't afford that.

Silver is the only one who knows who I really am. She warned me to keep my mouth shut about it. The more people looking for me, the more likely my fairy will find me.

If people knew that I was the old king's daughter, and that I was still technically alive, the Dark King and anyone else who hoped to win the king's favor would come after me. Greed springs eternal, and there's no hungrier need than a noble's greed for power.

"Do you think Malyn will dethrone the king?" I ask.

"I do." There's conviction in Dahlia's voice. Fear, too.

"It won't improve things, will it?"

"No."

"What are the odds that the king will squash her first?"

"Everyone knows it's lethal to underestimate the Dark King," says Dahlia. "But like everyone else, he underestimates the princess."

I gently rub ointment on a gash over her nose.

"She has more power than anyone thinks." Dahlia looks around cautiously, even though it's her own dream. "I've seen her..."

"It's all right," I say. "There's no one here but us."

Dahlia takes a deep breath. "She has a mirror."

"The broken one."

"Yes. You've seen it?"

I nod.

She swallows. "There's deep power in that looking glass."

"What if the king takes it? Would that make her helpless?"

"I don't know. I've seen her talk to it."

"Have you heard it talking back?"

"No. But I swear there's something in it that looks out at me sometimes."

"What do you mean, looks at you?"

"It's not something I see. It's just a feeling of being watched. Evaluated. Like when you know that someone suspects you of something when they're talking to you. It's like that. Only, there's no one in the mirror." She shivers.

I felt that too.

"What else could the king do if he wanted to kill her?" I ask.

"He'd have to surprise her. Catch her asleep, so to speak."

Goosebumps sprout all over me at those words. Malyn never sleeps, according to my nanny's version of my curse. Nevertheless, I've seen her in the Dreaming. I don't think she's a dreamer, exactly, but she is visiting the land of dreams. She's not a specter, either. Like me, she doesn't fit into any group.

"Does Malyn ever sleep?" I ask. "I'm not talking about seeing her in bed. Does she *sleep*?"

Dahlia thinks about that for a long time. "When she first came to the castle, she would wake in her bed as the servants came in with her breakfast. She always looked perfectly fresh and ready for the day. No need to wash or fix her hair. I always thought that was odd. It felt like she was pretending. But now that you mention it, she no longer bothers with that. She's always awake no matter the hour."

Just as my nannies said, Malyn does not sleep. But that doesn't mean that she gets that power from cursing me. She might just have an extreme version of fairy insomnia.

Regardless of the reason for her not sleeping, I know she visits the Dreaming. Would it be possible for me to kill her when she does?

I have no idea what happens to people if they die in the Dreaming. There's also the fact that I am not a killer. But maybe I could learn to be one if it means saving the kingdom.

Despite Silver's combat training, I've never actually killed someone. When I lived in the Waking, I was a princess who was sheltered and protected by the royal guards.

I dab ointment on poor Dahlia's face. But my mind is haunted by a question.

Could I manage to kill the evil fairy through her dreams?

CHAPTER 20

lean against the wall in front of Malyn's chambers. I'm just watching, learning. I don't know much about our new princess. Maybe if I knew her better, I'd have a better idea of what I could do.

Does she visit the Dreaming often, for instance? Can she still move in the Waking while she's visiting the land of dreamers?

Could life be that easy? Not that it would be easy to lure her into sleepwalking out of a tower window, but it'd be good to know if it was possible.

There's a lot I don't know about the Dreaming or what I can do in it. I was asleep for years before I even became aware that I was dreaming. And who knows how long it took before I learned to begin navigating it?

I tried a lot of things in those early years, wondering if I was nothing but a ghost in a world full of real things. As far as I can tell, my tower is the only place where I can be both in the Waking and be a spirit. Everywhere else I've managed to go has been in the Dreaming.

Don't get me wrong—I'm thrilled to be able to do what I

can. Anything's better than being stuck in that bed. But I can't feel the breeze, and I can't smell the rain, and I can't pick anything up, even in the tower.

It took me forever to learn that I can change things in the Dreaming. And even longer to learn that I can change my appearance to look like whoever I want when I present myself to the dreamer. The wolfkin and the Order of the Midnight Rose were incredibly excited when they found out what I could do.

I thought they were going to wet themselves with excitement when I figured out how to join dreams to bring people together. They declared me their secret weapon who could spy on the enemy and organize secret meetings where no one could ever catch us.

In reality, it doesn't quite work that way. People forget the details of their dreams far more often than I'd like. They also make stuff up when they're dreaming, so any information I get is always suspect.

Still, no one else can do what I do, and I'm always learning. So can I learn another trick? Can I learn to assassinate a member of the Dark King's family?

First step is to learn as much about Malyn's life in the Dreaming as I can. I watch everyone who goes in and out of her chambers.

As far as I can tell, they're all either dreamers or specters. None of them is Malyn.

There are a lot of anxiety dreams around her chambers. One lady-in-waiting shows up naked, looking scared to walk into the chamber. Another runs out desperately mumbling something about misplacing the princess's shoes.

There are a lot of specters running around too. Most are dressed far nicer than the dreamers themselves. Many of them look disapprovingly down at the dreamers. It's amazing how much insecurity there is among the nobles and their servants.

Many of them won't say her name. They just refer to her as the princess. The Dark King is so secretive that he fosters a culture of people referring to the royal family only by title. He believes that there's power in knowing names.

But even the king couldn't keep people from knowing the princess's name. She freely announced it to anyone who asked. The nobles and servants in the castle still seem to call her by title, though. I wonder if that's habit or superstition?

Things were simpler in my time, when everyone, even the lowest peasant, could call me Princess Briar. Well, it bothers me that I have to think of this evil fairy, usurper of my mother's chamber, as "princess."

"What does the prince call the princess?" I ask a lady-in-waiting dreamer who is trying to get up her nerve to walk into the chamber.

"Frightening," whispers the dreamer. She looks at me as though hoping that I'll take her away from this hallway and save her from having to enter the royal chamber.

"What name does he call her?" I try to be patient. It's possible that the name Malyn uses in her intimate circles is more of a true name than what the commoners call her.

The little lady-in-waiting looks around, obviously worried about being overheard. She's shrinking as we speak, getting younger and younger until she looks about eight summers old.

"The prince calls her Malyn," says the dreamer. "But only when he has to."

She looks like she regrets telling me as soon as she says the name. She looks around, then runs off back down the torchlit hallway.

So it's superstition that keeps people from saying Malyn's

name. People do the same with demons and powerful fairies. No one wants to call their attention.

Hovering outside the door isn't going to do much good. I gather my courage and walk into Malyn's chamber.

The chamber is crowded with dreamers. How could so many of the castle's inhabitants dream about one person? Apparently, once someone gets to know Malyn, she dominates their thoughts.

Like last time, Malyn sits at her vanity with her back to the door. She holds the cracked mirror in her hand. She must like to look at herself.

"Please forgive us, Lal—Your Highness," says a woman dressed as a kitchen worker. There's a dim glow around her, marking her as a dreamer.

That's odd. Usually, dreamers dream about the people in their lives. I would expect a kitchen worker to dream about impressing the cook, not the princess.

"Go away, Mama," says a young woman in a ball gown as she brushes Malyn's hair. "Can't you see that I'm becoming friends with Lal—the princess? You're embarrassing me."

The young woman is a specter, but I can learn even by watching specters. That's the second time someone has stopped themselves from calling Malyn by another name. That's enough for me to know that Malyn is just a made-up name, the kind that fairies use.

I shake my head. Do I need proof that she's a fairy? If I didn't already know it in my heart, would I be here at all?

Malyn ignores the women fussing and arguing around her. She's busy staring into her mirror. Does she ever leave it? She must. I can't imagine her going to supper with it.

Luckily, this time, she's busy and doesn't seem to notice me.

She's not glowing. I've been fooled by that before, though.

I think I need to assume that the usual signs I rely on to tell a dreamer from a specter are meaningless for her.

"Does the princess sleepwalk?" I ask the dreamer. Of course, I don't expect Malyn to sleepwalk, since she doesn't sleep. But I might as well start with the easiest scenario.

The women stop bickering and notice me. The older one in rags assesses my dress as though she has any right to assess anybody. The younger one in her ball gown does the same. I can see the resemblance between mother and daughter.

I draw myself up into an intimidating queen. There is no queen in this kingdom, but that doesn't matter in dreams. I channel my mother. She could be quite intimidating when dealing with wayward nobles.

Mother and daughter exchange glances.

"We don't know if she sleepwalks," says the mother.

"I don't think I've ever known her to sleep," says the daughter with a frown.

"How long have you known her?" I ask.

"We came to the castle with her," says the mother, puffing up with pride. "She wouldn't be here if it hadn't been for us."

"And all that time, you've never seen her sleep?" I ask.

Malyn angles her mirror to look at my reflection, not bothering to turn to face me. I see her ice-blue eye through the cracked glass.

A chill grips my heart at the possibility of someone like her being in my Dreaming, yet being wide awake.

Malyn's cold eye seems to be laughing at me. It is encased in a shard in the mirror, while the rest of the pieces reflect the chamber. It's just as creepy as it was the last time I was here.

My mind tells me that Princess Malyn has to be a specter because she's not glowing. But my instincts know that she is present. I can feel her awareness of me.

There's no denying that there's something odd about her. Why is she always sitting here with that eerie broken mirror in her hand? And how is it that she always notices me when most dreamers don't?

I walk around to try to look directly at her. It unnerves me to look at her through that cracked mirror. There's nothing stranger than seeing yourself in fragments.

When I walk around to the side of her, I gasp. My hand flies to my mouth in surprise.

I've seen a lot of strange things in my life. I do live in the Dreaming, after all. But this is one of the strangest, and it disturbs me beyond description.

Malyn has no face.

CHAPTER 21

*M*alyn sits in front of her dresser, holding that mirror.

All this time, I thought the looking glass was reflecting her face. I thought it was a coincidence that her eye happened to be reflected in that same shard both this time and last. But that wasn't what was happening at all.

Malyn is looking at me *through* the mirror. She's in the Waking, peering into the Dreaming.

I sit down on a bench so hard that someone might say that I collapsed onto it. They wouldn't be wrong. My knees—ghostly as they are—practically give out on me.

I stare at the cracked mirror. The faceless princess has turned it so that I can see her ice-blue eye watching my reaction with amusement.

Why didn't I see it before? That sense of disorienting carnival of reflections. It's off. Jumbled. It's so weird to look at that I didn't realize that there was more to it than dream distortion.

How many times has she seen me? Did she see me with

Dahlia? I frantically rummage through my memory, trying to figure out what I said and did near Malyn.

Did I say or do anything that gave her a clue about my tower's location?

Panic washes over me and I have trouble breathing. The thought of my body back in my tower having trouble breathing makes me even more panicked.

There's something naked and vulnerable about being seen in your dreams. Whether I'm a dreamer or not, this is all part of my Dreaming. And she has no right to be here.

I jump away from the bed and run out of the chamber, all the while feeling her sharp eye watching me through her shard.

It's Midnight dark. There's a wet sheen on the ground from some light source that I can't see.

All around me, there are islands of dreams, but they are in the distance. I shoved them back as far as I could so that I could hide in the corridors of darkness in between the dreams.

My breath comes in harsh gasps and my heart races so fast that I worry about my body back in my tower. I need to calm down.

But how can I calm myself when the fairy who cursed me can *see* me?

When I first woke, my greatest wish, other than to have my body awake, was to be seen by people. Real people in their real lives. I wanted to be part of the Waking, not trapped as a specter in the Dreaming.

For a long time, I wandered around in a crowd of dreamers, completely alone, totally isolated. It's better now that Silver and the wolfkin know about me, but I can never get past the fact that they leave me here when they go back to their waking lives.

Now that someone else can see me, though, all I want to do is hide.

I hug myself in the darkness. I could search for a comforting space. A big chair with a nice cushion. A window overlooking a garden. But none of that would be real. Sometimes, I just need something real.

The closest I can get to the reality of the Waking is to be alone in the dark. What a miserable thing that is. If I was being honest, I'd admit that the closest I could get to the Waking is to go back into my body and be trapped there.

I sigh, watching my breath stream out in a cloud. The hell with the Waking and reality. I need to go home.

I make an opening to my tower. The tightness in my chest eases at seeing the familiar comfort of my tower through the rip in the fabric of the Dreaming.

I sense something behind me. I pause, turning to look.

It's not quite a sound and it's not quite a touch, but it's as though I detect both. A ripple in the darkness.

Someone is walking toward me. A shadow among shadows.

Dreamers can't walk out of their dream islands. The islands can drift close to each other and a dreamer can hop from one island to another. That happens all the time. But I've never seen a dreamer walk out of her own dream.

I let out a deep breath, trying not to panic. I can't help but feel like something is invading my home. The Dreaming is the only home I have left.

When the shadow walks past a lit island, I get a better look. A noblewoman's dress, long hair, a hand-held mirror.

When the light hits the woman's face, it only shows the blank contours where a face should be.

Nightmare Malyn walks like a sleepwalker, slow and

steady, away from the castle island toward me. I'm frozen to my spot.

She lifts and angles the mirror so that I can see the broken glass. It's faintly glowing with its own light. In it, Malyn's frosty eye looks at me.

In the cracked pieces next to her eye, I look like a cut-up doll who could never be put back together again.

A scream gets caught in my throat. No sound comes out even though I need to scream. I've seen a hundred dreamers do this in their nightmares, but I've never experienced it myself.

I spin and step into my tower. As soon as I'm in, I swipe to shut the opening as fast as I can.

But it's too late. Malyn already saw my tower.

CHAPTER 22

$\mathcal{I}$ curl into a ball with my back to the curved wall, expecting to see Malyn come into my tower at any moment. On the bed, my body breathes fast and shallow. I know my heart must be thumping like mad.

I can't actually feel anything when I hug myself. My dream self is as ethereal to me as I am to everyone else. There is no satisfaction to curling up or hugging myself. I only do it because it used to be something I did when I was corporeal.

I crawl over to my bed. Then I do something I didn't think I'd do again. I settle into my body.

Outside, the sun sets forever on the Waking.

I feel my heart pounding. I can feel it when I'm out of my body, but it's not a physical sensation the way it is when I'm wrapped in flesh. I hear and feel blood flowing too. Rushing in my throat, on my face, in my feet.

I am alive.

I exist.

A tear slips down my cheek. I can't remember how long it's been since I felt that.

I lie here as my tower gets dark, frozen on my bed, wondering when the evil fairy will come for me.

I lie in my body all night, wondering how long it will take for Malyn to find me.

At first, I'm convinced that she'll come crashing through at any moment. I huddle in my warmth of flesh and blood, trying to get some comfort from being real.

Eventually, I come to understand that it'll take some time before she can find me. Yes, she saw me go home. Now, she knows I'm in a stone chamber. She probably saw my window and knows I'm in a tower somewhere in the forest. But the forest is a large place—not as large as all the basements and caves and hidden places in the world, but it's large.

The problem is that the forest is the home of wild fairies. They know it better than any other creature, except maybe for the wolfkin. And if Malyn manages to kill off the Dark King, she'll have an army at her command to look for me.

I lie in the dark, listening to the ogre grunt and roar in his pain in the courtyard. He's getting closer. If he keeps this up, Malyn may have competition to be the first to reach me.

It's one of the longest nights of my life, and not just because the nights are getting longer.

I finally gather enough courage and resolve to get up out of my body. The wicked fairy would love to see me cowering like this. She would want me to experience every moment of my meat prison.

Malyn might have beaten me in the Waking, but I won't let her beat me in the Dreaming. I won't let her enslave my mind the way she has enslaved my body.

I calm myself enough to sit up without feeling trapped. I push through the resistance of my flesh not wanting to let me go, pushing through the stickiness as my bones and veins cling to me. I've had enough of lying down and feeling helpless. It's time for me to take action.

And what better action than to help the king kill Malyn?

I may not be a killer myself, but I can't just lie around while I'm being stalked and cursed, now, can I?

Silver and her lessons must be getting to me. Just the thought of letting that wicked fairy continue to do what she's been doing to me infuriates me enough to unstick myself from my body and drag myself out of bed.

The rising sun lends me some courage as well. The sky turns from gray to rosy beyond the woods.

It won't actually turn into daylight. It'll simply shift from night to dawn to twilight. Then it'll eventually move from twilight to night and back all over again. I can't remember the last time I saw the sun.

Below, the ogre continues his frustrated and pain-filled roars.

I walk over to the window. The ogre has moved a few feet from the last time I saw him. It must be like swimming through amber, if amber happened to cut, slash and pierce.

"Why won't you go back home?" I call down to the courtyard.

I don't expect him to hear me.

"Nothing to go back to," he grunts.

I blink in surprise and stare down at him with a frown. Just one more reminder that my tower is at the border of the Dreaming and Waking. I shake my head at the wonder of him hearing me. Can he see me too?

He doesn't look up at me as he pushes his way farther into the brambles, slashing with his sturdy stick.

"Aren't you tired?" I ask. I'm not inclined to ask him to look up at me. I'll take what odd company I can get right now.

He grunts, making it clear that he is tired.

I sigh. "Can I ask you something?"

"Why not?" he growls. "I got nothing better to do."

He hits his stick hard against the brambles, and when the thin branches don't break, he kicks it in his frustration. All that does is get more thorns into his foot. He growls at the brambles as if he thinks he can intimidate them.

"Do you think killing someone who wants to kill you is so terrible?" I ask.

He stops and looks up at me. His nose is bulbous, his eyes wide pools of grease. The rest of his face is streaked in blood. There are so many thorns sticking out of him that he looks like he has thorns for hair.

"Why would you want to kill someone?" he asks.

Apparently, he can see me too. I marvel at that, even if he is an ogre.

"This person stole my life," I say.

"Vengeance?" He has no judgment in his voice, just curiosity. Not surprising, since ogres probably kill for any kind of annoyance.

"Not vengeance," I say. "She certainly deserves it. But I think it's just that...I'm afraid. Afraid of what else she might do."

It feels very strange to say that out loud.

"Are you telling me this because you think I won't live to remember this conversation?" asks the ogre.

He sounds quite human in that moment. But all I have to do is take another look at him to know that's just my ignorance of ogres. There are lots of stories of their horrific crimes, but I admit that this is the first ogre I've ever spoken with.

"Perhaps," I say. "Your chances of survival will be much greater if you—"

"Turn around and go back."

He sounds like a boy mimicking his elders. He pushes toward my tower and growls at the pain. It's a fierce sound that makes me glad to have so many thorns between us.

"Who is this person who frightens you?" he asks.

"Someone very powerful. Someone very evil."

"Can you match his power?"

"I can ally with someone who matches her power."

"Oh, it's a woman."

He swipes at his brow, trying to wipe the blood streaming down his face. But all that does is scratch his brow from the ends of the thorns sticking out of his hand.

He's hard to look at. It's like talking to a torture victim while he is being tortured. I harden my heart, though. If he makes it to my chamber, I'm the one who is going to be tortured.

"Is she a witch, your enemy?" he asks. "Or is she merely a village girl?" He sounds casual, as though he expects me to confess that all my enemy did was to spread some embarrassing gossip about me.

"She's a powerful fairy who is determined to enslave me." I don't bother to go into details of how she's already enslaved me.

He squints up at me. It must be difficult to get a good look at me up here in the tower.

"You should forget about the fairy," he says. "You can't win against that kind of power. Stick to your lady friends and the protection of your family."

I cross my arms. "Just where do you think I keep my lady friends and my family? Here in the tower?"

"Oh. You're in the tower."

"Where did you think I was?"

"Somewhere." He waves his hand vaguely. "The others I've talked to aren't here. Most of them are back home, enjoying their parties and lavish meals."

I frown. Apparently, he's been having dreams or delusions. I suppose it's all the same when you're in this twilight space.

"All right," I say. "I need to go now. Enjoy your parties and lavish meals."

"Wait." There's urgency in his voice as he looks up at me.

"Yes?"

"Is the sleeping princess up there?"

I consider what to say. He doesn't realize that it's me. I can't begin to guess what goes on in an ogre's head or what motivates him, but I might be able to save both of us with a little lie.

"No. There's no princess up here. I heard there's one in that direction." I point past the courtyard wall. "Just a few days' walk. I hear she's in a tower a lot like this one, but without the thorns. She's supposed to be asleep. Under some curse or something. Is that the one you're looking for?"

"Yes, that's her." He sounds relieved.

"Well, you'd best get going. You don't want some other ogre to find her before you, do you?" I try to sound friendly, getting into my mode of nudging dreamers. I'm getting pretty good at it.

"Yes, I'd better hurry." The ogre pushes even harder into the brambles toward me.

"Not that way. Over there." I point to the courtyard wall where he came from.

"You're just one of the many tricks and traps protecting the sleeping princess. I've been through plenty of them, and the closer I get, the more tricks and traps there are. So I know I'm on the right track."

He shoves mightily into the thorns. He has his arms up, trying to protect his face.

I can't bear to look anymore. I turn away from the window. I have my own quest to deal with.

I let myself feel the borders of the Dreaming. It's like water lapping at me. When I feel it, I step out of my tower.

CHAPTER 23

Strangely, I step out of my tower only to end up back in my tower.

I frown, puzzling over what is happening. There are a lot of odd things in the Dreaming, but I've never been trapped in my tower before.

Trapped.

That word sends shivers down my ghostly spine. I was encased in my unmoving body for far too long to ever feel comfortable with the idea of being trapped.

I'm about to turn and try to leave my tower again when I notice that the sleeping girl on the bed isn't me. She has golden hair flowing all around her like a peacock's tail. I've never had hair like that.

I move toward the bed to take a closer look. She's radiantly beautiful and definitely not me. Her hair is perfect, her skin is perfect, her lips are rose-red and her cheeks a dusty pink.

I stand over her with my hands on my hips, wondering what in the Dark King's name could be going on. Just as it dawns on me that this is strangely dreamlike, the top of a head rises from the other side of the window.

All I can see is a dark crown of hair until a pair of hands reach up to grab the windowsill. Both the hair and the hands glow faintly.

Outside, the sky is blazing with the brightening sky of morning.

It's never daytime in my tower. I must be in a dream.

And the dreamer is climbing through the window.

I frown so hard that the lines between my brows pinch and press against my nose. No one dreams about my tower because no one is supposed to know about it.

Sure, people can dream about a place they haven't visited, but what they envision is usually different from what's in the Waking. I glance back at the girl on the bed with her golden hair and perfect everything.

All right. I can accept that this is someone's dream. It's not surprising for someone to dream of a tower chamber that looks like mine. All the tower chambers I've seen look pretty much the same. It's round, small and made of stone walls. It's the furniture and windows that change.

There's just my four-poster bed and a single window in my tower. That's not so hard to dream up.

The man climbs through the window. He is handsome, with broad shoulders and a muscular chest. He's tall and strong, with clean lines and even features. I have no idea if the dreamer actually looks like this, but if he doesn't, he did a good job of conjuring himself a great body.

"She's beautiful," says the man.

I glance at the girl on the bed. "I suppose she is, if you like the golden, fluffy kind of girl."

"You don't think she's breathtaking?" He looks at me. He doesn't have a single scratch or hair out of place. His clothes look new and fashionable, as though he is attending a social event.

I'm a little surprised that he's talking to me. Often, dreamers are so engrossed in their dreams that they don't even notice me, even if I talk to them.

I shrug. "There's more to a person than her appearance. She could be empty inside, and no amount of beauty could make up for that."

"Why would you say she's empty? I spent all this time looking for her." He brushes imagined dust off his shoulder. "Risked my life to reach her. And now that I'm finally here, you're putting doubts in my head about what she might or might not be like."

"Oh, sorry. All you have to do is kiss her, then you'll find out."

I could leave him and go about my own business, but other than Silver's dream of me as a child, I've never been in a dream about me before. I can't help but watch.

He just stands there by the window, looking at the girl on the bed as her chest steadily moves up and down. He watches but doesn't take a single step toward her.

"What are you waiting for?" I ask. "She's not going to wake herself."

"You're right. I don't know her at all. What if she's no better than the ladies at court who mindlessly chatter all day?"

"She's not. I don't know why I said she might be empty. Empty-headed, I mean. She's great. I've met her. She...might not be as pretty as you think she is, but that doesn't matter. She'll be thrilled to meet you."

"Not as pretty? What do you mean?"

"How could that matter? She's fine. Go on. Kiss her."

"Don't rush me." He rubs his thick hair. "It all matters. I'm committing myself to spend the rest of my life with her, and everything about her will matter."

"Didn't you already commit to that when you embarked on your quest?"

"That's different."

"How?"

He sighs, and his voice loses all its bravado. "I didn't expect to find her."

"Then why did you go on the quest?"

"It's what everybody expects me to do. My father and all ten of my brothers and sisters would have to die before I inherit a title. I may be from a powerful lineage, but soon, I'll be a nobody. My father's title and lands will go to my eldest sister. This is the only thing of value being offered to me."

"So you're a pauper prince. She won't care. Just wake her and ask her."

He looks down at the girl on the bed. "I think I'll wait and think on it."

Where is this lordling in the Waking? Is he on the journey to search for me? Or is he simply dreaming about going on the search?

"You'd better not dawdle for too long," I say. "There are other suitors on your heels, you know." There's been not a single prince who has come this far, as far as I know, but he doesn't have to know that.

He nods, but he doesn't move.

"She has a legitimate claim to the Kingdom of Midnight," I say in a singsong voice. "If you wake her, you might get your own kingdom."

"True. But the kingdom is in tatters and the Dark King rules it. The chances of me taking it from him are laughably small and tremendously dangerous." He shakes his head sadly.

No wonder no princes have come my way. There's not much incentive, it seems.

"Still," he says. "She is comely. And having a claim to a kingdom—even if it's Midnight—is better than nothing, I suppose." Then he looks at me. "How about a little tryst before I wake up my bride-to-be? There's no harm in a little fun before waking her up, eh?"

I wrinkle my nose. "You are becoming less handsome by the minute." Without thinking, I shove him out of the window.

I watch as he falls with a shocked expression on his face. He pinwheels his arms as though trying to fly. I'd feel bad, except all I'm doing is giving him a bad dream. He'll most likely wake in his silk sheets when his servant brings him breakfast in bed. After this, I'm pretty sure that he'll decide not to go on the quest.

I may have destroyed my one chance for a nobleman to finally embark on the journey to rescue me. I doubt that he would have made it to my tower window anyway. It takes indomitable courage to find my tower. After that, it takes even more determination to make it through the brambles.

The lordling lands in the courtyard thorns, shooting thorns every which way as he crashes down.

"Hey!" the ogre roars as he shields his face with his muscular arms. "Watch where you're throwing out your trash!"

"Sorry," I call out as I lean over the window. "Didn't see you there."

I'm only a little surprised that the ogre is in the nobleman's dream. But since this place is in both the Waking and the Dreaming, it shouldn't surprise me. The ogre is no more of a dreamer or a specter here than I am. I suppose we have that in common, at least for now.

"Some of us have to go through life one step at a time,"

says the ogre, "unlike this lad." He slashes at the branches in front of him with a sturdy stick.

"Well, I suppose that was smart of him to start at the window instead of in the middle of the brambles," I say as I lean out the window.

"Smart has nothing to do with it."

"If you say so."

I'm ready to leave this dream when I realize that I should try harder to talk the ogre out of reaching me.

"You're midway in the courtyard," I say. "It'll take you just as long to reach the tower as it will for you to reach the wall. Don't you think it's a good idea to get out of the brambles before they kill you?"

"No." The ogre struggles painfully against the thorns, stubbornly pushing his way closer to me.

"Why not?"

"I'm on a quest."

"I see that. But quests can be abandoned."

"Not for me."

"Even if it kills you?"

"It won't." He swipes his stick and pushes against the brambles even though thorns pierce his arms, chest and face.

"How do you know it won't kill you?"

It's hard to watch him being mangled by the thorns, so I turn away from the window and stand with my back to the wall. His voice wafts up from the courtyard.

"I'm the only hope she has. I won't let her down."

CHAPTER 24

*I*n the darkness between dream islands, I take a couple of deep breaths and gather my courage. Then I head back to Midnight Castle again.

This time, I'm heading to the king's chambers. Unfortunately, it's not as far away from Malyn as I'd like, but neither is the far side of the moon.

This part of the castle is dominated by everything war. Instead of tapestries, the walls are decorated in armor and weapons. The hallway hasn't been scrubbed in a long time, by the look of the soot marks staining the walls. Clearly the Dark King doesn't care much for having a bright and clean castle.

As I near the king's chambers, memories come flooding back. I didn't visit my father often when these were his chambers, but I have clear memories of the times I did. Back then, the walls were lined with noble tapestries full of color and artistic designs.

All my memories of walking down this hallway are filled with sunshine streaming in through the arched windows. I wonder if the sunshine still fills the Waking hallway, or if the Dark King had his sorcerers banish the light.

Here in the Dreaming, the place is empty of dreamers. It's morning in the Waking and most people in Midnight get up early. Of course, there are always exceptions, especially the nobles. But it seems that no one is dreaming of being near the king's chambers this morning.

So it's a surprise when I see the lone guard in front of the king's door.

The castle has countless guards, most of them bored and thinking about something other than their duties, but this one is different. He's alert and sees me immediately. It's as though he's expecting an attack.

He wears a helm and the usual crimson cloak of the Dark King's personal guards. He carries a spear and a sword, looking ready for battle.

"Halt, who goes there?" he asks. I can't see his face behind his helm, but he's tall, with a broad chest and shoulders. He sounds confident and commanding.

A lot of guards are so young and untrained that they barely even know what end of the sword to hold. I know, because I've seen plenty in my time both in the Dreaming and the Waking.

This one has a seasoned air about him. I suppose any guard who gets assigned to be the king's personal guard must be good at what he does. Of course, this could just be the kitchen boy who dreams of being the king's only personal guard. I like to think that I can tell the difference, but I have no way of knowing for sure.

"I'm just here to deliver breakfast to the king," I say, pretending to hold a tray laden with food.

It appears in my hands a moment after I pretend it is there. Dreamers are so susceptible. Whatever they imagine, it appears in their dream. All I have to do is nudge them. I'm now in a royal servant's uniform.

He blinks a couple of times and looks closely at me. Aside from his eyes, the only other part of his face that I can see is his jaw. It's square and clean, and looks as hard as his armor.

I put on a flirty smile. "You know, breakfast. Even a king must eat."

"You mean to say, 'His Majesty.'"

"Sure, that." I nod. I should behave more appropriately, but honestly, it just about kills me to call the mad dog who murdered my father "His Majesty." It's too hard to force the honorific out of my mouth.

"His Majesty is not to be disturbed," he says. I notice that he doesn't sheathe his sword.

"He called for breakfast. What is your name? I'm certain that he'd want to know who kept him hungry."

His eyes narrow. "You don't speak like a servant."

"I am no ordinary servant. I serve breakfast to the king. In his chambers. How many other servants do you think are allowed to do that? Now, please get out of my way. I'm sure the king is as hungry as one of his own subjects."

There's a pause as he stares me down.

"You shall not pass."

"Do you think I'm going to murder him? Harm the king with a fork? Or strangle him with his napkin? Isn't your job to protect him from big, bad enemies and not a serving girl who is desperately trying not to get in trouble with the cook?"

"I've seen you before." He looks closely at me with heightened suspicion.

I get that a lot. Sometimes, I take on the form of someone the dreamer knows. It used to happen inadvertently all the time before I figured out how to manage it. Now, I use it when it suits me.

The problem is that I didn't turn myself into someone he knows.

"We both work at the same castle," I say. "I bring the king breakfast. Of course you've seen me before."

"The king does not eat breakfast." He watches my reaction carefully.

"Of course he does. I mean, I'm new, so I don't know how long he's been eating breakfast, but what man doesn't eat breakfast?"

"A man who stays awake all night and sleeps through the daylight hours." The guard is like a wall between me and the king's chambers.

I sigh, tiring of the game. I can't stay here all night arguing with a dreamer.

"You're probably not even this tall," I say as I drop the tray. The food splatters all over the hall. "What are you, one of the stable lads? Why don't you go back to your pathetic little dream of impressing the kitchen girls and let grownups conduct their important business?"

He says nothing. He simply holds his weapons out in front of him, ready to skewer me if I make the wrong move. He doesn't seem to care about the splattered food, and I can't get him to move away from the door.

That's when we both hear the cry coming from the king's chambers.

The guard spins and crashes through the door. I dart right in behind him.

CHAPTER 25

The king retches over the side of his bed. Beside the bed is a steaming pool of half-digested slime. Long strings of drool hang off his mouth.

He is just as disgusting and repulsive as I've always imagined. Until now, I've done my best to avoid him. How could I watch the killer of my family and usurper of my father's throne without wanting to strangle him? It was just best to avoid any contact with him.

He's not as big as I imagined him to be. He leans back onto his pillows—an aging man with sagging skin and thinning hair. His bed is an impressive four-poster with a fine linen canopy. He leans against oversized and colorful pillows made of animal skin.

The grandeur of the royal furniture only serve to make him look even smaller, frailer. A part of me is glad to see him groaning and shriveled in bed. Another part of me, though, is disappointed.

This is the man who murdered my father and took the throne? The mad Dark King who thirsts for blood and tortures people for entertainment?

I realize that he's only dimly glowing. He's only partly dreaming. He probably has indigestion and is likely tossing and turning in his shallow sleep.

The guard, though…he's glowing too.

I frown. Whose dream is this?

It's not that dreamers can't be in the same dream. I nudge people into it all the time. It's just that it rarely happens naturally.

Then I notice something else. There's a patchwork cloak hanging on a stand beside an armoire. It's also faintly glowing.

Is there anything about this situation that isn't strange? How could a cloak be dreaming?

I drift over to it while the guard tends to his king. This is the infamous Cloak of Souls. It's trimmed in luxurious fur, but that's where the sense of luxury ends.

The cloak is made of many patches of hide. It's crudely sewn together, almost as if the person sewing it had palsied hands. Maybe the seamstress was trembling.

The patches are mostly various shades of hides ranging from milky white to dark leather, but there are a few patches that are a dull blue or green. I put my hand out to touch it, but stop just short of touching the hide.

The cloak is lightly glowing, but it doesn't glow as a whole. The patches themselves glow individually. Several of the patches don't glow at all. When two patches glow next to each other, I can see a faint border where the color and texture of the glow is slightly different.

The Dark King took over the throne while I was asleep, before I managed to get out of my body. But Silver told me what happened, and I picked up enough clues from other people's dreams to know what questions to ask of her.

People say that the king's cloak is made of the skin of fairies that he slew during the Wild Wars. Silver thought that only a few of the patches were actually fairy skin, although she admitted that no one knew for sure. The rest of the patches were likely from his human enemies.

But humans don't dream after they've been cut into leather patches and sewn into a cloak. Can fairies dream after they die?

From the look of the glow, more than half of the patches are from fairies. Maybe the Dark King's reputation really is based in truth.

On the bed, the king belches. I make a prudish face in response.

"Bring me some wine," the king commands the guard. He looks like he might throw up again.

"That's what servants are for," says the guard to the king.

I can't see the guard's face behind his helm, but I swear his voice sounds like it has a sneer behind it.

That gets my attention. Guards don't talk to royalty like that, especially the Dark King. Dream or not, people rarely stray from their real social position. When they do, the overwhelming result is to dream of being lower on the social ladder.

The guard doesn't fawn over the ailing king, nor does he seem particularly concerned about his illness.

"Have you been poisoned?" he asks. "Or are you drunk?"

"Poisoned," says the king, rolling on his side. "That bitch is trying to kill me."

"So kill her first," says the guard.

"My thoughts exactly. You"—the king points to me—"get me some wine."

I remember that I look like a servant and curtsy. I don't leave, though. Dreamers often forget their line of thought, so sometimes, I can get away with simply agreeing and then ignoring whatever I agreed to do.

"Aren't you supposed to protect me?" asks the king.

"You're doing a crap job of it. You should have known that the bitch was poisoning me and stopped her."

"My charge is unharmed," says the guard. "Your indigestion is of little concern to me." He turns to leave the chamber.

"Your charge has been cut up and sewn to the bottom of my cloak. I piss on her sometimes, you know, when I'm drunk."

A muscle on the guard's jaw twitches. He's barely holding on to his temper.

I reassess him. He's not protecting the king after all. But it doesn't make any sense to protect a piece of skin from a dead person.

I glance back at the cloak. Is he protecting one of the fairy patches or a human patch?

"You did a terrible job of protecting your mistress," says the king. "Now that she's dead, you're pretending to be the vigilant guard?" He laughs. It's a mean, mocking sound.

The guard doesn't respond. He merely turns to go.

"What if I tear your mistress into shreds with my knife? What would happen then?" asks the king.

"Then I would be free." The guard throws him a backward glance. "And you would be dead."

I expect the king to order the guard to be executed, or at the very least to mock him. Instead, the Dark King shrinks into his oversized bed. He crawls over to the other side and retches.

This is the king who I'm hoping will free the world of a powerful fairy?

CHAPTER 26

J lean against the stone wall outside the king's chambers. The stone behind my back is cold and so is the air. It's nowhere near winter, yet I swear the temperature has dropped.

The guard goes back to standing in front of the door as though nothing happened. He doesn't even look at me, which gives me a chance to look at him.

His helm and uniform are the same as the king's other personal guards. I saw the king from afar during dreams of festivals and parades. And, of course, there were endless dreams of the prince's wedding that were dominated by the king.

In all those dreams, the Dark King was always surrounded by guards who looked just like this one. But this guard doesn't seem to belong to the king.

"Who is the lady you're protecting?" I ask.

He doesn't answer. He doesn't seem to care what I do or say, so long as I don't barge into the king's chambers without permission.

"Is she...*was* she a fairy?" I ask.

He still doesn't answer.

"I can talk all night," I say. "Tonight, tomorrow night, and every night thereafter. Unlike you, I have nowhere else to go, no one else to bother."

"What makes you think I have somewhere else to go?" he asks.

"Ooh, Tall, Dark and Mysterious talks. When you wake up, you'll no doubt have a hundred places to go. You can't be on duty all the time."

"I am."

"You are what?"

"On duty all the time."

I frown. "That's just when you're here, in the Dreaming. When you wake up—"

"Stop talking," he says.

"That's rude."

He looks at me. He seems to really see me for the first time. He looks right into my eyes, and I can feel his sudden curiosity and interest.

"Stop. Talking." He stares intently at me.

"Why should I? I don't take orders from you."

His lips part a little. His mouth is dream-perfect. This guard must have a high view of himself to be so perfectly formed in his dreams.

"Ugh." I frown my disgust at him.

I turn and walk away from the king's chambers.

I had intended to talk to the king, to tell him that Malyn is going to attempt an assassination. But it seems that he already knows that. The king dreams of being poisoned by her. He dreams about being stuck in bed, shriveled, helpless and retching all night.

Warning him is pointless. What he needs is protection.

I feel sick at that thought. Not that I can protect him.

What am I supposed to do? Stab the faceless Malyn until she drops her mirror and stops coming after people?

I don't have that kind of power. I'm just a sleeper who can navigate dreams.

"Wait."

The guard comes trotting up to me. I look around to see if he's still talking to me.

"I thought you wanted me gone," I say.

"I wanted you to stop talking. But you didn't."

I shrug. "Maybe you should have asked nicely."

He grabs my arm. His grip is hard enough to be painful.

"Hey." I jerk out of his grip. "What are you doing?"

"How is it that I can touch you?" He sounds genuinely puzzled.

I frown. It's not impossible for a dreamer to touch me, but it's rare. Silver is the only one who does it regularly.

"Well, you put your meat hooks around my arm and squeezed. I suppose that's how you managed to touch me."

"How are you able to resist my commands?"

I put my hands on my hips. "Are you crazy? Maybe you should just wake up. There's something not right about you."

He stares at me for a tense moment.

"You're not an ordinary dreamer." His voice comes out soft and full of wonder. "You're not a wisp, either."

"What's a wisp?"

"A dream person made by a dreamer."

"A specter?" Now, I'm staring just as intently at him as he is at me. "How do you know about specters?"

I hear his breath catch. He takes a half step back as though afraid he might catch something from me.

"You're like me," he says.

"Believe me, I'm not like anybody."

"You live in the Dreaming. And you can't wake your body." He swallows. "Just like me."

CHAPTER 27

My ears ring. Everything is still as it was a moment ago. The night wind is still blowing outside. And the hallway in front of the Dark King's chambers is still cold. But now, there's a ringing in my ear.

I shake my head like a dog. I must have misunderstood what the guard just said.

"You think you're like me?" I say. The words come out in an awed whisper.

He blinks, as though unable to believe it himself. Then he nods.

For a moment, I reel with the possibility. I'm not alone. There are others—or at least one other—who are like me.

A tightness in my chest loosens at the thought of no longer being alone. No longer abandoned in a wide world full of people who don't even know that I'm here.

Then I come to my senses. I've been fooled over and over again in the Dreaming.

All dreamers fully believe in their dreams. Their dream life, their history, their friends and enemies—they believe in all of it. Their conviction is so strong that it's hard not to fall for it.

Over the years, though, I've learned to be jaded. I've learned to understand that their reality is not mine.

"Not even in your wildest, craziest dreams could you be like me." I poke his chest. "And thank your lucky stars for that, my too-handsome friend. You don't know how fortunate you are."

His chest feels as solid as the stone wall in my tower. I look at my finger, wondering if there is something wrong with it. Even Silver always feels a bit squishy when she hugs me.

I poke him again. His chest feels just as hard as the last time. And his hand felt firm enough to hurt when he grabbed my arm.

We both look up from my finger on his chest and into each other's eyes. His eyes are as dark as mine. As surprised as mine.

"When you wake up, you probably won't even remember me," I mumble.

"What I can't remember is the last time I woke up."

He sounds serious. I have to remind myself yet again that reality is funny in the Dreaming. Every dreamer thinks their dream is real and eternal.

I sigh. I'm not an amateur. I know better than to believe what a dreamer tells me. But I still find it hard to walk away.

"All right." I cross my arms. "Where is your body sleeping?"

"I'll tell you if you tell me where *your* body is sleeping."

Obviously, that's not happening. "What are you doing here? If you're like me, you can go anywhere in the Dreaming. Why stay here to guard a door?"

"I'm not guarding a door. I'm guarding my mistress."

"Who is a patch of skin on the king's cloak?" I feel ridiculous even saying it.

He nods.

I fidget, trying to figure out what questions to even ask.

"Why? Isn't she dead already?" It's a complex question because I did see the glow around some of the patches in the king's cloak.

"Possibly. But not all of her is dead. The king tore a piece of her and captured that piece in his cloak."

"So you protect that piece of…what, her soul?"

He nods.

"What are you protecting it from?"

"Whatever threatens it."

"And what is that right now?"

"Princess Malyn. She covets the Cloak of Souls."

I wrinkle my nose. "Why would anyone want that nasty thing?"

"Because it's a patchwork of powerful fairies. The Dark King doesn't know how to tap into the power that's still there, but the princess does."

"You know what she is?"

"If she kills the king and gets the cloak, everyone in both the kingdoms will know what she is."

"Both kingdoms?"

"Midnight and the fairy kingdom."

I'm realizing that I may have an ally. It makes me uncomfortable to forge a new alliance when I have my own, but the wolfkin and the Midnight Rose have made it clear that they won't help me protect the king.

"Your mistress is a lucky lady to have such a loyal guard." What I wouldn't give to have a guard in my tower as loyal as this soldier.

"I'm not loyal." He sounds like he's talking through clenched jaws. "I'm enslaved."

My brows shoot up. "Enslaved? By a patch of fairy skin?"

"The fairy enslaved me before she was vanquished. But once the king defeated her, I found myself here. I suppose I would have died had he managed to kill her outright."

"So if your patch of fairy skin is destroyed, you'll die too?"

"Perhaps."

"What's the alternative?"

"I might wake up."

I feel the weight of that statement in my chest. It causes a mix of complex emotions to bubble up.

"How long have you been asleep?" I can't think of a delicate way to broach the topic.

"I don't know. Do you know how long it's been since the king collected the patches for his cloak?"

I have a vague concept of how long it's been, but since everyone I used to know is dead, I haven't paid much attention to the happenings of the kingdom for years.

"It's been less than a lifetime...but longer than you might like."

He nods. I can't see his expression behind his helmet, but I imagine he's not happy.

"What happens to you if Princess Malyn gets control of the king's Cloak of Souls?"

"Then I will become her property."

"Her slave," I say.

"Yes. Unlike the king, who does not understand the power he has in his cloak, the princess will be able to command the cloak. And through it—me."

I'm doubly glad I haven't revealed much about myself. Even if I could work with this guard as an ally, he could end up being my enemy at any moment. I'll have to watch myself carefully so as to not give him any information that could lead to him getting me killed.

"I hate fairies," I say. "Maybe we can help each other."

"How?"

"Can you affect anything in the Waking? Can you make someone walk in their sleep? Or maybe scare them so much that their heart stops?"

"I can kill someone with my spear and sword."

"Will they die in the Waking as well?"

"Yes."

"How do you know?"

"Because my mistress forged these weapons specifically so that I could kill her enemies in this manner."

"You're a dream assassin?" I try to sound casual about it, but I don't think it works to keep the awe out of my voice.

"Of course. Aren't you?"

CHAPTER 28

I'm not a dream assassin. But I don't want to tell this stranger that I'm cursed and that my body is lying helpless in a tower somewhere.

"You're not a captive soldier." He sounds breathless, as if he can't believe it. "How are you here? Are you a witch?"

"No. Definitely not a witch." When I can't come up with a better answer, I finally mumble, "I'm cursed."

"To be here, in the Dreaming?"

I nod.

"For how long?"

"Long. Long time."

"And you can't get out?"

I shake my head.

It's technically not true. I can get out into the Waking, but as far as I can tell, I've only managed to do it in my tower. It's possible that I can do it in other places, but I haven't managed it yet. Maybe the tower is special because it was the place I first stepped into the Dreaming.

I'm not about to tell him any of that, though. The less he knows, the better.

He just looks at me with what I have to assume is pity.

"You're stuck here too," I say. "Don't look at me as though you're any better off."

"I'm just surprised."

"There aren't others, are there? No other assassins sneaking around?" I glance around at the torchlit hallway, wondering if I mistook dream assassins for ordinary dreamers.

"You think it's easy to create a dream soldier? If it was, every fairy would have an army of them."

"Why did your mistress even need a dream soldier? Aren't fairies deadly enough without one?"

"I was supposed to be her personal guard to complement her waking-life defenses. Those defenses failed her while she was awake. But I'm still here in the Dreaming."

"So you're doomed to guard the cloak." I'm beginning to grasp the horror of his situation. "And the safest place for it is with the king because he doesn't know how to use it, and he's powerful enough to keep others from getting it."

He nods.

"If Princess Malyn lives, she will end up with the cloak," I say. "Either she'll kill the king or he'll eventually die of old age. The prince isn't going to want a hand-me-down cloak made of the skin of his father's enemies, so he won't care if his wife claims it."

"She won't be easy to assassinate."

"I'll help you," I say.

"Why?"

I can tell by the tone of his voice that this is an important question.

I have a choice. I can either continue my ruse and try to deflect from my true story, or I can tell him the truth.

"Malyn is the one who cursed me."

He's silent for a moment. I brace for more questions. He

seems like the type to interrogate. He won't get more out of me, though. I've already said more than I should. But without Silver and the wolfkin backing me up, I'm out of friends and allies.

"How can you help me?"

He's not digging into details. Maybe this is the way assassins work. You don't dig, I won't dig. I like it.

"I'll distract her. She watches me when I'm nearby. Her creepy dream puppet follows me around." I shiver at the memory.

"Dream puppet?"

"You've seen her, haven't you? She has no face. I don't think that's actually her. It's like she uses a puppet and she's not really here..."

It dawns on me—how can we kill her here if she's not actually here?

I sigh. "I suppose you can't kill her if she's just a puppet, can you?"

"Do you know that it's only a puppet? Everyone sleeps, even fairies."

I shrug, trying not to give away more information than I already have. "She has no face. And she looks out through a broken mirror. It's as though she's peering in from the Waking."

"But she must sleep. Everyone needs rest." He leans against the wall as though getting weary just thinking about it. "Unless..."

"What?"

"Unless it's a spell."

I try not to show concern. It's a good policy to never trust a stranger in the Dreaming. "Of course. Fairies and their spells."

"Spells are not limitless, though. Just as everyone needs to sleep, a waking spell needs a source to draw from."

"A source?" I can't help the concern in my voice. I rack my mind for a new topic to try to distract him, but he's too fast.

"A source. The kind that sleeps." His voice is full of meaning as he watches me.

I do my best to turn my surprise at his sharp deduction into a look of incredulous injustice.

"She's drawing on my sleep to stay awake?" My face heats up with anger, as it does every time I think about it. "That can't be right. It's too powerful."

My misdirection seems to be working because he doesn't seem suspicious.

"The best spells strike a balance," he says. "It's hard to sustain otherwise. Fairies can do it briefly, but it's a constant drain on their powers. How long have you been asleep?"

"Too long. Wait. If what you say is true—which I don't think it is—would that mean that if she dies, that I'll wake up?"

I hadn't thought of that before. I almost tremble with the possibility.

"I don't know. I'm not a sorcerer."

"Can you do it? Kill her?"

"She's stronger than I realized. I'd need to watch her before I could tell if she's vulnerable to an attack."

"Well then, come on."

I turn and walk down the hallway with him following me.

CHAPTER 29

There's an edge of tension in the way the guard moves through the castle corridors. It reminds me that he's a trained killer.

I slow down so we can walk side by side. I don't want him behind me. Not that he couldn't kill me if I could see him, but I'm not entirely defenseless.

I can reshape the dreamscape, at least to a point. I'm still learning, but I'm getting better at it. That could be handy if I suddenly need to protect myself.

Besides, I've been trained by Silver. Her physical training isn't as helpful as it could be, considering the laws of the Waking don't work the same here. But Silver is always saying that the mental training will hone my edge.

The most powerful force in the Dreaming is the power of belief. Silver doesn't even live in the Dreaming, but she knows it better than I do in some ways. She's always encouraging me to try things out, to see what works, to push my limits.

I'm still getting used to the idea, but if I believe my abilities have limitations, then they do. Likewise, if I can convince myself that there are no limitations, then I can do anything, create anything, destroy anything.

That's the theory. I'm still learning. I won't be surprised, though, if I wake long before I ever get near that kind of all-powerful state.

"Can you change your appearance?" I ask. "I don't know if she'll spot us if we're in disguise."

"We have to assume she will."

He didn't answer my question. Is he, perhaps, planning for his inevitable turn to the other side?

I mentally kick myself as a firm reminder that he's not a friend like Silver or the wolfkin. I don't even know him and likely never will.

"Can you change your appearance?" I ask again.

"Can you?"

"Yes." I hate giving him information about myself, but I can't see another way to get him to tell me about himself.

"I can too," he says.

"All right. Can you turn yourself into an ordinary guard? Maybe she won't notice a guard outside her door. I'll be a servant and hope she doesn't notice me."

I know I don't sound confident. Malyn has noticed me before when I appeared in her chamber in that guise.

"How about we travel as birds?" he asks. "Maybe we can peer in through a window without her noticing."

A bird?

All this time in the Dreaming, and I've never tried turning into anything other than another person. When I lived in the Waking, I never had a dream where I was anything other than a person. So it never occurred to me to try to shape myself into an animal.

I reel at the thought. Haven't I made fun of dreamers for appearing so close to their waking selves in their dreams? It probably never occurred to them that they could be beautiful or wealthy or a member of a powerful family in their dreams. Just as it never occurred to me to turn into an animal.

No matter how much I learn, there always seems to be more.

The guard changes into a raven. He's in the air almost before he finishes changing.

I watch him fly out of an arched window into the night sky. It dawns on me that there are no dreamers in sight. If what the guard told me is true, he's no more a dreamer than I am.

That means that he turned into a bird without the aid of a dreamer's imagination. Excitement bursts through me at this revelation. I've always thought that I nudged dreamers into changing my appearance. Could it be that it's *me* who is powering the changes?

I don't want to look like an amateur, so I hurry to change into a bird. With my shift in thinking, I have a hard time believing that I can make the change on my own.

At first, I hop around on one leg with only one wing and an arm still attached to me. When I try to commit, I manage to turn my arm into a second wing.

I flap around, hopping on my one still-human leg. When I finally manage to change that into a skinny bird leg, I end up flying haphazardly into a wall.

Flying into a wall feels exactly as hard as I would have imagined. I reel back drunkenly, trying to regain my breath.

I fly in a zigzag until I somehow manage to fly out of the window.

Outside, the night air is cool against my feathers. The moon is full, as it almost always is here. I'd say that it's full two-thirds of the time and the other third, it's a crescent moon. Funny how people only dream of dramatic times.

I manage to catch up to the raven. Only then do I realize

how tiny I am. I seem to be a little sparrow while he is an oversized, glossy raven.

I follow him as he lands on a branch outside a castle window. Landing is a scary thing and harder than I ever imagined. Who knew how many things have to coordinate in order for a bird to land?

By the time I do it, I'm so flustered that I barely remember why I'm here. The raven, though, is intently watching through a window into the castle. I suppose there was a reason why he was chosen to be an assassin even in an unpredictable place as the Dreaming.

I'm disoriented, and I've been here for most of my life. I bet he used to be an assassin in the Waking too. His intensity and focus is too strong for an ordinary guard.

When I finally adjust to the gently rocking branch, I peer into the window. Now, I see why the guard is so intense.

Malyn is sitting in front of her looking glass. She sits stiff as a statue as she holds her mirror in front of her, but of course, she has no face to look at.

She's so still and absent that it's like she is sleeping. I shiver, my feathers fluffing as they shake.

Just because Malyn isn't moving doesn't mean there isn't movement in the antechamber where she sits. The mirror doesn't show her eye for once. This time, it shows the room.

Well, the reflection shows Malyn's room but it's not the antechamber that's in front of me.

The room in front of me is empty except for her sitting like a statue. There's nobody else in there. Nothing moves, not even a fire in the fireplace.

But in the mirror's reflection, something else is happening. There are people moving about in the room who are only in the mirror.

One of them is Silver.

CHAPTER 30

*I*t's not real.

I mean, it's not the real Dreaming that Malyn's mirror is reflecting. It's the Waking. I'm sure of it.

It's a broken, shattered reflection, but I can see Silver speaking to Malyn. I can't hear what's being said, but I can see her expression. Silver is cautious, polite, formal.

Not surprising, since she's talking with the princess of the Kingdom of Midnight. Why is Silver there? And what are they talking about? Is she all right?

I don't think she's a prisoner. The conversation doesn't seem hostile, just tense. After a while, Silver hands Malyn a vial.

Malyn smiles. She looks smug and satisfied, like a cat who managed to eat the prized bird in the gilded cage. Silver, on the other hand, doesn't look happy but maintains a polite expression.

She bows stiffly and leaves.

Malyn turns sharply, as if sensing that she's being watched. I tense, ready to fly away. But Malyn simply looks out the window.

She looks out her window in the Waking, where we don't exist. I hold my breath, wondering if she'll look in the mirror. I'm pretty sure she'll see us there.

I want to fly away into the cold night. I'm about to open my wings when Malyn holds up her vial. She smiles at it. Then she turns and leaves her chambers.

The mirror shows nothing but an empty room now. I keep expecting the Malyn puppet in the Dreaming to turn and catch us watching, but she doesn't. She continues to sit like a statue while her owner gallivants around in the Waking, using the strength and alertness that should be mine. She doubles her life while I sleep for her.

If I had an arm, I would throw something. It wouldn't be as satisfying as throwing a real item, but it'd be better than nothing.

Thoughts of the Waking inevitably bring up thoughts of me in the tower. I wonder how things are going there. How far has the ogre gone this morning?

The raven guard flies into the night sky, and I follow.

We circle the castle, looking down on the dreamers and their specters. There's a formal ball happening in the Midnight Castle of the Dreaming. Nobles and servants are in their best and shiniest dresses. Bright specks move below us.

In the center stands the dreamer. She's wearing dirty undergarments and seems full of distress as she tries to find a way out. The nobles and even the servants laugh at her, pointing their long, crooked fingers at her.

Why don't people have restful dreams?

We circle back to where we started, and I follow the raven back into the king's hall. As soon as we land, the guard turns back into himself.

He's good. He's obviously more comfortable here than I am. I'm a bit ashamed that I haven't practiced more, but to be fair, I've never needed to be a spy before.

My landing and transformation are rougher than his. I almost crash into the wall after just barely making it through the window. After I land, I stumble about on one leg as I change back into human form, one embarrassing limb at a time.

"What was that about, do you think?" I ask as soon as I manage to change back into me. I brush feathers out of my hair with my fingers.

"Poison." He sounds sure.

I almost say that I know Silver, but I stop myself.

"How do you know?" I say. "It could have been a vial of perfume."

Behind the door, the king retches. He's having a tough night.

The guard looks at me, and I can just imagine his eyebrow arching behind his helmet.

I have to admit, it's looking plausible that Silver is supplying the princess with poison to kill the king.

"Why would Malyn need someone to supply poison?" I ask. "Don't evil royalty come with their own poison?"

He doesn't answer me. Instead, he throws me a look that tells me that I should think before I let words come out of my mouth.

"All right," I say. "Sure, someone has to make the poison." But why Silver? There must be poison makers who can squeeze the juice out of... Then I understand.

Flowers.

Some of Silver's most popular flowers are poisonous. No one can grow flowers like Silver. Maybe Malyn insisted on the freshest flowers for the most potency.

And maybe Silver didn't mind so much, considering that the Midnight Rose decided to back the princess over the king, should it come down to that.

"How do we defend the Dark King against poison?" I ask.

"We don't." The guard sounds awfully calm for someone who's about to become a slave to an evil fairy.

"Then what do we do?" I ask.

"We assassinate her." He takes out his sword and runs his finger along the edge.

"It's a dream sword. There won't be nicks in it unless you put it there."

He looks up at me. It feels good to catch him off guard. I swear he looks a little sheepish, but it's hard to tell behind that face-shielding helmet.

He slides his sword back into his scabbard.

"Was that habit from your Waking days?" I ask, curious as to what kind of life he led.

"What do you know about that looking glass?" he asks.

"Has anyone ever told you that you rarely answer questions?"

He doesn't answer.

I sigh dramatically. "She looks out through that mirror. She can see me, but I don't think she's here in the Dreaming. I think she's looking at me from the Waking."

He thinks about that for a moment. The full moon shines bright, highlighting his broad shoulders. He looks like a warrior of old. My father used to have a tapestry of ancient warriors in his dining hall, and I swear they looked like this guard.

"Do you think that if I threw my spear at her through the mirror, it would hit her in the Waking?" he asks.

I can almost see it. This guard would throw it with power, almost one with the spear until it left his hand. It would shoot in a perfect arc through one of the shards in the mirror...

I can't picture what would happen after that.

"I don't know," I say with a frown. "Do you think you can do it?"

"I can try." He sounds doubtful.

I nod and put on a bright smile. "I have an idea."

It's not a great idea, but sometimes, you just have to go with what you've got.

CHAPTER 31

We head toward Malyn's part of the castle. This time, we walk in our human form. It's faster to fly there as birds, but I'm not confident about my landing and transformation enough to risk it in enemy territory.

"So if I'm going to trust you to save me while I run screaming away from a faceless evil fairy," I say, "don't you think I should know your name?"

"I'll hear your screams. No need to call me by name."

I can't tell if he's joking. "Well, I'm Briar. Can you take your helmet off so that I can see you? I think you just spoke in jest, but it's hard for me to imagine you having a sense of humor. I'll have to see it to believe it."

"No."

"No, you won't take your helmet off? Or your name is No?"

"You can call me Sentry."

"Sentry. Really? Do you know how many people in the castle would answer to 'Sentry'?"

"Doesn't matter."

"Why not?"

"Because if you're calling me, I'll be the one smashing your attacker. There won't be any confusion as to which one I am."

I like the image. I haven't had a personal guard since I fell asleep under the curse. Of course, I know he's not *my* guard, but even jokingly hearing that I *might* have a protector makes me feel a little better.

"You're just saying that to convince me to stick with the plan," I say.

"Perhaps."

"Can't you at least leave me with my heroic fantasy of playing my role in all this without actually getting harmed?"

"You can dream about safety all you want after today."

We're more than halfway through the castle. The dreamer who dreamt the masquerade has moved on to other nightmares. There are still a few guests of the grand ball wandering around in the walkways. By their wispiness, I can tell they're specters who are about to be forgotten.

"What do I do if you can't kill her?" I ask.

"Run faster."

I look sidelong at him. He does have a sense of humor. But it's a bad one.

We near Malyn's chambers. There's a small alcove lit by two torches on either side of it. Sentry snuffs out a torch, then the other. He slips into the shadow of the alcove and leans his spear against the wall.

"Make sure she's close when you run past me." He draws his sword and flattens his back against the stone wall. "I won't be able to see how far behind she is. If she's too far away, she'll see me and have time to prepare."

"You said nothing could survive an attack with your sword. What does it matter if she sees you?"

"That's soldier talk before a battle, Briar. Have you never been around soldiers before?"

The wolfkin and the Order of the Midnight Rose are the closest to soldiers that I've been in my life. They're pretty fierce, but my part of the mission is usually solo. I take care of the Dreaming while they take care of the problems of the Waking.

This is the first time I've had a mission where I wasn't by myself. Soldier talk, huh?

"I'm going to run circles around her." I take a deep breath. "Maybe I'll bash her faceless dummy body myself and kick her into her broken mirror."

He just gives me a disparaging look. He doesn't look at all impressed, nor does he look at me like his partner in crime.

"Never mind," I say quietly. "Just nerves."

He jerks his head toward Malyn's chambers.

I take another deep breath, wondering what would happen to my body if I died in the Dreaming. My head wants to split just thinking about it.

I glance one last time at him. Sentry looks confident and ready. Every muscle is tensed as he holds his sword back, ready to chop someone's head off. I just hope it's not mine.

I move toward Malyn's doors. Those doors never looked this menacing when it was my mother's room. Now, *she* was a good queen—gentle and kind. I hate the thought of Malyn having her chamber.

I slam through the door without knocking.

The room is a twilight version of my mother's old antechamber. Malyn's puppet sits at her vanity with her back to me. She looks like a statue in front of the empty frame where the vanity mirror should be.

The hand mirror shows Malyn holding a dress up to herself in her chamber in the Waking.

"I know who you are," I say.

The cracked glass shows Malyn in the Waking turning to look at the mirror.

"I know *what* you are," I say. "And I'm going to tell the world about you before you can kill the Dark King."

Malyn walks to her looking glass and peers through it at me.

Her dream puppet gets up stiffly and turns toward me as if she's used to the habit of looking even though she has no eyes. I wonder if she's used to talking even though she has no mouth.

I spin and run.

Glancing back, I see that the faceless puppet is moving faster than I thought she could. She holds the mirror before her like a candle in the dark. She seems to be using it as her eyes.

I almost trip on my own feet as I watch her come after me. There's something about her faceless body that disturbs me all the way to my core. They say you can see a person's soul through their eyes, but that's for people with souls. I know without a doubt that this thing has none.

I race down the hall, remembering to slow down just before I reach the alcove. I pretend to stumble again. That slows me enough for her to almost reach me.

She's so close that I feel her nails rake through my hair.

Then I'm past the alcove.

I hear a grunt. Then a thud.

I look back, then stop.

The Malyn puppet stands in the hallway holding her cracked looking glass. Her head rolls on the floor.

There is no blood. Malyn's nightmare puppet stays standing for a moment. I expect her to topple without her head, but she doesn't.

The headless body pulls back her mirror and swings it at Sentry.

Sentry ducks.

Dropping his sword, he spins and grabs his spear.

Malyn's bloodless, headless body raises the mirror again and swings at Sentry. As she swings, I catch a glimpse of Malyn's ice-blue eye watching through a shard.

With both hands gripping his spear, Sentry stabs into the mirror.

CHAPTER 32

The mirror shatters.

A thousand shards explode in all directions.

I duck and cover my face with my arms. A shower of shards fly toward me. I brace to be hit, but at the same time, I instinctively envision an invisible umbrella to protect me.

I have no expectation of it working until I realize that I'm not getting cut to bits. I can't believe it actually works. A few shards get through, but the bulk of them miss me.

By the time I look up, the glass shards are being sucked back into the gilded frame.

So is Sentry.

The nightmare Malyn puppet is still on her feet, headless and holding the frame in front of her, mirror-side out. Sentry leaned in as he speared into the glass, putting all his weight into it. Now, he can't pull back.

His muscles strain to pull away from the looking glass, but his feet slide forward.

I try to project my umbrella shield in front of him. But it's too late.

The spear jerks into the gilded frame as though someone is yanking on it. Sentry flies into the mirror with his spear.

"Sentry!" My cry is too late. He isn't in the hallway anymore.

The remaining shards fly into the golden frame and the mirror pieces itself back together.

There are more cracks in it now, but it holds its shape. The shards are still large enough for me to see the reflections of the Waking.

The looking glass shows Sentry crashing onto the floor on the other side. Malyn's silver slipper steps up to him.

I don't see much after that because the headless Malyn puppet raises her looking glass in an arc and aims it right at me.

I turn and run.

I make it to the corner and turn to see how close she is. She's still at the alcove. She gropes around blindly until she finds her head. Then she puts it on top of her severed neck.

The head is sideways and her blank face is turned toward me. Then she turns the head into place and screws it back on.

I run down the narrow stairs. No need to wait to see if the puppet's head sticks on.

I hear her footsteps behind me.

The stairs are narrow and uneven, so I can't run very fast. I could try to change it to something easier to run on, but the castle is a place that has been built by generations of dreamers. Thousands of people have reinforced the architecture and agreed on what the place is like.

I can't just change that, especially while I'm running for my life. Why couldn't Malyn's puppet be in a cottage on the outskirts of the village where no one visits? I may have been able to change a place like that.

I wish I could just disappear and reappear elsewhere. Maybe one day I could—it's on my list of things to try.

Instead, I have to run out of this dream and either into another dream or to my tower.

The last thing I want to do is to lead Nightmare Malyn into my tower. Having her see it the last time I did that was bad enough. This time, she might be able to come through with me.

I race out of the castle.

Luckily, I don't need to get out of the castle proper. There are parts of the castle that sit on the ragged edge of the dream island. I can simply walk right through the wispy wall in those places and end up in the dark place between islands.

As I run out, I turn to see if she can see me.

Around the curve of the stairs, Malyn's hand sticks out, holding the mirror. Her vicious eye looks right at me through one of the shards.

Beside her eye, several of the pieces show a dark-haired man on the ground. He's bleeding from his forehead, blood streaking down his face. Beside him is Sentry's helmet, empty and rolling on the floor.

He scrabbles back away from something. Something big.

I leap out of the castle and into the dark.

CHAPTER 33

I run through the dark, scared to go to my tower until I'm absolutely sure that Nightmare Malyn won't follow me.

In my panic, I scan the nearby dream islands as I run, hoping to see a way to lose the puppet. One of the islands is in sunshine while the rest are in either twilight or full night.

It's Silver's cottage, sitting in sunlight like a nugget of gold.

I run there. Silver will know what to do. If she's there, that is. A place can be dreamt by anybody.

Before I step into her yard, I take a quick look behind me. Once I'm inside a dream, I can't see outside of it unless I poke my head out. Hopefully, the creepy faceless puppet is stuck in the castle, trying to figure out how I left.

I don't see her, so I step into Silver's dream.

The warmth of the sunshine instantly melts my panic. It feels so real that I'm sure this must be Silver's dream. She has a way of remembering the true reality of good things.

Her garden is full of flowers. Some are exotic while others are the ordinary flowers that used to grow like weeds back when I was a little girl. Now, I hear that those flowers have died out. Some people say it's due to lack of sunshine, while others blame the Dark King.

Silver's yard is full of color. Bright dahlias, orchids, tulips and roses all grow side by side in her yard. I sometimes wonder if that's just her dream of how her yard could be or if she really does have a cottage full of flowers. I'd give anything to find out for myself one day.

Silver kneels on a mat in the soil, planting new flowers. She doesn't seem to notice me.

That's unusual. Silver is the most keenly aware person I know. She must be deep in her dream.

"Silver," I say, panting. "Malyn just kidnapped my friend. I think she pulled him into the Waking."

She pauses and continues to stare at her flower.

"Silver?" I take a step closer, expecting her to get up and give me a hug like she always does when we're alone.

She looks up at me.

She is faceless.

There are two dents where her eyes should be. There's a small bump where her nose should be. She is missing her ears and mouth. There aren't even holes in her nose. Her entire face is skin.

She gets up and takes a step toward me.

I stagger back, unable to stop staring at her, yet not wanting to see her blank face at all.

I spin and run back into the darkness.

CHAPTER 34

T run into my tower. My knees are shaky, I'm drenched in sweat and I feel gutted.

The girl on the bed sleeps peacefully as though mocking me. Her breath is coming a little faster than usual and she has beads of sweat on her brow, but otherwise looks normal.

"Do something!" I want to kick the girl on the bed. "Wake up! Don't just lie there, being useless."

I try to rattle the bed but my hands just pass right through it. I try to yell something more, but what comes out is a broken sob.

I break down and crumple beside the bed, bent double with my sobs.

"Stop yelling at my princess," says the ogre from the courtyard. He sounds angry.

Having someone listen to me cry is like cold water on my face. I'm so used to being alone here that it's a little disturbing to know that another living creature shares my keep. Oddly, it's a little comforting too.

"She's not your princess," I say. An ogre is not my first

choice of company, but I could use a little distraction right now.

"She's not yours, either," says the ogre.

"I'm afraid you might be right." I sigh.

"Get used to it."

"Used to what?"

"Me being right."

I pick myself up and move to the window to peer down at him. There's a tremor to my hands, and I'm sure my face is red and streaked with tears. I take a deep breath and try to calm down.

The ogre has made some progress toward my tower, but otherwise looks the same as before. He's almost buried in thorns. There are so many rivulets of blood streaming over him that his head looks like a grim holiday ornament.

"I don't think you should be bragging about your superior thinking," I say, wiping my nose. "You're wading through a sea of thorns. That's not exactly the best decision making, you know."

"Aren't you supposed to be taking care of the princess?" He pauses in his efforts and looks up at me.

He's hard to look at. Even without the blood streaming over his face, he must be the ugliest ogre in the forest.

"What makes you think I'm here to take care of her?" I ask.

"Why else would you be paired with her? You take care of her and she takes care of you."

"She's not doing anything right now."

"She will. As soon I kiss her awake." He resumes his painful push toward my tower.

"Doesn't that hurt? Don't you care that you're going to die by a million cuts and stabs?"

"I care deeply." He swipes his stick and pushes his way

one step further into the brambles. "That's why I'm annoyed and grouchy." He glances up at me. "What's your excuse?"

"First of all, I'm not grouchy. Secondly, if I was, I'd have good reason. My friends are being snatched by an evil fairy."

"The same fairy that you told me about?"

I'm surprised that he remembers. I've never heard of ogres having much of a memory or holding a conversation. "Yes. The same one."

"What are you going to do about it besides crying in your tower?" He hacks at a branch, causing thorns to spray.

"What can I do?"

"Only you know that. What *can* you do?"

I know how Silver would answer. She'd say that I can do more than I think. She'd say that I am the master of the Dreaming and can make miracles happen.

I take a deep breath, feeling stronger. "Thank you."

"For what?" He swings his stick mightily, chopping off another branch and getting sprayed with thorns for his trouble.

"For talking to me."

"Anytime." He must have lost his patience because he roars and charges into the thorns.

I can't look anymore. Besides, talking to the ogre was just what I needed to regain my courage.

No more cowering in my tower. I need to get back into the Dreaming and see if there's anything I can do to help my friends.

CHAPTER 35

*E*verywhere I go, there are faceless people. The tavern, the village market, the chapel—at least one out of five are faceless.

It takes visiting three dream islands before I realize that the specters still have faces, but many of the dreamers don't. The specters' faces are uniformly bland and their stares are more vacant than ever, but at least they have eyes. They're not talking with each other, though, which is odd.

Usually, specters have their own lives during a dream. They talk with each other, they fight, they probably even fall in love. When a dreamer visits, the specters are fully alive with their own independent lives.

But something is missing today. They walk around lifeless, bumping into each other, standing and facing the corner, sitting and staring out to nowhere.

The faceless dreamers wander around aimlessly. It's as though they know something is missing but don't know what or how to look for it.

I constantly look behind me. It feels like I'm being

followed, but with this many faceless dreamers, I'm not even sure who is my enemy and who is not.

What is happening?

I rack my mind for possibilities. Is there some strange disease that's spreading among the dreamers and it's affecting their dreams? Did Malyn cast a spell over dreamers? For what purpose?

No matter where I wander and what strange possibilities I come up with, I can't escape the coincidental timing of Sentry being sucked out of the Dreaming and so many dreamers of the realm becoming faceless.

But what possible connection could there be?

I step out of the twilight market where far too many faceless dreamers roam. It feels like they are homing in on me. That could just be paranoia, but I swear they turn their blank faces to me when I'm near.

I could also swear that they drift toward me as if they all have orders to "look" for me. I can't tell for sure because I don't stay long enough to find out.

I run from dream island to dream island until I'm sure no one is following me. Then I head into the darkness.

My plan is to go back to my tower and think. That seems to be my fallback whenever I'm in trouble. It's a dangerous one, since my body is so vulnerable. For all I know, someone following me could recognize something out the tower window and know where my keep is.

I'm tempted to visit Silver again. Maybe that wasn't her. Maybe she's awake and Malyn inserted an impostor Silver.

I wander around in the dark. There's one other place I could go to, but I'm afraid to go there. If I find the wolfkin faceless too...

Breathe.

Calm down.

The wolfkin aren't normal dreamers. They're considered

monsters in the Waking and they sometimes manifest as monsters in their dreams too. They're too strong to fall under a fairy spell...I hope.

The thought of them being faceless and lifeless makes me feel trapped and helpless. Silver and the wolfkin are my only true contacts with the outside world. They're not just dreamers, they're aware of me as a living being who happens to visit them in their dreams.

How can the Dreaming be so enormous and yet feel like a coffin at the same time?

I rush past island after island until I find the wolfkin den. It's a mansion in the forest. They're my last hope of helping Sentry and figuring out what's happening.

I step into the mansion grounds from the darkness. The full moon beams down, bright enough for me to see everything the way I can in daylight. It's beautiful in the same haunting way that my tower is beautiful.

The mansion is another place where enough people have dreamt it so that the details are stable. It's overgrown, and the forest is always on the verge of taking it over. It's empty, though.

There's no one in the howler yard where the Dark King's experimental subjects are normally chained. There's no one in the flower garden where Silver often comes to replenish her flower supply. I hear nothing but the sound of the breeze rustling the branches.

I drift up the steps to the front doors. They are grand and ornate, obviously carved by a master craftsman. Like everything else at the mansion, the doors are exquisite.

They're also ajar.

Now, if there's one thing I can say about the wolfkin it's that they take their security seriously. It has something to do with protecting the pack and defending their den. I'm pretty sure men have those instincts too, but it's pronounced in the wolfkin. The doors would either be wide open or shut tight, never ajar.

I push the door open slowly, not sure what to expect. It's been a pretty rough day so far, so I'm not expecting anything good.

Sure enough, a bloodied wolfkin growls at me from the shadows. I freeze, trying to figure out if it is someone I know.

When a wolfkin is in wolf form, he's much larger than a natural wolf. A wolfkin is like a wolf in the same way a wolf is like a dog—that is to say, they're clearly in the same family, but there's a world of difference between them.

Mostly, I gauge the difference by my instinctive reaction. I'm fairly relaxed around a dog, but around a wolfkin in wolf form, I have to fight my instincts to run as far away as I can. That happens even with wolfkin I know.

And this is no exception. I know I can't outrun a wolfkin, even in dreams. They're creatures who are predators right down to their claws, and they know it even in their dreams.

The wolfkin steps out of the shadows.

His mouth is stained and dripping with blood. The moonlight above shows his white coat splattered in more blood.

I take a step back, my heart pounding in my ears.

"Ketter?" My voice comes out in a squeak.

He growls as he stalks toward me.

CHAPTER 36

*T*here are dark shapes lying on the floor and stairs around Ketter as he takes another step toward me. They're so still that it's easy to mistake them for shadows. But these shadows are in the shapes of wolves. Wolves lying as still as stones in all sorts of unnatural angles.

I take another step back. Can I make it out of this nightmare before Ketter rips out my throat?

"What happened?" My mouth is so dry that I'm surprised I can get the words out.

Moonlight streaming in from the ceiling windows hits Ketter full in the face. He's bloodied, but I'm relieved to see that he has a face.

Ketter snarls but stops stalking me. I take courage from that.

He may be dreaming in wolf form. Usually, I can only access people dreams, so I'm not used to seeing any of the wolfkin in their animal form. I suppose everything in the Dreaming is strange right now, so I shouldn't be surprised.

"Did you...kill them?" I ask.

Ketter growls loudly, wrinkling his snout and baring his

enormous fangs that couldn't possibly be that lethal in the Waking.

I put my hand out in a peace gesture. "Of course you didn't. Sorry. Who attacked the den?"

He stops growling and hangs his head. It looks like all the fight drains out of him.

"Look, it's all right, Ketter."

Ketter snaps his head up, looking like he's ready to tear into me.

"It's a dream. You're having a bad dream. Your pack is all right, probably all sleeping in a pile in the garden, dreaming of chasing giant rabbits. You're just in the wrong place, that's all."

Ketter paces agitatedly. He paces to one wolf body after the other. Only now do I see how many of them there are. It must be his entire pack. He's dreaming of being the last survivor.

Some people might consider it good to survive a massacre, but to a wolfkin, it's probably their worst nightmare. A wolfkin needs to be with his pack, dead or alive.

"It's all right." I keep my voice gentle and soothing. "Ketter, can you turn into a man? We can talk then. I need your help."

Ketter sighs as though he's breathing out his last energy. He walks toward me.

I back away, not sure what he's doing.

He walks past me, out the door, and lies down at the top of the steps overlooking the garden. He moves as though all the fight has been drained out of him.

If I didn't know better, I'd say he was depressed. Do wolves get depressed?

"Ketter, can you change? We need to talk."

I have an eerie thought. What if him changing into a man makes him become like the other faceless dreamers?

"Wait," I say.

He lies there, just looking at me.

"Maybe you should stay in animal form. Look, strange things are happening around here."

The words come tumbling out—faceless Malyn, her broken mirror, the guard, and the now-faceless dreamers. By the time I finish telling him about my day, I'm the one who wants to lie down and stare depressively at the garden.

"So I think it may be best for you to stay in wolf form. Do you think it's possible…" I trail off, not wanting to bring up the possibility that the rest of his pack might have been dreaming in human form. Who knows what can happen to a sleeping wolfkin when a spell is cast on dreamers?

Whatever is happening, I'm sure that it won't help for me to bring up the possibility that his pack might be dead. He's already living that nightmare.

"Something happened here after my friend Sentry got pulled through Malyn's mirror. Can you see if you can find him in the Waking?"

Ketter tilts his head.

"I'm serious. Whatever is happening here might have something to do with him. He got sucked out of the Dreaming, then faceless dreamers started showing up and following me around. I swear they see me, even though they don't have eyes. Malyn is up to something."

I can't shake the feeling that this has to do with me. Why do those faceless dreamers sense me close by? Why do they gather around me?

The dreamers always had a glow around them. They gave off a sense that they were alive while the others were mere specters.

Malyn took that away from the dreamers and more. They're now blind and voiceless, airless and unidentifiable. They've had their souls stolen.

I shiver in the warm night.

"Can you rescue Sentry?"

Ketter chuffs.

"You've managed this sort of thing before."

Ketter chuffs again.

I sigh. "Can you at least find him? Let me know if he's alive?"

I pace in front of the doors, trying not to see the bodies of wolfkin lying in the foyer. I try to make sense of it all, but it's all jumbled in my head.

I glance into the foyer at the shadowy lumps lying on the floor.

"Find out if Sentry is alive if you can, Ketter. I'll see what I can do on my end."

Ketter makes a noise that I take as agreement.

"Also, can you check in on Silver?"

He sits up, alert. Silver is essentially an honorary member of his pack.

"She's one of the faceless dreamers."

Ketter gets up and walks down the steps.

"And tell your pack mates to sleep in wolf form until we figure out what this is. I think their chances of being safe are better if they're not dreaming as a person."

I'm not sure if Ketter heard me. He keeps loping out of the mansion grounds. I watch him go out through the gates and disappear into the woods.

I try not to fret over how much of this he'll remember. I never have control over that and often don't even find out if dreamers remember anything at all until someone tells me.

Once Ketter is gone, I feel my neck prickle with the knowledge of dead wolfkin at my back. Their stillness and the unnatural angles of their necks and legs give me the creeps. I follow Ketter in a rush out of the mansion grounds.

CHAPTER 37

J don't want to go back to my tower. I also don't want to go back to Malyn's chamber either, but I do.

The way I figure it, the fairy magic is in that looking glass. Sentry went into it. And I hate to even think about it, but I'm guessing the only way for him to come back is through that mirror again. Of course, I could be wrong.

He could simply fall asleep like any other dreamer and come into the Dreaming that way. But there's too good of a chance that he might become faceless and soulless like the other dreamers. I don't want that for him.

There is the nagging problem that he *wanted* to leave the Dreaming. If I manage to miraculously bring him back, he'll be stuck here again.

And if my guess is right, whatever evil magic Malyn is doing in the Waking would suddenly be missing a key ingredient.

Sorry, Sentry. I know you want to get back to your life in the Waking. I don't blame you. I do too. But you being yanked through those broken shards into Malyn's chambers is like me being woken up by an ogre prince. It's not the way either of us want to enter the Waking.

I sit perched on a branch as a little bird outside Malyn's window. There's only a single candle lit in her chamber, and it reflects fractured light off the broken mirror.

Does the Malyn puppet just sit there holding the looking glass all day? From what I can tell, that's exactly what she does. The only times I've seen her moving is when she's coming after me.

How am I supposed to get to the mirror if she never leaves it?

I sit on the branch and watch her for hours. Not only does she not move, no one comes into her chamber. Nobody is dreaming of her. And by the looks of the still castle, no one is dreaming of being in the castle either.

If the dreamers weren't so creepy right now, the natural thing for me to do would be to nudge a dreamer into distracting Malyn. But the castle is eerily quiet, so I simply sit and watch.

Over time, I finally notice that the motion in the glass shards aren't just the reflections of the flickering candle. All this time, I dismissed the tiny motions in the shards as flickering shadows, but the more I look at it, the more I see that the pieces have life in them.

I'm in my sparrow form, and apparently, sparrows don't have eyes that are better than my usual ones. I open my wings and fly off the branch. I climb high into the night sky where nobody can see me.

There, I slowly grow my wings as well as the rest of me. Since I'm new to this, I change slowly, almost imperceptibly. The last thing I need is to fall out of the sky.

I change into a hawk. We'll see if hawks can live up to their reputation of having excellent eyesight.

I know that if I can make myself believe that sparrows

have excellent eyesight, I wouldn't need to change into a hawk. But it's far easier to go with my established beliefs than to try to convince myself of something new. Sometimes, my mind just won't stretch that way.

Besides, one of these days, I'll reach my limit of what I can do in the Dreaming. I'm not eager to see what that is. I know—it's cowardly to resist doing something just because I don't want to learn my limitations. But that kind of behavior is a nice reminder that I am still human.

A human who can change forms like an all-powerful magician. Midair, no less.

While pondering the philosophical aspects of my powers, I think I've succeeded in changing into a hawk. Of course, I won't know unless I see a reflection of myself. For all I know, I could look like a sparrow with the head of a hawk. But I don't have the luxury of worrying about that right now.

I fly down to my branch outside Malyn's window. Unsurprisingly, she's still sitting at her vanity, holding her mirror as though she's looking into it.

With my new eyes, I can see the reflections in each shard. Luckily, her eyes aren't peering out at me in any of them.

There are too many shards to look at all at once, so I have to look at them one at a time. In one, there is a perfectly red apple. That both confuses and comforts me. It's such a mundane thing to see in an evil mirror.

In another shard, the Dark King sits at the head of a banquet table. He's wearing his Cloak of Souls and looking like he's heading to battle instead of heading a royal banquet.

In the third shard is Malyn herself. I'm not sure which is more disturbing—seeing her without a face, or seeing her with a sweet, innocent one. She's also sitting at a banquet table, and I have to assume it's at the same banquet headed by the Dark King.

There are noblemen sitting around her. All of them fawn over her. All but the crown prince.

The prince sits beside her, stiff as a servant in his royal finery and his circlet crown. He eats his meal mechanically, never making eye contact with anyone.

In his own way, he reminds me of a dreamer. I'm not sure which is more disturbing—seeing a dreamer without a face, or seeing the heir to the kingdom with a face that looks lifeless.

Everyone around Malyn is talking animatedly. Malyn herself seems pleased. She glances surreptitiously at someone outside my view. I wonder if she's glancing at the king.

What devious misdeed does she have planned? Is she about to poison the Dark King? He knows it's coming, or at least has been worried over the possibility, since he's been dreaming about it.

A motion catches my eye elsewhere in the mirror.

The king staggers up out of his banquet chair. His eyes are wide and bulging. He gasps for air as his face turns red.

He claws at his throat then lurches into the servants, who rush in to try to help.

Chairs and goblets tumble to the floor. People step away from the staggering king, as though afraid to be blamed for whatever is happening.

The king tumbles forward onto the banquet table, gripping the table cloth like a drowning man. He sweeps silver dishes piled with food, gold utensils and jewel-studded goblets off the table.

His eyes gloss over. It looks like he's fading inside.

He slowly slides down the table and slumps onto the floor.

The nobles and servants all stare in shock. A stunned hush comes over the crowd.

In a separate shard, I can see Malyn watching the king from her end of the banquet table. The men who had been competing for her attention only a moment ago are now all staring in horror down the table.

Malyn is having trouble keeping a smile off her face. She doesn't even seem to be trying that hard. She picks up her jewel-encrusted goblet and takes a sip, managing to almost hide her smile.

The crown prince stares blankly beside Malyn. When he finally moves, he scoops another mouthful of pudding into his slack mouth.

CHAPTER 38

I'm breathing quickly and shallowly, even for a bird. My battle is lost. The evil fairy who cursed me will become the queen of the kingdom.

I can't even fathom the horrors she'll inflict on the people. Not to mention that she'll be able to send an army to search for my tower.

My head is feeling light with all the ramifications of what occurred tonight. I don't know what being a frantic bird does to my sleeping body in the tower. So I force myself to slow my breathing to give my human body a rest.

I need to think without feeling so lightheaded that I risk falling off my branch. I try to focus on something other than Malyn's murder of the Dark King, just for a moment's respite to calm myself.

And that's when another shard catches my eye in the looking glass.

There, water splashes on a prisoner's face. The prisoner is in a guard's uniform.

He's being propped up by rough hands while someone throws water on him. The prisoner looks exhausted and desperate for sleep. His eyelids keep closing even though the men shake him.

They splash more water on him. He startles awake.

A guard's helmet lies beside the prisoner. The face shield of the helmet is ornate and familiar.

It's Sentry. It has to be.

How long has he been in the Waking? Has it really been long enough for him to look that tired? Or are they just having trouble waking him?

If they let him fall asleep, will he come back into the Dreaming?

I take a deep breath, trying to think straight.

I could go to the wolfkin and see if they can help him. I can't tell where he is, though.

As I have that thought, I catch sight of fur in one of the other mirror shards. A pack of wolfkin in wolf form sniff the air at the edge of the forest. In front of them is Midnight Castle. The moon rises in the background, giving the castle an eerie glow.

As though sensing drama happening inside, the wolves pause in silence with their ears perked and their snouts in the air. Did they hear the screams? Smell the poison? The castle must be churning with activity.

The wolfkin turn and disappear back into the shadows of the forest.

So much for their help.

In the mirror, the king lies on the floor among spilled platters of fish and fowl and spreading pools of wine. Even though his eyes are open, it's obvious that there's no one there anymore. They are blank and staring into nothingness.

I rack my mind for something I can do. If the king is dead, the prince will take the crown. But that doesn't bring me any comfort. One look at the prince makes it clear that it'll really be the new queen who will rule the kingdom.

The soon-to-be Queen Malyn takes another sip of her wine while everyone else stares in shock at the dead king.

It occurs to me that no matter what, Malyn will be busy for at least an hour or more. I don't know what happens when a king dies, but whatever happens next will require attention from the remaining royal family members. She can't simply get up and retire to her room at a time like this.

I have at least an hour where Malyn is not paying attention to her mirror or her nightmare puppet. Could there be something I can do to help my friends or Sentry? Can I help the dreamers?

When Malyn is busy and away from her looking glass, I wonder if her puppet in the Dreaming becomes unaware.

I test it out by flying back and forth in front of the window. It would be hard not to notice me, even for a puppet.

When the faceless Malyn doesn't move, and no pair of eyes appear in the mirror, I make a shriek loud enough to wake the dead.

Nothing. No reaction from the nightmare puppet. Even better, the Malyn in the Waking doesn't look at me through the mirror either.

If there's anything I can do to help any of the people I care about, this may be my only window of time to find out.

I gather my courage and spread my wings. Then I fly through the window into Malyn's chambers.

CHAPTER 39

I'm careful not to land too far into the room. It shouldn't be hard to fly right back out should the nightmare puppet try to grab me.

But the faceless Malyn doesn't move, just as I suspected. She sits like the lifeless puppet that she is.

I think about changing back into my girl form, but decide I'm better off being able to fly out of here if need be.

I hop carefully toward nightmare Malyn. One small hop after another. She doesn't react.

I get bold and begin cooking up a plan for turning back into human form, then reaching into the mirror and pulling Sentry out. It's a vague plan, but if Malyn can pull Sentry into the mirror, maybe I can pull him out of it.

I hop around on bird legs, looking for a rope or something that I can use to pull Sentry out. I'm not used to such an expansive view of the floor. I'm so small that the room looks enormous, and it takes me a moment to adjust perspectives.

Fast as a striking snake, nightmare Malyn shoots her arm toward me.

Before I can comprehend what is happening, my left wing jerks away from me, and I'm dangling from her hand. I thrash and flap like crazy, pecking her with my powerful beak. She seems not to notice.

I swear that she looked like a statue even as she grabbed me. Her arm was the only thing that moved.

Now, she's fully animated.

Nightmare Malyn cruelly grips tightly to my left wing, dragging me like a rat she's caught by the tail. My wing joint feels like it's going to rip. The more I thrash, the more painful it becomes.

I can't believe how fast she moved. I've seen her run, so I thought I knew her speed, but I didn't count on her reflexes being lightning fast.

She puts her mirror down on the vanity. This is the first time I've seen her put down that mirror. She caught me one-handed without even needing to free her other hand.

But now, apparently, she needs both hands. Despite the pain, I thrash harder.

My instincts are to make a lot of noise, but I clamp my beak down unless I'm biting her. I'm scared to make noise in case the real Malyn notices what's happening in the Dreaming.

Nightmare Malyn walks me to a shelf. It's a shelf full of platters covered in glass domes, like the kind that might hold cakes and pies.

Instead of cakes, though, the platters hold rats. Most have one rat on a platter, but a few hold two rats. Could she be so fast as to catch two rats at one time?

Most of the rats are alive and active. A couple of them look dead, though, and I have to wonder what she's doing with them.

She dumps me on a platter. Before I can leap off, she traps me under a glass dome.

The dome might be all right for rats, but it's not all right for a hawk. I barely fit. There's no room for me to spread my wings.

I'm about to thrash when Nightmare Malyn turns away to go back to her vanity. I make myself go still.

I may be too big for this trap. I might be able to thrash enough to push the glass dome off the shelf and hopefully fly away. But with Nightmare Malyn's reflex speed, I need her as far away from me as possible when I do it.

She sits in front of her vanity again and picks up the mirror to her blank face. She goes back to being so still that I would have assumed she was a sewing dummy if I hadn't just been caught by her.

CHAPTER 40

 have to admit, I have a better view of the mirror from under my glass dome than I did outside the window. With my hawk eyes, I can see everything it reflects.

One of the shards shows Malyn standing over the dead king while the prince continues to eat his meal. The other nobles look too afraid to say anything as they stare.

Malyn has taken charge of the castle.

She directs servants and nobles alike. I can't hear what she's saying, but it's clear that she's giving commands. The nobles jump to do anything she says, even if it's to wipe the floor of the spilled food and wine from around the fallen king.

In another shard of the mirror, Sentry is being beaten by a brute of a man.

Every hit makes me flinch, but Sentry hardly seems to notice. His eyes are barely open and his jaw is slack.

At first, I think they're beating him senseless. Then I wonder if maybe they're trying to beat him into awareness. He might be falling asleep.

My heart thumps in my little feathered chest at the

thought of Sentry being able to come back into the Dreaming. Will he come back faceless? And what will happen to his body while he's gone?

I flinch again when another fist hits Sentry. He's going to have serious bruises.

I look at Sentry's surroundings, hoping to get a better idea of where he's being held. There's a stone wall with a torch mounted on it. That doesn't mean much, but I'm guessing he's in the castle somewhere.

The bruiser who was hitting Sentry drops him on the ground. My view changes so that it follows Sentry as he lies slumped against carved stone.

Curious—the stone isn't the typical pieces of a wall. It's carved in straight lines and swirls. It dips and protrudes into a design that I can't see fully. And is that dirt I see at the edge of the mirror?

Two pairs of meaty hands grab Sentry beneath his arms and pull him up. The view through the shard stays with Sentry's face, showing me what's behind him.

It's a crypt.

They're inside a crypt. There's one below the castle on the other side of the dungeons.

A face is carved in the wall behind Sentry. It's the chiseled face of an angel. Maybe it's the angel of death, because it seems to have no mercy as it looks down at the men.

The angel's face seems vaguely familiar and I realize that it looks like Sentry. There's a resemblance in the stone features that makes me think that this could be his family's crypt.

I'm too far away to see the names. I wonder which family it is. Only the wealthiest of nobles have crypts. Everyone else simply gets buried in the dirt alongside the road or maybe burned to ashes.

I tear my eyes away from Sentry when I hear a woman's

voice. One of the shards now shows an ice-blue eye peering out.

"Go get me a rat," comes the voice from the mirror. "A big one."

Nightmare Malyn comes to life. She's been so still until now that I almost began to think of her as part of the furnishings. She puts the gilded frame down on the vanity and gets up.

I can't breathe for a moment while I watch this monster creature turn her blank face my way.

Nightmare Malyn walks toward me. Without eyes or her mirror, she could easily mistake me for a rat.

She walks to my shelf and reaches out. Her right hand touches my glass dome while her left touches the dome beside mine. There's a fat rat in my neighboring plate, moving agitatedly as Nightmare Malyn stands over us.

There's a moment of indecision. I hold my breath and try to be as still as possible even though I can feel my feathers ruffling.

The rat squeaks.

I have no idea if Nightmare Malyn can hear, but regardless, she takes her hand off my dome and picks up the rat's plate. I let out a long breath as she walks away from me.

She takes the plate and holds it up to the mirror. Then she lifts the glass dome from one side like a mouth opening.

The rat squeaks and tries to run away from the looking glass. A hand reaches out from the mirror and grabs the rat. The rat squeaks in panic and frantically races its legs.

The hand that comes out of the mirror is fractured, like the glass. It's made of shards of flesh that don't quite seem to fit together, yet the flesh stays in the shape of a hand.

The hand pulls back into the gilded frame, taking the rat with it.

I hear a lot of squeaking. It's amazing how a little creature like a rat can still convey so much panic and terror in its screams.

Then the noise dies down.

Something is tossed out of the mirror and lands on the floor. It's a pink blob with little legs that still twitch as though it's trying to run.

Before I can fully comprehend that it is a skinned rat, Nightmare Malyn leaps on it. She grabs it and stuffs it into her mouthless face.

The skinned rat squeaks with surprising force. It's not moving very much now, though. Malyn has no mouth, but she presses the rat where her mouth would normally be. The rat begins to dissolve and spread into the blank canvas where her face should be.

Then Nightmare Malyn silently sits back down in front of her vanity and calmly picks up her looking glass.

She sits there, holding the mirror in front of her, looking like a statue.

CHAPTER 41

I didn't know that birds could tremble this hard. I do my best to stay still, but my feathers shiver and my skin feels like it's prickling all over. I have to make an effort not to flitter around desperately under my glass dome.

I don't want to do anything that attracts Nightmare Malyn's attention. Not after seeing what she just did. Whatever I do to get out of here, I need to do it right, because I'll only get one chance.

I really, really don't want to be eaten by the faceless nightmare.

Maybe I'd die.

Or maybe I'd still be conscious inside Nightmare Malyn —trapped in the same way that I was in my sleeping body.

Just the thought of it is enough to make me panic. I tighten my muscles, trying to stay still. I look around to distract my thoughts, tearing my eyes away from the eerily still Malyn.

Of course, my eyes go to the mirror. I can't help it. There's color and motion there that draws my attention no matter where I look. I might have been calmer if I continued to stare at Nightmare Malyn.

In one of the glass shards, a pair of ice-blue eyes are staring right at me.

I want to duck and hide, but there's nowhere to go.

I remember that I'm in hawk form. She can't see my real self.

But no matter how small and unnoticeable I try to make myself, I'm the only creature under glass that isn't a rat. Nightmare Malyn might not be able to see, but those ice-blue eyes sure can.

I realize I'm staring at the eyes like a person in shock. I move my head back and forth, hoping I look like an ordinary hawk.

Nightmare Malyn stands stiffly. She holds the mirror facing me and begins walking.

I instinctively raise my wings to fly away. The glass traps them so that I can't even open them.

I slam my beak into the glass, hoping for it to shatter. The glass is thick and even my powerful beak does no damage.

I slam my body into the glass, trying to knock the dome off the shelf. But it doesn't budge.

I'm trapped.

I'm breathing so fast that I might pass out.

Calm down! I shriek into my glass prison.

Usually, screaming at myself doesn't do much good, but this time, something clicks inside my head.

This is not the Waking.

This is *my* world.

I am not the helpless girl lying frozen in a tower. I'm not even a bird fluttering weakly in a glass cage.

I'm in a glass prison because I'm convinced I'm in one. I can't move the glass because I *believe* it's as strong as a stone wall.

Nightmare Malyn walks steadily toward me. The frosty eyes stare at me through the looking glass with keen interest.

I open my beak and shriek. The sound comes from deep inside me. It's filled with the intention to shatter every belief I have about my powerlessness.

Nothing happens.

I shriek again. This time, I swear the glass dome rattles.

I shriek a third time. A fourth. A fifth.

All the while, I think of the things that hold me here. The glass. The fear. The curse. Malyn. My belief in all those things holds me here. And biggest of all—my doubt in my abilities holds me hostage.

Nightmare Malyn is completely unfazed as she moves toward me.

I shriek with all my fury and frustration at being trapped. At being helpless. At being cursed.

My shriek is long and loud, and I swear my head is about to burst with it.

I keep telling myself that I believe. That I am convinced. And then I stop thinking about it and just throw my entire being into my shrieking.

The glass rattles.

Then the domes to either side of me begin to rattle. I'm encouraged by the sound and the vibration of the shelf below me.

I shriek more fiercely, feeling the blood pound in my head.

Then the glass shatters.

Not just my own glass dome, but all the glass domes. The shards explode outward in blinding, swirling waves of shrapnel.

My delicate ears are shocked by the unending cracking of broken glass. It sounds like the Dreaming itself is shattering.

The chair in front of the vanity topples and tumbles away. The vanity itself shivers and drags on the floor.

On either side of me, rats scurry out in panic. Nightmare Malyn reflexively grabs for one as a rat runs past her. She's so fast that she catches it.

I get past my shock of what just happened and open my wings. I leap off the shelf, careful not to fly anywhere near Malyn's creepy puppet.

Her face is covered in bits of glass. Dark goo seeps out of her flesh where the shards stick out. She doesn't seem to notice.

She smears the rat into her face. The poor thing squeaks and thrashes as it melts into what should have been Malyn's face.

The looking glass in her hand still faces me. I can feel the eyes in the mirror follow me as I shoot past them.

I dart out the window and flap my wings as fast as I can to fly to the edge of the castle. I need to get out of this dream island.

I make it out, but my heart continues to flutter as if I was still trapped. It doesn't matter that all I see is the soothing darkness of the place in between islands.

I fly as far away as I can.

No matter how far I go, though, I can't shake the feeling that Malyn—the one who watched me through the mirror—saw who I really was inside the hawk form.

I keep looking back to see if those icy eyes watch me from the dark. But all I see are the islands behinds me, full of dreamers without faces.

CHAPTER 42

I lurch through the thin barrier between the Dreaming and the Waking and stagger into my tower. The air feels warm even though the gauzy bed curtains flutter in the breeze.

Leaning against the stone wall, I slide down and hug my knees on the floor. The wall behind me feels slightly warmer than the air, as though the stones have been absorbing sunlight all day. I've never noticed that before, particularly since sunlight never beams into my chamber.

It calms me, giving me comfort. I'm back in my sanctuary. Still, I have to hold my knees tight to keep my hands from trembling.

What happened back there? I flew as a bird. And made glass explode into a million shards.

Can I truly do those things? The vast possibilities scare me almost as much as Malyn. I know that I should be excited, and I am. But it turns out that even good things can be frightening sometimes. A normal girl might dream of having this kind of power, but I dream of just being a normal girl.

The ogre roars outside my window. I'm glad for the distraction. I push myself up off the floor.

"You're still alive." I walk over to the window.

"I plan to stay that way."

He's hacking at an especially tangled portion of the brambles. Beside him are the remnants of an ogre who came before him. Until now, that ogre had made it the farthest of all the ones who climbed over the wall.

I should be nervous about this new ogre getting past the last skeleton, but I'm not. It must be a sign of how bad my day has been, because it's nice to have company who can't harm me. If he keeps at it, he'll fall into a different category altogether, but for now, I'm a tiny bit glad he's still here.

When you've been around as long as I have, and have lived the kind of surreal life I have, anything you can do to ground yourself is good. Talking to someone else—someone real—falls into that category, even if he's an ogre who might kill you tomorrow.

"How do you do it?" I ask. "How do you keep moving forward through the pain, especially when you feel trapped and helpless?"

"I'm not trapped. And I'm far from helpless." He whacks the thorny branches with his stick.

I'm not sure he understands his situation. The brambles that he hacked away are already regrowing behind him, cutting off his exit. The new growth slithers toward him like a nest of snakes. A normal person would have seen it, but I'm not sure this ogre has ever turned to look back.

"How do you do it?" I ask again.

"Focus. On. The. Goal." He hacks with every word.

"What goal is that?"

"Rescuing the sleeping princess."

He pauses for a rest, bending to lean his hands on his

knees. His bloody shoulders heave up and down with his breathing.

"Why? What about her keeps you going? You've never even seen her."

He looks up at me with his bloody face. His eyes are the only part of his broad face that's not red. "I know she needs me."

"For what? You think you can kiss her awake? *You?*"

"Why not?"

"Only someone who is fit to be her consort can wake her."

"I'm fit."

The stories my nannies told me clash with what Malyn showed me. When my nannies told me I would be kissed awake by a prince, I always assumed that he would be human. And that the kiss would be a mere introduction, albeit a rather forward one.

Malyn's version has to be some kind of evil joke. It must be. What kind of a horrible fairy would even come up with such a curse?

I do my best to believe in my own arguments, but it doesn't stop me from believing the worst.

"The princess will hate you," I say.

"She'll love me."

"She won't."

"She will."

"What makes you so sure?"

"I just am."

"That's nothing but your self-assurance. It's founded on nothing. And you think that's good enough?"

"Of course."

"Your belief is that powerful?"

"*Yes*. That and my annoyance at these blasted thorns. I will not let these thorns get the best of me."

He swings his stick and begins chopping again. Despite a

thousand thorns prickling him, despite the odds, he's one more step closer to his goal.

This ogre will surely eat me for lunch, or worse, if he ever climbs in through the window. He still has a ways to go, though. He'll have to make it through the rest of the court-yard and then climb my tower. There's a reason why no one has made it yet.

He won't be the one to make it. He can't be that strong. I try to reassure myself, yet I can't quite believe it. Even worse, I have to shove down a grudging respect that's growing for him for making it this far.

"What should I call you?" I ask from my window.

I've only named two others who tried to reach my tower. One was an ogre, and the other was a prince. In my imagina-tion, the prince was as handsome as could be, but I never got a good look at him. He was short, and the thorn branches swallowed him so that I could not get a good look.

He died a painful death halfway across the courtyard. Only then did I realize that his face was too broad, his head too big, and his hands too stunted to be human. He might have had some human in him, I suppose.

I named him Charlie. Charlie is nothing but bleached bones now. That's an improvement over the phase when he was covered in squirmy bugs.

I sigh. This new ogre is not only past Charlie, he's now passing Grunt. Grunt was my scariest ogre until now. Maybe they just get scarier as they get closer.

The ogre below me roars as he yanks at a particularly clingy branch of thorns that has managed to wrap itself around his leg. His bald, oversized head is shiny with blood and sweat.

"Shall I call you Sweaty?" I nod. "It suits you. Or how about Roar?"

"Bronson."

I frown. "Bronson? Your mother named you Bronson?"

That sounds like a person's name. Are there ogres who aspire to act like people? Perhaps he named himself after a person he ate and is now pretending to be human. Maybe that's why he's here—taking over the real Bronson's quest of rescuing me.

"I'll call you Roar. It's more noble than Sweaty." I feel magnanimous.

"Bronson."

"Oh, fine. I suppose I should be glad that you don't insist on being addressed as Lord Bronson or Your Highness."

I roll my eyes and turn away from the window. It's a waste of time talking to the ogre. But I'm strangely grateful to him for distracting me from the near-miss I just had.

I stand over my sleeping body and watch my chest rise and fall.

I'm still alive. Despite everything, I'm still alive. I hold on to that fact the way a child might hold on to a stuffed toy.

I lie on the bed beside the sleeping girl. I suppose I could go inside my body to rest, but the thought creeps me out. I know it's really my soul "possessing" my body, but it often feels like my body is possessing *me*. So I don't go in.

This seems like a good place to think through my options, though.

What would have happened if I'd grabbed the mirror and run off with it? Would it have exploded the way it did when Sentry stabbed it?

What would have happened if I jumped through it?

The thought of possibly being lost in whatever worlds the shards harbor makes me immediately shy away from that idea. I think that Sentry is in the Waking being tortured with lack of sleep, but I don't know for sure.

I can't just sit around and let Malyn turn dreamers into

faceless slaves. There must be something I can do. This is the only world I have left. I can't lose this one too.

Every path leads to Malyn and her mirror.

And the change happened after Sentry got sucked through the looking glass. So that means that the solution has to do with that mirror. Break it, use it, or steal it.

But here's the thing—I'm terrified of it. I saw it shatter and come right back together again. I watched it suck Sentry into it. And what's it doing with rats?

I suspect it just likes to torture creatures. Doesn't matter if it's a rat or a person.

There's one more thing about that mirror. I've been trying to bury the thought, but it keeps coming back and won't leave me alone.

When Nightmare Malyn was coming for me when I was under the glass, I saw something. Something I've been trying not to think about. Something that claws at me like a trapped animal.

I saw my tower nestled in the forest through one of the mirror shards.

CHAPTER 43

I will not be afraid.

I have no choice but to take action, so what's the point of being afraid of something I'm going to do anyway?

I curl my hands into fists to stop the trembling. I have to squeeze pretty hard before I begin to feel the determination of my fists rising up my arms and into the rest of me.

Stepping out of the safety of my tower, I go back into the Dreaming.

I walk alone in the darkness, watching my boots make ripples on the wet ground. Hugging myself, I hunch my shoulders against the chill. There's no wind here between the dream islands, but it's always a little colder than it should be.

Malyn knows where my tower is. If she doesn't, then she will soon, I'm sure of it. The mirror will show her.

Does she feel the urgency to find my body?

I can't get rid of the feeling that it won't be long before either Malyn finds me or the ogre reaches me. Despite all my efforts to reassure myself that the ogre won't make it to my tower, he could be the one.

He's moved steadily without signs of slowing. And his grunts and frustrated yells only prove that he's got energy to spare. The others faded out long before this. Even Grunt hardly whimpered by the time he reached where Bronson is now.

If he reaches me, the rest of the curse will play out one way or the other.

And if I wake, Malyn will lose the power she draws from me.

She's practically living two lives while I sleep for her. How much more scheming and power-mongering can someone like her do when she is awake all the time?

Will she need to catch up on her sleep if my curse is broken? I have lovely fantasies of her sleeping for years.

I walk out of the dark and into the torchlit hallways of Midnight Castle.

This is the last place I want to be, but the source of all the problems are here—both mine and the kingdom's. I'd rather hide in another form, but I don't dare sit outside Malyn's window as a bird again. She's probably ready to capture any bird she sees now.

I can't get rid of the image of Nightmare Malyn shoving that rat into her blank face.

That won't be me. I swear it. I haven't spent decades trapped in the Dreaming just to be eaten by a nightmare. I have skills now that Malyn never predicted when I was a child.

I squeeze myself into the shadows. I'm at the alcove where Sentry attacked Nightmare Malyn. There's no blood on the floor, even though by all rights, this area should be drenched in it.

There is Sentry's sword, though.

I pick it up and feel the heft of it. It's a short sword, well balanced. It feels good in my hand.

I swipe at the air for practice, reminding my muscles of the drills Silver taught me. I imagine Nightmare Malyn's head being sliced off and falling with a satisfying thud.

When that happened last time, all she did was put her head back on. But she had to grope around for it first. That could leave plenty of time for me to grab that mirror out of her hand. I can do this.

I might even get the satisfaction of kicking her head and watching it bounce off the wall. That would be an added bonus.

I take a deep breath. Yes, I can do this.

Doing my best to ignore the eerie, prickling sensation of the gaping darkness of the hallway behind me, I gather my courage. I stride right up to the doors. I'm gripping Sentry's sword so tight that my hand is practically being forged into it.

Shoving my way in, I expect to see her at her vanity.

There's nobody here.

The vanity is blank, with not even a single perfume bottle on the rich wood surface. The empty frame of the vanity mirror has a disturbing sense to it. The missing mirror is an indication of a world not quite right.

That eerie sensation grows and gnaws at my gut.

With my sword ready to slice, I carefully stalk over to the archway leading to the bedchamber. It is smaller than the antechamber, with nothing but the bed and a bench at the foot of it. The bed looks like a showpiece—never touched, never slept on.

I look around the bedchamber, but there's no one there. The bed reminds me of my own back in my tower. There's something uncanny about the similarity. It makes my spine crawl.

I step back into the antechamber. The only motion is the

scurrying of rats under glass on a shelf. The tiny sound of their claws scratching against the glass grates my nerves.

I'm tempted to let them out. But if I do, Malyn will know an intruder was here. I can't afford to raise her suspicions.

The shelves are fringed with deep shadows along the corners. The longer I look, the more it seems the shadows are churning. It's a bit mesmerizing, imagining something in those shadows.

I blink hard. I'm about to turn away when something jumps out at me.

I only have a moment to take in what's happening. The impression I get is Nightmare Malyn coming at me.

But it's a version that's not entirely formed. Like a wisp of a nightmare coming together. She's in a black, shapeless dress that could be made of tattered shadows. There's no color, no jewelry.

If this creature had a face, it would be contorted with evil right now. Her jaw pulls down, tearing an opening barred by streaks of black where her mouth should be.

Instinctively, I swing my sword. My blade slices right through her. A puff of black smoke swirls as my sword passes.

The only good thing about this horror is that her hand passes right through me. I imagine feeling something, but there's not enough time to think about it.

In one hand, she holds the mirror. It's dark and looks dead. The gilded frame is shadow-black rather than its usual gold.

I sidestep and swipe at her. Again, my blade cuts through her the way it would cut through mist.

Her head begins to turn solid. Color begins to wash down her face, her feet and her hands. The mirror also begins to solidify, and color flows down the gilded frame, turning it into the familiar gold.

The wisps of shadows are turning into a true nightmare. Is that how I look when I step out of my tower into the Dreaming?

I swing my sword, putting my entire body into the movement. I aim for the solid portion of her head and feel a deep satisfaction when my blade strikes something hard.

The top of her head slices off and slips down to the floor. There's no blood, but the rest of her stutters in her motions.

Using my momentum, I swing my blade around and slam down her solidifying hand. Her hand thumps down on the rug.

I expect it to crawl around, but it looks like a lump of dead flesh. Nightmare Malyn twists her head, looking like she's howling in pain. Her jaw dangles by the gummy threads of her flesh, but no sound comes out.

I swing my sword and chop her head off. I flinch, still expecting a spray of blood, but of course, there is no blood. Nightmare Malyn's head falls off silently and thuds on the rug.

Her lower legs topple. Her remaining hand drops to the floor, along with the bottom half of the mirror that it holds. The top half of the looking glass is still smoky.

The rest of Nightmare Malyn is still a dark, churning mist. Instead of forming into her body, it thins and loses the shape.

Then it fades away altogether.

None of Nightmare Malyn's parts move on the floor. They are lifeless, waxy pieces, just like the bottom half of the mirror in her hand.

In one of the shards of the looking glass, a startled eye opens in shock.

I lift my sword high above my head. Then I slam it down with all my might.

The tip of my blade pierces the eye.

CHAPTER 44

The glass shatters into a thousand fragments.

I shut my eyes against the explosion of glass. I can feel the powder spraying on my hair and face.

The bigger pieces land and break into smaller pieces, causing tiny explosions everywhere.

I wipe the dust off my face, shaking the sparkles off my hands. Nightmare Malyn's severed feet and hands are covered in sparkle dust, making the macabre parts look weirdly enchanted. I don't even want to look at her head pieces.

The dark fog that was forming into the rest of her is nothing but broken wisps of mist now. The bits drift in different directions, fading as I watch.

I did it. I killed Nightmare Malyn.

And the mirror—I destroyed that too. At least, I destroyed the Dreaming version of it. I can hardly believe it.

My ears ring like an echo of a scream. And my heart races so fast that I feel the need to run just to use up its power. I let go of the sword, knowing if I move my hands on it, I will grate my flesh on the glass powder and fragments stuck to it.

I turn and run out of the chambers. I don't stop until I'm outside the castle. It's nighttime and there's a mad thunderstorm blowing through Midnight.

The wind is icy and my clothes become instantly wet and sticky. But I'm so busy running that I hardly notice. The sound of the rain and thunder blot out all else, and I keep looking behind me in case there's something chasing me that I can't hear.

I only slow once I'm far enough away from the castle that I feel safe. Letting the rain wash over me, I wander through the countryside. I'm so hot from running that the rain feels good.

Miraculously, the glass powder is washing off, slipping along my skin and hair as the rain pounds against me.

It's hard to believe that I escaped unscathed. I stop myself mid-thought. I need to believe that I *did* escape unharmed. I need to envision all the glass fragments melting off my skin, my hair, my clothes.

And so it does. I can see the sparkling dust dripping off me. I look at my arms and hands being cleansed by the rain.

A tiny trickle of blood streaks down my hand. I trace it back to the source, trying to see where it comes from.

I can feel a tiny sliver that has pricked my finger.

Lightning streaks across the sky, and I can see the details of my finger for a moment.

I grab and pull out the sliver, being careful not to stick myself again with it. I drop it on the ground like a poisoned dart.

A bright drop of blood bubbles out of the meaty part of my fingertip.

My feelings roar up in a jumbled sense of dread. The last time I pricked my finger, I fell asleep and got trapped in a body that might as well be dead.

I take stock of how I'm feeling to predict whether I'll drop as I walk. I have this unshakable fear that I'll fall asleep.

That's ridiculous, of course. I'm already asleep. I'm already cursed. I'm just a spirit. How could I fall asleep?

Still, I can't shake the sense of heavy dread as I start running again. I need to get back to my tower. It may be my prison, but it's also my home—the only place where I feel safe.

I race through the night as the wind and rain lash against me, picking up speed until I leap out of the storm.

CHAPTER 45

*M*y tower feels cool as the twilight deepens outside. The window has no shutters or covering, so the wind and chill come in at all hours. The sounds come in too. That means whenever Bronson the ogre curses down in the courtyard, I hear it.

I'm too tired to care. I nearly fall into bed.

I snuggle up good and close to my warm body. I get as close to it as I can without actually going inside. I'm no longer wet—I dried as soon as I crossed the barrier—but I'm chilled all the way through.

No matter how cold it is outside, my body seems to be enchanted to be warm. I've never seen gooseflesh on my arms or seen my lips turn blue, even in the coldest of winters.

I look at the prick on my finger. There's still a dried smear of blood on my fingertip.

It seems incredibly unfair that I could prick my finger even in dream form, even when I'm just a ghost. But there it is, blood and all.

Did I kill Malyn?

I let the thought roll around in my head, savoring the thought. I wish it was true, but it doesn't feel like it. I'm pretty sure I destroyed her creepy puppet. She was a creature of the Dreaming.

But the mirror is probably in the Waking as well as in the Dreaming. I feel confident that I destroyed the Dreaming version of the mirror. Maybe I even damaged the one that lies in the Waking. But it's too much to think that I destroyed both Malyn and the mirror in the Waking.

Still, a victory. The shocked look in that ice-blue eye when I slammed my sword down on it is enough to warm my heart for the moment.

The throbbing in my finger gnaws around the edges of my victory, though. What can piercing my finger do to me that hasn't already been done?

Unease feels heavy in my gut. I try not to think about it.

I watch and listen carefully to my body breathing. It's steady, like it always is. I can hear my heartbeat when I put my ear to her chest. The regular beat comforts me.

The sound of my breathing and the steady rhythm of my chest rising and falling make me drowsy.

Funny, I don't remember ever feeling drowsy outside my body. I can sleep—that's how I have my own dreams—but I rarely do it. I'd rather be a visitor in someone else's dreams than be the victim of my own nightmares. I get enough of that in my daily life.

Besides, what if I never wake up? It's bad enough for my body to be asleep forever, but to have my soul asleep too?

I cringe at that thought. But I can't stifle a yawn. My body is warm and comforting, and Bronson's grumbling in the courtyard is not enough to pull me out of my drowsiness.

I look again at my pricked finger and wonder. Am I doomed to always fall asleep whenever I prick my finger?

As soon as the thought enters my head, it fades like wisps of smoke. Wasn't I wondering about something?

My breath matches my chest's rise and fall—in, out, in, out...until my eyelids droop over my eyes.

And then I fade into slumber.

CHAPTER 46

I'm in a dark chamber.

I can hear labored breathing before my eyes adjust to the dark. I'm afraid to move until I know where I am. At the very least, I want to be able to see.

My eyes adjust painfully slowly. When they finally do, I see that I'm in a dungeon cell.

Behind me, the labored breathing hitches. I turn to look.

It's Sentry.

His head is hung low between his raised arms. His arms are shackled to the wall.

The chains are too short to allow him to sit, and he is obviously too exhausted to stand. So he slumps, pulling his entire weight on his wrists, making them bleed with the rubbing of the shackles.

I thought I saw him in some sort of crypt earlier. They must have dragged him here to torture him. There probably aren't too many shackles in a crypt—at least, I hope not. The kingdom has enough problems without worrying about the dead coming back.

Sentry's eyes are closed, and I can't tell if he's trying to sleep or on the verge of becoming unconscious. Perhaps he's dying.

I hear his labored breathing, so I know he's still alive. I rush over to him and reach out to lift him by his chest to take the pressure off his wrists.

My hands flow right through him.

I'm confused. I look around, wondering where I am and how I got here. I have no problems lifting things in the Dreaming.

A certainty sneaks up on me. It's one of those things you just know in a dream. No one has to tell you. And the thing that I know is this—I'm no longer in the Dreaming.

I frown.

If I'm not in the Dreaming, where am I?

I've never managed to be in the Waking anywhere other than in my tower. I look at my finger. There's still a smear of blood on my fingertip.

Could being pricked by the mirror sliver in the Dreaming make me fall awake? Maybe it makes me transition from one place to another. If it pricks me while I'm in the Waking, it puts me into the Dreaming.

Am I dreaming?

I look at my hands. They're not glowing, so I'm not a dreamer. But can a dreamer see her own glow?

I'm lost. I can't tell if I'm dreaming that I'm in the Waking or if I really am "awake."

I run my hand through Sentry. It flows through just as it always does through my own sleeping body.

My heart races at the thought that I'm in the Waking. Sure, I'm still a ghost here, but I'm here nonetheless.

Men grumble behind me. I walk right through the cell bars to look. Two men walk down the row of cells—one holding a torch in front of him. The smoke from the torch is so black that it's hard to see their faces.

I wave my hand to clear the air. Nothing happens. I try again. The smoke doesn't change. It's like I can't even generate a breeze.

If I was in the Dreaming, that smoke would clear. In fact, now that I think about it, there's never been smoke around the torches in my world. The torches provide light and nothing else. They've never provided heat or smoke.

I must be in the Waking.

CHAPTER 47

J want to run, but I force myself to stay still and watch the two men walk down the aisle of the dungeon.

One of them coughs and waves his hand in front of him, disturbing the torch smoke. All that does is make it swirl around his head. They somehow manage to make it to Sentry's cell despite the smoke.

The Waking is far grimier than I remembered. The walls are charred and sooty. The floor is wet and the whole place reeks of things I don't want to think about. People cough listlessly and moan softly down the hall.

The men unlock Sentry's cell and come in. They both carry buckets. The one carrying the torch walks up to Sentry. For the first time, I see Sentry's face up close.

His helmet is still beside him. It lies face-up like a head that's been chopped off. Even without the helmet, Sentry's face shows the outline of it as though he still wears it. The long center of the helmet's nose guard is lighter than his cheeks and chin. I'm not sure if that's from the sun baking his skin or from soot.

The second man stands in front of Sentry with his legs braced. He grabs the bucket with both hands and swings it back.

"Stop it!" I yell.

Nobody hears me.

I try to grab the bucket as the man swings it toward Sentry, but my hands go right through it. He doesn't seem to notice any resistance.

The water splashes on Sentry's face so hard that it jerks his head back. He startles awake, bursting out of his daze like a drowning man.

Water drips down his clumped hair and into his once-crisp uniform. He begins to shiver immediately. I see now that he's slumped in a puddle that was there even before these men splashed the bucket of water on him.

How long have they been keeping him awake?

The guard grabs the second bucket and tosses more water on Sentry.

"What'd you do that for?" says the man with the torch. "We'll just have to haul in another bucket."

"One's not enough. Look at him." The other man lifts his hand toward Sentry. "He's still drowsy."

"He don't need to be fully awake," says the torch man. "Our orders are to keep him from sleepin'. That don't mean we need to wake him."

"What are you going on about, talking nonsense? The man's either wakin' or sleepin'."

"He's not sleepin'. Look at him. His eyes are open and he's shiverin'."

"He don't look awake to me. He's not even looking at us. He's still seeing dreams or something."

"Don't matter. What matters is that he's not sleepin'."

They're right. Sentry isn't looking at them.

He's looking at me.

I look around, trying to see if there's anything else for him to stare at. There's nothing to see but me.

I wave my hands in front of him and hop a little. He squints, shaking water out of his eyes. I could swear he's watching me.

"Are you all right?" I ask.

Of course, I don't expect him to respond. He won't be able to see or hear me any better than my sleeping body can.

"What are you doing here?" he asks. His voice is raw, as if he's been screaming.

For a moment, I think he's talking to me. But he can't be.

"See? I told you," says the torch man. "He's not sleepin'. A babbling man can't be sleepin'."

"My pa used to babble in his sleep."

"Run," says Sentry. He makes a fist, jangling his chains. He manages to push himself up onto his feet.

"First, he sleeps like he's dead, now he's telling us to run?" says the torch man. He shoves the torch into Sentry's face.

"Stop!" I rush over to try to stop him, but my hands flow right through his arm.

Sentry jerks back, the flames nearly scorching his face.

The torch man laughs. "Fire and water. The new queen has a sense of humor, that one."

"She won't be laughin' if she sees you hurting her prisoner without her permission."

"What, you think she cares?" asks the torch man. "Maybe we just kill him off and be done with it. I'm tired and want to go home to my Betty. Do the fancy nobles want us to stay up all night? Don't they know that it's just as much torture for us to stay up all night as it is for him?"

"The queen wants him alive. She's got questions she needs answerin'."

The torch man shoves his face close to Sentry's. "Why

don't you just tell her what she wants to know, and we can all get some sleep?"

"Don't know where the girl is," croaks Sentry.

"Yeah, sure you don't," says torch man. "Just make somethin' up. Worry about what other lies to tell her later, *after* we all get some sleep."

He shoves the torch toward Sentry's face again, nearly scorching him.

I try to lift the empty bucket to hit him with, but to no avail. I stop when I notice that Sentry's eyes follow me.

I look at him with my head tilted. He looks right back at me.

The two men continue to grumble to each other as they step out of the cell and lock the door. Their voices begin to move farther away, and still, I stare at Sentry.

"Can you see me?" I ask.

"Aye," says Sentry. "Shouldn't I?"

"I… No. I mean, yes." My tongue feels thick, and I have a hard time accepting that he can see me. "How can you see me when no one else can?"

"I see you," he says. "But you don't belong here."

I snort softly. "Don't I know it."

"How did you get here?"

It takes me a moment to remember. I show him my finger. "The mirror. A tiny shard pricked me."

"And you woke?"

I shrug. "I suppose not, since I would wake in my bed in my own body if I did. Instead, I'm here." I look around at the dank cell. "What are *you* doing here?"

"I'm a prisoner."

"I can see that. Why won't they let you sleep?" I have a suspicion about that, but I need to hear it.

"The new queen doesn't want me to sleep."

"The new queen." My blood runs cold just saying these words. "Has it happened then? Is the Dark King truly dead?"

"He is." Sentry looks grim.

"What happened to his cloak?"

"I assume Queen Malyn has it."

"Are you going to protect Malyn now?" The words come out in a whisper.

He doesn't answer. Instead, he says, "I need to sleep."

"Why is she afraid to let you go back into the Dreaming? She has your body, so what does it matter if you sleep?"

"She thinks I know something. She doesn't want me to escape into the Dreaming. She can't make me tell her what she wants to know if my body is asleep and she can't wake me."

"What does she want to know?"

He looks intently into my eyes. "The location of the fabled sleeping princess."

CHAPTER 48

I can only stare at Sentry, my thoughts racing. "But...you don't know where the sleeping princess is, do you?"

"That's what I keep saying," says Sentry. He jangles his shackles for emphasis.

"Sleeping Beauty is just a fable. A story for children."

"The queen doesn't think so."

"Does Malyn have any idea where the princess is?" I ask, trying to sound unconcerned.

"In a tower. Somewhere."

That mirror saw far too much. But seeing my tower in the Dreaming and knowing where it's located in the Waking are very different things. At least, I hope so.

"What else does she know?" I ask breathlessly.

"She thinks it's in the forest."

My heart sinks. The forest is large and deadly, but I don't think that matters much to a fairy. One of the reasons why the dark forest is so dangerous is that fairies live there.

"Anything else?" I ask.

"You're beginning to sound like her. If you're a spy for

her, tell her I don't know anything. It's the truth, I swear it. I'm only here to protect the king's cloak."

"I'm sure that'll go over well with her."

"I don't need your sarcasm. I need your help." He rattles his shackles. "Get me out of here."

"I can't." I demonstrate by waving my hand through the bars of the cell door. "I can't affect anything in the Waking. Normally, I can't even *be* in the Waking."

"Shh." Sentry lifts his head, listening intently.

Down the hall, the sound of feet shuffling floats toward us. There's no talking though, which makes me think it's not the guards.

I remember that no one but Sentry can see me. I walk through the bars to see who's coming.

It turns out that it *is* the guards.

One carries a bucket full of water that he holds with both hands. It's tilted, and water dribbles out with every step. The other guard holds a flickering torch that casts dancing shadows over them.

Their faces are so strange that it's hard to look at anything else. I can see a hint of eyebrows. There are holes where their gaping mouths are, but the color of their lips matches their skin, making them look lipless.

Their feet shuffle, meandering this way and that. They're generally headed this way, but one of them bumps against the bars of a cell. He slowly careens off the bars and bumps into his companion.

The two guards meander toward us in this manner, red shadows flickering from the torchlight against their faces.

"It's your friends, coming to wake you," I say. "There's something wrong with them."

"Can you get the keys?" Sentry whispers.

"I told you, I can't touch anything."

"Try."

I know it won't work.

But maybe that's the problem. When I first woke in my tower, I tried so hard to move my body, to lift something, to be a part of the Waking. When nothing worked, I gave up. I became firmly convinced that I couldn't move anything—that I couldn't affect anything.

But that was a long time ago. I'm no longer the helpless, sheltered princess that I was then. I've learned that belief can trap you or free you. And I'm tired of it trapping me.

I walk up to the two empty men. That's how I think of them. Like the faceless dreamers, they seem to be empty of any independent life inside their bodies. If my own body got up to walk while I was here, this is how I imagine it would move.

These men are soulless. If I'm a spirit and my body a shell, then these men have lost their spirits.

I shiver at the possibility of people in the Waking becoming like the faceless folk in the Dreaming.

I try to grab the keys dangling in a guard's hand. My hand goes through. I try again but to no avail.

I kick the guard out of frustration, envisioning a painful hit. I get no satisfaction out of that, either. My foot simply goes through the man.

He grunts, though.

I stop and stare. Did he just grunt in pain? Or was that the grunt of a mindless, soulless man?

I kick him again. He grunts again.

My foot floated through him, but I could swear that he took a step away from me. Like a drunken man, he continues to meander to Sentry's cell.

The guard mindlessly lifts his hand to open the cell door. To do so, he lets go of one side of the bucket, spilling water onto his breeches and boots.

He doesn't seem to notice. He continues to hold on to the

almost empty bucket with one hand as he unlocks the door. His companion pushes it open.

I run at the guard and slam into him.

I feel a jolt as the ickiness of going through him hits me. He's slimy and sticky inside. I want to throw that bucket of water onto myself by the time I end up on the other side of him.

The guard lurches a little.

He catches himself and manages to stay upright. He keeps moving until he's in front of Sentry.

"He felt you," says Sentry.

The guards don't respond. At least I'm not the only one they're ignoring.

The guard raises his bucket as though it's still full of water. The keys dangle from his hand as he does so.

"Sentry, grab his keys if you can." I dive in and shove the guard's arm as he raises it.

The hand holding the keys jerks up and toward Sentry. Sentry makes a grab for it, swinging his entire body to swipe at the keys.

His fingertips touch the ring but slip off them.

The guards don't seem to notice. The one with the bucket throws a small amount of water onto Sentry. It's barely a pint.

As if he thinks he's carrying a full bucket of water, he swings it again. Meanwhile, the guard holding the torch jabs the flame toward Sentry's face. Their fractured minds must be replaying the last time they were here.

This time, I slam my shoulder as hard as I can against the bucket-carrying guard's arm. I try to shove it up and toward Sentry's shackled hands.

The guard's hand jerks up, almost dropping the keys. I reach for the ring, trying to catch it.

Sentry snatches it. The key ring dangles precariously on the tip of his finger. One tap and he'll drop it.

But he doesn't. He manages to firmly grab it before the bucket guard bumps up against him.

The guards don't seem to notice or care that their prisoner has their keys. They open their mouths and mumble unintelligible words. Are they mimicking their last conversation here, when they were fully human?

Sentry fumbles with the keys while the guards turn to leave his cell. I wish I could help, but I've done more than I thought I could.

Dragging his bucket, the guard shuts the cell door and mimics locking it even though he no longer has the keys. They then shuffle their way down the hall away from us.

"Well, that was creepy," I say. "It competes with the strangest dreams I've had the misfortune to be in."

I'll admit it—I'm spooked. I can handle all kinds of nightmares. It freaked me out when I first encountered them, but now, I keep my head low and have a good instinct as to which dream islands to avoid. Usually, the screams are a good clue.

But this isn't the Dreaming.

That's what's got me spooked. This is the Waking.

"I'm having a hard time telling the difference between the Waking and the Dreaming," I say. "And I don't like it."

Sentry's face is all concentration as he weaves a key into the lock of his shackles. The chains don't give him much room to work with, but he manages.

The key doesn't fit. He tries another one. Then another. Eventually, he manages to unlock the shackles.

"Do you have a place to go?" I ask.

I think about mentioning the crypt I saw him in but decide against it. If his body rested there before Malyn's henchmen dragged him out, I doubt if he'd want to talk about it any more than I want to talk about my tower.

"I'm already where I need to be, Briar."

"In the dungeon?"

"In the castle."

"You're going after Malyn?" Even though I say the words, I don't believe it. "That's what got you here in the first place, remember?"

Sentry rubs his wrists. They're raw and bruised. "I remember."

"But you're going to find her anyway? She's the queen now."

"I know."

"What are you going to do when you find her?"

"Kill her."

He marches out of the unlocked cell as though it's a royal chamber and he a prince.

CHAPTER 49

*A*fter knocking out a guard and stealing his clean uniform, Sentry looks like he belongs in the castle again. He holds his pike like he was born with it.

The guard still had his normal face. Whatever is happening, it's happening only to a select few.

I run after Sentry down the twilight halls of Midnight Castle. Of all the places to be during this eerie night, the castle is probably the scariest.

A woman drifts on by. Her eyes are closed and her lips are the color of her skin. My blood runs cold as I recognize Dahlia.

I hold myself from calling out her name. Silver drilled into me the dangers of revealing other people's secrets. These days, even a hint of an accusation is enough to get a person killed.

Besides, Dahlia wouldn't hear me. She no longer has ears. Sentry would, though.

I trust him. I really do. But until Silver herself tells me to reveal the identity of the castle agents, I'll die with Dahlia's secret.

I can't help but stare, though, when she walks by. It's still her, but her motions are dreamlike, her face only vaguely resembling Dahlia's.

I want to give her a hug and tell her it'll be all right. We have to fix this. *I* have to fix this.

But I'm just a girl sleeping in a tower.

The clock tower chimes. I expect it to ring something dramatic, like twelve times, but it's twilight, so it only rings three times.

I remember a time when sunset didn't happen until after supper. But that was long before the Dark King started flinging dark magic in his war against the wild fairies.

Sentry marches through the castle, ignoring everyone and everything as if he really is one of the queen's drones. The only difference is that his eyes burn behind the face shield of his helmet. They burn with such intensity that it makes me shiver.

I'm glad he's not coming after me. He's not someone I'd like to anger.

The castle has people buzzing about, but no one pays us any attention. Everyone looks nervous and avoids eye contact. Most of them still have their faces. They watch the faceless ones out of the corners of their eyes, as though afraid that it could happen to them at any moment.

I see a group of people who are dressed in much finer clothes than the rest. One has a crown on his head, and it takes me a moment to realize that this isn't a jest.

The prince—who, I suppose, is now the king—is silently shoveling manure onto a wagon. His guards and the fine nobles who might ordinarily be fawning over him are also shoveling manure onto the wagon.

They all still have their faces, but their actions make a clear statement. In case there was any doubt, everyone in the castle is getting the message about who is in charge and who is not.

It's also a clear statement about how much power Queen Malyn has.

I have a bad feeling about this. How can Sentry—who's barely awake with nothing but a pike and a ghost—beat someone like Malyn?

There's a beautiful lady in the middle of the courtyard who is wandering around, looking shocked. She moves like a dreamer who is having a nightmare.

The castle dwellers must be so used to random acts of terror by the Dark King that they're probably used to staying quiet and out of sight. But this lady is wandering around so freely that I imagine she must have had a favored position in the Dark King's court. Looking at the horror on her face, though, I'm guessing she doesn't feel so favored anymore.

She's trapped in a living nightmare that she can't wake from. I'm sure that's what she thinks is happening. Do I look like that sometimes when I wander around in the Dreaming?

I try not to think about it.

Sentry walks straight to the queen's chambers. She has guards, of course. They wear helmets that don't allow me to see their faces, so I can't tell if they're entranced or not. They look exactly like Sentry.

Sentry marches straight to the queen's doors. Two of the guards cross their pikes across the doors. They look stiff and mindless, like they're made of stone. It's clear that they won't let Sentry through.

"I have an urgent message for the queen from the king," says Sentry.

The guards pause for a moment as they gauge him. Their eyes are dark and intense. There's a tension in those eyes that reminds me of that poor woman in the courtyard. These guards are afraid.

The queen's guards aren't supposed to be afraid of anything. They have a reputation for being almost inhuman in their fearlessness.

"The queen is not to be disturbed," says one of the guards.

"The new king demands to see her. Are you going to go tell the king what he can and can't do?"

No reaction from the guards. I imagine they're calculating their best odds of survival. If they're smart, they'll side with the queen.

"Surely, the queen didn't mean for you to guard the doors against the king."

"You are not the king," says the guard.

"The king does not need to come to the queen. He can simply send me to fetch her. Now, move aside, or bear the wrath of the Dark King's heir."

There's a tense moment when I worry that the guards will call Sentry's bluff.

But the moment passes, and the guards raise their pikes.

"That was almost too easy," I say.

Sentry behaves as if he doesn't hear me. He opens the door and steps into the queen's chambers.

CHAPTER 50

$\mathcal{T}$he two guards walk into the queen's chambers behind Sentry. It suddenly looks like he is a prisoner and they are his guards.

The queen's chambers look the same in the Waking as they do in the Dreaming. The only difference is the light. I'm used to seeing it with a gray tinge, almost as if the colors had leached out. Here, though, the colors are as vivid as they are in my own tower.

The new queen sits at her vanity as though it is her throne. She's facing us, though. I've gotten so used to seeing her as Nightmare Malyn that it's strange to see her perfect features.

Behind her, the vanity still has its mirrors attached to it, unlike its counterpart in the Dreaming. It reflects the room—the window with the darkening sky, Sentry looking tall and handsome, the two guards in their crimson uniforms.

Her hand mirror sits on the vanity. It is cracked, but otherwise looks whole. I may have destroyed its counterpart in the Dreaming, but it's still gleaming and golden here in the Waking.

For once, Malyn is not holding it. Instead, it's propped against a jewelry box at an angle that shows its cracked glass. Even here in the Waking, it's strange. Though it lies angled toward the window, it reflects other parts of the room rather than the window.

It reflects me.

It takes me a moment to realize that's what I'm seeing. No one else can see me, but the cracked mirror shows me hovering beside Sentry.

The only reason Malyn hasn't seen me is that for once, her back is turned to her looking glass.

Malyn is not alone. Beside her stands a witch.

There's no mistaking what she is. The witch is covered in a black cloak with the hood drawn over her face. I catch glimpses of a large nose and claw-like hands.

In the cracked mirror, the witch's reflection glows gently, as if her power is too large to contain. Strangely, her hands look ordinary in the glass rather than claw-like. Could it be a glamour?

Usually, glamours make people look more beautiful. I've never heard of using one to make yourself look uglier. Maybe it's a curse.

There's a young woman kneeling before Malyn and the witch. She looks up to the women as though she expects to be anointed.

Beside her is the king's patchwork Cloak of Souls draped over a chair. Even now, that cloak exudes unmistakable power. The patches of hide are roughly cut, as if the knife was wielded to rip and tear, causing as much pain as possible.

The queen holds a torn piece of the cloak. A patch of robin's-egg-blue hide is stretched in her hand. It looks like we interrupted her in the middle of...something.

A part of me expects the girl on her knees to be sobbing in fear. There's something about this situation that feels ritualistic. These days, it's wise to run from anything that smacks of ritual in the Kingdom of Midnight.

The maiden's features are barely visible. I can see the half-moon of lashes defining her closed eyes. She still has a nose and lips, but all color has drained from her face. She's not quite faceless, but she's fading. She trembles in silence, looking paralyzed with fear.

Malyn does not look pleased about the interruption. She hardly looks up at us before putting out her hand to silently stop the intrusion.

Everyone stops.

One guard slowly begins backing out of the chamber. The other follows almost immediately. Sentry holds his ground but doesn't approach.

The witch is mumbling. Her voice rises as she raises her hands.

Her words are nonsensical. At first, I think she's speaking a foreign language. But as the only child of the king, I was taught all the languages in the nearby kingdoms, and I'm at least familiar with how they sound.

This is no foreign language that I've ever heard. This is a spell in progress.

"Sentry, it's a curse," I say.

He looks mesmerized, and I can't tell if he heard me.

CHAPTER 51

The witch raises her hands in the air as though raising something from the floor.

It isn't the floor, though, that responds. It's the bluish patch of the Dark King's cloak in Malyn's hand. Malyn holds it in front of the kneeling girl.

A wisp of smoke rises from the patch of bluish skin. It writhes like a snake, shifting this way and that as if there's a slight breeze. It floats as though it comes from a flickering flame, slithering up into the air.

It meanders over to the girl's face. It shifts around to one side of her face, then moves to the other.

The witch chants louder, more forcefully. It sounds like a command.

The smoke wafts into the girl's nose and mouth, beneath her lashes and into her ears.

My heart pounds so loud that I almost can't hear what's happening. I look at the mirror.

The reflection of the girl shifts. She wavers, becoming smoky, then settles back into a solid reflection.

I look away from the mirror to see the girl's face re-form-ing. I expect her face to become blank, but I'm wrong.

Color flushes back into her cheeks and lips. Her lashes begin to flutter. She begins to look like a girl again. A noble-man's daughter on the verge of being old enough to wed, perhaps. Her face is pretty and fresh with youth.

In the mirror, though, the girl's face doesn't transform the same way. Rather than becoming fresh and healthy, her lips turn black. Rips appear in her cheeks and down her neck. Black ooze drips out of the rips in her skin, looking like clotted blood that doesn't have enough liquid to flow properly.

I look away from the glass. The girl in front of me takes a deep breath and sighs. She stretches her rosy lips into her cheeks, showing her white teeth. I don't even want to see what that smile looks like in the mirror's reflection.

The two guards, who had been inching toward the door, pause. I can almost hear them thinking that perhaps they were wrong about the new queen. Maybe she wasn't doing something as horrible as the Dark King would do. Maybe she's just trying to save her subjects from some other dark force that's causing the horrors of the night.

"Rise," commands Malyn.

The girl gets up, a little unsteady on her feet.

"She's weak," says Malyn like an accusation.

"She'll find what she needs to regain her strength, Your Majesty," says the witch.

The girl looks everywhere but at Malyn. Her eyes flicker to Sentry, then to the two guards by the door.

Without warning, she moves inhumanly fast. In a blink, she's beside the guards.

I must have seen her move, but I can only remember it as a streak.

What she does next, she does at ordinary speed, though.

She stands on her toes and leans her head into one of the guards. She looks like she's about to kiss his neck.

In a swift motion, she bites into his neck and tears it out.

Blood sprays everywhere. He screams. The horrible sound is full of gurgles and bubbles.

The guard beside him gasps, then stumbles back through the door.

The girl laps up the blood through her victim's fingers as he tries to stanch the flow. Then she bites off one of his fingers and chews on it as she bathes in the spray of his blood.

She giggles and squirms.

"See?" says the witch dispassionately. It's unnerving to hear her disembodied voice coming from the darkness of her hood. "They know what they need to finish their bond with their new bodies."

"Are you sure she's not simply insane?" asks Malyn.

"Possible. Your people have been trapped for many years."

"Thanks to you," says Malyn.

The witch bows, making her face even more hidden in the shadows of her hood. "I am a subject of the kingdom as much as anyone else, Your Majesty. I merely do what I am commanded."

"In other words, you have no loyalty."

"I am loyal to the kingdom and will follow the commands of my liege."

Malyn sneers. "I am your liege now. And I command you to follow none other than me, even if you hear lies about my demise. Do you understand?"

"Yes, Your Majesty."

"Never forget that I saved you from the Dark King. You wished it. I granted it. In exchange, you are mine. Now and forever. You will take no other master, even if I'm thrown into a dungeon or captured by a usurper. Do you agree?"

"I do, Your Majesty." The witch bows again.

Of course she agrees. It's obvious that she has no choice.

In the cracked mirror, I look scared standing beside Sentry. A helpless ghost in a world full of real people.

I can hear Sentry's harsh breathing. He sounds like he's running. I'm guessing his heart is racing as fast as mine.

"Excellent," says Malyn. She looks pointedly at Sentry and says, "Shall we free another?"

Malyn slowly strokes the Dark King's cloak. She stops and tears out one of the patches. This patch has a violet tinge to it.

Sentry stops breathing.

He stares intently at the patch of fairy skin in the queen's hands. I can almost hear his heart pounding.

I look back and forth between Sentry and the patch in Malyn's hand. I try to come up with a harmless reason why he's staring at it so intently.

But every reason that comes to mind is ominous.

CHAPTER 52

*W*hen Sentry finally does start breathing again, it's faster than ever. A drop of sweat rolls out of his helmet and drops from his jaw.

I look at the patch of fairy skin Malyn is holding. Does it contain the soul of the fairy who enslaved Sentry?

I don't like that word, *enslaved*. I prefer *employed*, although I know Sentry's loyalty—or should I say bond?—goes beyond an employment relationship.

Malyn looks at Sentry. "Who should we bind this one to? A guard, perhaps?"

Sentry finds his voice at last. "I have a message for the queen." He bows, looking like the perfect soldier.

"Who dares interrupt me when I made it clear that I was busy?"

"The king, Your Majesty," says Sentry. "He wishes to see you."

"Why?"

"He did not tell me. He only commanded me to fetch you to his chambers."

Malyn's eyes narrow and my heart races.

"Wrong answer," I say. "The king is her puppet. He'd never fetch her. He'd come to her."

It still feels weird and uncomfortable talking in front of the others. A part of me is convinced that they'll hear me, while another is convinced that I'll be stuck forever as a ghost with nobody to hear me but Sentry.

Malyn steps toward him. He holds his position but bows when she stops in front of him. He holds his spear upright, and I wonder if he'll take this opportunity to stab her.

The queen's guards are outside, probably scared to death. The first freed fairy is rolling in a pool of blood, giggling beside the dead guard.

And who knows what the witch can do? I can't see her face in the darkness of her hood, but I get the prickling sensation that maybe she's watching me.

Malyn stops so close to Sentry that they could almost kiss.

"Come on, Sentry," I say, balling my fists. "Spear her. This is your chance."

He stands stock-still. Has the witch put a spell on him?

"I wonder what the king will say if I use you as the receptacle for my next child?" Malyn asks.

"I don't understand, Your Majesty," says Sentry.

"Of course you don't. I didn't order you to. You see that young girl on the floor?"

It's hard to miss her. She's rolling around, delighted to see the blood smear patterns she's creating.

"She is my child. She'll be the first of many. I admit, she's a little insane right now. But I was the same when I finally became free. She'll recover. Eventually. In the meantime, the king will gladly accept them all. He spoke incessantly of having a brood of children before we wed." She raises her brows as though just realizing something. "Not that he's said much about them recently."

"Perhaps it would be best if we brought in babies, Your Majesty?" asks the witch.

She apparently didn't realize that the queen was planning on treating these possessed bodies as her children.

The thought of babies being possessed by the newly freed fairies makes the back of my neck crawl. The thought of possession by any entity is bad enough, but everyone knows that wild fairies are as dangerous as can be.

It was the whole reason why the kingdom surrendered to the Dark King. People figured that being ruled by a sadistic king was still better than being enslaved by the wild fairies. I'm not sure that they were wrong.

"No babies," says the queen. "I'm not interested in children who need to be taken care of. I want children who can go forth and execute my wishes."

"She wants a fairy court," I say.

I swear I see a twitch in the witch's hood, as if she's looking toward me. I fidget, wondering if her witch powers give her the ability to see and hear ghosts.

Malyn sighs and runs her finger over Sentry's muscular shoulder. "As much as my next child would love to take over your body, I'm not quite ready to trust them in a strong one such as yours. You're too skilled in fighting techniques.

"Bring in the next one," she calls out loud enough for her guards to hear.

Two guards march in another girl. This one is about the same age as the first.

She has gold-streaked hair pulled up in an intricate pile on top of her head. She's wearing a fluffy confection of a dress. She looks like dessert dressed in lavender.

Her expression is one of terror, though. Her violet eyes are wide and on the verge of tears.

"Please, Your Majesty." The girl's voice is soft and well mannered.

She must be a highborn daughter of a noble. Normally, the daughters of noble houses would be protected. Even the Dark King couldn't harm the powerful families without economic or political ramifications. Not that it stopped him, but he abused them less. He pushed as much as any king, but even he had to tread carefully among his most powerful nobles.

"My father will be quite happy to discuss anything to do with me," says the girl.

"I'm sure he would." Malyn smiles. "The great Illiana family must treasure their only living child."

Illiana is a wealthy family line that goes back as far as anyone remembers. They were the wealthiest and most powerful of nobles when my father was king.

They presided over the lushest lands in the kingdom. Without them, half the people in the kingdom would have starved, including the soldiers.

My father spent a fair amount of time courting the Illianas. Those glory days ended for them when the Dark King took the throne.

I'm sure they managed a precarious dance of survival with the Dark King, though. Countless horrible things happened to the people of Midnight under his rule, but starvation wasn't one of them.

Does this outsider queen have any idea what a delicate balance she's messing with?

"My father will do anything to ensure my safety, Your Majesty," says the girl.

She looks right into the queen's eyes with more steel than I expect. Perhaps her upbringing wasn't all about how to catch the eye of a prince. There was much speculation that the daughter of the Illiana house would be selected as the next queen. That was all before the mysterious Malyn caught the prince's eye, of course.

"I'm sure he will." Malyn smiles. "But your father won't need to. Once we're done here, you'll have more than enough power to deal with life without your illustrious father."

Malyn's smile fades. "On your knees."

The guards let go of the girl's arms, allowing her to slowly get onto her knees on her own. The girl's eyes take in what's happening on the floor in the corner.

The first girl smiles at the Illiana girl with blood all over her teeth and jaws. She's smearing the blood on the floor as though it was a canvas and blood her paint.

"Please," says the Illiana girl. "I'll do anything you want. I'm no threat to you. I can convince my father of many things."

Queen Malyn holds up the violet patch of fairy skin.

"Why didn't you spear her when you had the chance?" I ask Sentry.

I want an answer but I know he can't tell me. He stares at the violet patch of fairy skin, looking mesmerized.

Could it be that he needs to step aside and allow the queen to free his liege?

I don't know what binds him to her, so I can't guess what's going through his mind. Does he want his liege saved? Or does he want her killed? Even if he wants her killed, he may be forced by the binding to protect her.

Being cursed, I know how complicated your inner landscape can get. I want to say more to him, but I don't, in case the witch can hear me.

"Do stay and watch, little soldier," says Malyn. "You can go back to my royal husband and tell him that you saw the birth of our children." She smiles as though she was speaking in jest.

"This girl is unsuitable," says the witch. "Her spirit is still occupying the body."

"Do it anyway."

"But, Your Majesty, her spirit will fight against an invasion."

"And who do you suppose will win?" Malyn lifts the patch of skin. "This is a fairy so powerful that the Dark King had to trap her in his cloak because he couldn't kill her. He took her and the others with him everywhere he went because he was afraid of letting them out of his sight, even after he'd vanquished them. Did you know that? Do you truly think that this girl who has known nothing but her sheltered garden and the latest fashion of the court can win over a wild fairy?"

"I have no doubts as to the winner, Your Majesty," says the witch. "But the madness phase of the transformation could be...unpredictable." She gestures to the first girl, who begins to cackle.

"You said it wouldn't last long."

"Unless there are unforeseen circumstances. An original soul has priority in her body. She could—"

"It'll be entertaining to see how my old rival does with such a situation."

"You were rivals? If I had known, I wouldn't have fretted so much about a smooth transition."

"It needs to be as smooth as it can be."

There's a pause as the witch thinks about it. "The best way to ensure a smooth transition is to find a near-empty body. There are plenty wandering around the castle."

"I need this one. There is only one Illiana child left alive. The future of her family clan lies with her. Her father and uncles will all do exactly as I say so long as I have control over this girl."

"Then perhaps you can perform the ritual to empty her?" asks the witch.

"Enough discussion," says the queen. "Get on with it."

Malyn cuts off the conversation so abruptly that I wonder

if she has enough power to do the emptying ritual on this girl. Power aside, I'm sure these curses are complicated. There are probably volumes in the sorcerer's tower filled with rules that must be delicately balanced for black magic to work. Malyn doesn't strike me as a scholar, but you never know what power-hungry creatures are capable of.

The witch takes a deep breath, obviously trying to gather herself despite her doubts. For the first time, I wonder if this witch was ever a normal person with emotions that I could understand.

The witch puts her clawed hands out toward the trembling Illiana girl and begins her curse.

CHAPTER 53

The witch chants in a droning tone and sprinkles something from her fingertips onto the violet patch of skin. The queen doesn't seem concerned that some of it falls onto her.

The patch begins to steam. The wispy mist turns into a steady stream of smoke that meanders toward the girl.

The Illiana girl screams and tries to run. The guards hold her still so that she can't even get up off her knees. She struggles with all her might, though, and almost manages to get away.

Almost, but not quite.

I'd do anything to help her. I run up and kick the guard as hard as I can. He grunts, probably thinking it's the girl. But whatever he feels, it isn't enough to get him to let go.

The smoke snakes into her nostrils, her eye sockets, her mouth, her ears. She still flails, but now, it looks like she's fighting herself rather than the guards.

She screams, every part of her going rigid.

The guards drop her and step back as though scorched. They look to the queen for instructions.

Malyn flicks her hand toward the door, and the guards rush out of the chamber. They look like they can't leave fast enough.

The girl's eyes roll. She begins to convulse, jerking uncontrollably on the floor.

"Is she dying?" asks Malyn.

"I don't know, Your Majesty," says the witch. She takes a tiny step back. Involuntarily, I'm sure, but it betrays her anxiety.

In the mirror's reflection, the Illiana girl has two different shades tumbling through her. One is violet-black and the other is white. These mists swirl and grapple, in and out and all around her.

"Come on, Illiana," I mumble. "Fight her off."

The girl screams again. A heart-wrenching, ear-piercing scream that lasts longer than anyone could have breath for.

When it finally dies off, it turns into a soft whimper. Then nothing.

She lies still and motionless on the floor, every part of her limp. Her hair is no longer coifed on top of her head in intricate curls. It lies as limp as she, pointing in every direction like snakes trying to escape the nest.

Just when I conclude that she must be dead, she takes a sharp breath. Her chest arches off the floor, almost to the point of looking like she's about to float. Then she falls back.

Heaving breaths, she gets up like someone who's had a night of too much debauchery and stumbles to her feet. She sways there as though she's drunk.

With her hair streaking over her face, she looks through the hair and glares at everyone in the room, one at a time. I'm relieved when she looks right past me.

There was a part of me that worried that reconstituted fairies could see me. But of course, since Malyn is a fairy, and she can't see me, there's no reason for me to think that another fairy could. Still, it's a relief nonetheless.

The possessing fairy stops her assessment and stares at Sentry.

"Watch out, Sentry," I say. "Remember what the last one did when she first took over a body."

I'm not sure that he hears me. He seems mesmerized by the Illiana girl.

The girl tilts her head to the side. "Sentry?"

Sentry immediately gets down on one knee with his head bowed.

I frown, my heart in my throat.

The girl begins to laugh. It's a throaty, mature laugh, not the high-pitched, carefree laughter of a sheltered girl.

She saunters to Sentry and stands over him.

"Be careful," I hiss. I can't help but think of what happened to the last guard. I rush over, even though there's nothing I can do if she decides to tear his throat out.

"Take off your helmet," she says. "Let me see you."

Without hesitation, Sentry takes off his helmet. His face is chiseled and handsome in a way that makes me ache. His dark hair is tousled and sweaty from the helmet, making him look painfully masculine.

I steal a glance at Malyn and the witch. Malyn could recognize him, but Sentry doesn't seem to care. He only has eyes for the Illiana girl as he looks upon her with adoration.

My heart sinks, feeling heavier than it has in a long time.

"My loyal Sentry." The girl touches his hair.

She strokes it as though he's her pet and she his master. There's tenderness in it, though. I suppose the master of a dog can feel tenderness toward her pet.

"Don't listen to her, Sentry." I move to his side, hoping desperately that some part of him can still hear me. "She's cast a spell on you. She doesn't care about you. You're just a toy soldier to her."

She continues to stroke his hair, and he continues to gaze at her with rapt attention.

"She's going to tear your throat out and roll in your blood any moment now. Can't you see that?"

"We should give her another guard to use so that she may complete her process of bonding," says the witch. "This one seems to have some meaning for her, or at least she thinks this guard is someone she used to know."

"Not likely," says the queen. "Not unless he's been kept alive all these years by magic."

Malyn squints at Sentry. "Have I seen you before?"

I understand her problem. Castle guards all look alike. Sure, they have different-colored hair and different-colored eyes, but unless that coloring is unusual enough to remember, one guard is interchangeable with another.

They all wear the same uniforms, they have the same manly build, they all behave in the identical manner that all royal guards do. That's the whole point of their training. If one falls, a replica takes his place. Us royals wouldn't know the difference from one to the other, despite the fact that they are with us day and night, every single day of our lives.

When I was a princess, I spent more time with my guards than I did with my mother, father and any single nanny combined. But now that I think of it, I can't name a single guard. Nor can I bring up a familiar face—just a generic one that represents "guard" to me.

Before Sentry can answer, the witch answers for him.

"He's a king's guard, Your Majesty. I'm sure you've seen him many times."

Malyn looks sharply over at the witch, making it clear that her opinion is of no consequence. If it had been anyone else, Malyn probably would have the offender's head. But she lets it go.

A sharp suspicion comes up. How many witches can perform this unbinding and binding, I wonder?

It must take a tremendous amount of power. Most likely, it also takes a special talent that a witch probably develops over years, perhaps decades.

I try to look into the dark cowl at the witch's face but see only shadow. I glance again at her reflection in the cracked mirror. The only parts that are different are her hands. They continue to look normal in the mirror while looking clawed and bony in real life.

Interesting. Her hands are the only part of her that I can see clearly. The rest of her is well hidden beneath her cloak and dress.

The witch bows to the queen. "I'll fetch someone in case she needs it, Your Majesty. Not everyone goes temporarily insane when they're freed and immediately bonded to a new body, but it's better to be ready."

Malyn nods, giving the witch leave to go fetch someone. They both walk to where Sentry is kneeling.

The queen stops beside the Illiana girl while the witch walks past us to the door. As she walks by, I swear I hear the witch mumble something.

"What did you say?" asks the queen.

The witch pauses on her way to the door. "I was saying an incantation to clear the room of uninvited spirits, Your Majesty."

I get a prickling sensation along my spine. I'm sure that my sleeping body is getting goosebumps right now.

"Why?" asks Malyn.

"Habit, Your Majesty. It's best to clear the room now and then. Otherwise, a chamber can fill with restless spirits who aren't invited nor wanted. And when that happens, a conversation must be had with the spirits to see what they want."

"Oh." Malyn sounds uninterested.

She's clearly more interested in the girl-turned-fairy in front of her than in hypothetical spirits who may or may not clutter up a room.

The witch leaves the queen's chambers. I look at Sentry, then at the closing doors.

There's nothing I can do to help Sentry, especially if he's so enchanted that he's not even listening to me.

I hurry after the witch.

CHAPTER 54

*T*he guards are gone from the hallway outside the queen's chambers. There's no one there but the witch.

"They ran like frightened rabbits," says the witch. "You can train a soldier to kill, but it's a far greater task to train them not to run."

I realize she's talking to someone. I look around. There's nobody but the two of us.

But she's not looking at me. She's looking down the hall.

"So, spirit. Why are you here?"

She can't see me.

"Can you hear me?" I ask.

"I can."

Blood rushes to my head. A thousand questions jam up in my mouth. Does she understand what is happening to me? Am I stuck here like a ghost forever? Can she reverse the curse and wake my body? And if she does, will I go back to my body?

"Before I banish you, tell me why you're here," she says to the window even though I'm standing beside her.

"I'm not sure how I got here," I say.

She doesn't turn toward me. I suppose my voice isn't directional.

"Why are you releasing the fairies?" I ask.

"It's the queen's will."

"What does she plan to do with them?"

"It's not my place to ask."

"But you have guesses."

She nods. "I do. I presume the fairies will owe the queen favors. Perhaps more than favors. Freeing them from eternal bondage is likely to be worth a full pledge of loyalty to her."

"And if they swear fealty? What does she want with them?"

"Peace and prosperity for all?" Her voice drips with sarcasm. At least she isn't enchanted the way Sentry seems to be.

"Is the kingdom in danger?"

She actually barks a laugh at that. "The kingdom has been in danger for more than a generation. Are you that old of a spirit that you don't know the atrocities that the Dark King committed during his reign?"

"I mean, does the queen have a specific plan that she's intending to carry out with these fairies?" I don't bother to keep the frustration out of my voice.

"You seem very involved for a spirit. What matter is it to you?"

"I have family and friends who are still alive." My body could be considered family, couldn't it? "I want to ensure their safety."

"Wouldn't you rather be free of all worldly cares and go to the afterworld? The afterworld isn't such a terrible place compared to Midnight. I can summon a guide who can show you the way."

"No, thank you."

The last thing I want is to be taken to the afterworld. Being a ghost in the real world is bad enough, and being a non-dreamer in the Dreaming is about as far as my mind will stretch.

Besides, like everyone else, I'll have plenty of time to explore the afterworld when it's time. I'm also skeptical enough to question whether my life in the afterworld would be any better than it is now.

The witch sighs. "I don't know what the queen has in mind. It's nothing good, though. I feel that in my bones. I just know that she's not used to this much power. That can be a dangerous thing."

"What do you mean? She's always had power."

"Not this much."

True. Malyn would have enslaved her enemies a long time ago if she could have.

"What's giving her more power?" I ask.

The witch shakes her head. "Something that keeps getting stronger. Something that allows her to reshape the world."

"The looking glass?"

The witch shivers a little and looks away as though afraid to talk about the mirror. "Something else. I don't know what. I just know that it keeps her from having to sleep."

My breath catches.

"And lately," says the witch, "that source has been making her more powerful. What you see now are the queen's new abilities. Her power is growing, but there's more for her to take."

"What do you mean?"

The witch shakes her head. "She's trying to find something, something not of this realm. She wanted me to help her command dreamers to find what she's looking for." She shakes her head again. "But that sort of power is beyond me. And from what I can tell, she's new to it herself. She's flexing her new powers. Trying them out here and there on servants and guards."

Who else could Malyn be looking for in the Dreaming but me?

There's a power connection between me and Malyn. I know that she's probably using me to sleep for her. But it never occurred to me that she might tap into more than my sleep.

Did she get a power boost when I became aware while my body slept? When I managed to get out of my body? When I stepped into the dreaming without being a dreamer?

Has she been getting a boost to her power every time I've grown my abilities in the Dreaming?

Of course not. It can't be.

But if she can use dreamers to do her bidding in the Dreaming, why hasn't she done it before? Why hasn't she turned people in the Waking into faceless puppets until now?

Maybe she wasn't aware of the boosts to her power until she saw me in the Dreaming. Maybe she didn't know that I'd moved past beyond just sleeping.

I thought the changes to the dreamers had something to do with her kidnapping Sentry. It never occurred to me to correlate my new ability to change into a bird to Malyn's new powers.

Perhaps it isn't a coincidence that Malyn took over the kingdom during the time I was learning to navigate the Dreaming. That means that if I don't wake soon, Malyn could learn to do in the Waking what I can do in the Dreaming.

I reel from the thought.

It can't be true.

It can't.

But I know that it is.

CHAPTER 55

"*W*e have to stop her," I say, pacing around the witch in the hallway.

The witch snorts.

If anyone saw her, they'd think she was mad. How could it be otherwise with her snorting and talking to herself in a dark corridor?

"Isn't there something you can do?" I ask. "Malyn relies on you. Can't you botch a transfer or something?"

"I can certainly botch all kinds of spells and ceremonies. But if I do it in front of the queen, that will be my last mistake. And I fully intend to make many more in the years to come."

"Please. I can make sure you get paid for your troubles."

She snorts again. It's an indelicate sound that matches what I assume she looks like inside that dark hood.

"No need to pay, child. I never volunteered to be in the service of royalty. It's never good when they darken my doorway. I am a simple woman with simple needs. One of those needs is to survive, I'm afraid. And so, I do what they tell me to do, when they tell me to do it."

"So you're nothing but a victim?" I let the sarcasm drip in my tone.

"I'm far more than a simple victim. Otherwise, kings and queens would not seek me out. However, even I am powerless against an army."

"Can you work your position to our advantage? Can you help the people of the kingdom by subverting her plans? Whatever she does, it will not be to the benefit of the people. I fear that she may be worse than the Dark King."

The witch is silent for a moment. I wish again that I could see her face. It's difficult to gauge someone when you can't see their eyes.

"Follow me," says the witch.

"Where?"

"Back into the queen's chambers. I'll see what I can do. Do exactly as I say, even if it doesn't make sense. I'll have to do some fast thinking on my feet, and that might mean you'll have to trust me no matter what goes on in that chamber. Can you do that?"

I hesitate, then nod. I don't know her, but I have no choice but to believe in the kindness of strangers. She may be just a pawn like the rest of us, being forced to do things she doesn't want. Or she could be a murderous fiend who doesn't care much about anything other than herself.

Either way, I'm out of choices. Besides, I'm a ghost that she can't even see. What can she do to me?

"Are you still here?" asks the witch.

"Yes, I'll trust you."

"Then follow me." She turns back to the queen's door.

"What are you planning?" I trot along behind her, getting excited to be able to do something, anything. Hopefully, it'll be something that helps Sentry.

"I'm not planning anything. I'll simply figure it out as I go. But no need to worry. I have exceptional instincts."

The witch pushes through the door without knocking or announcing herself. It's a very intimate servant who walks into the queen's chambers without asking for permission.

That nagging doubt tingles more emphatically. But there's nothing I can do about it. Walking away is my only other option, and that means leaving Sentry behind with that creepy Illiana fairy. It also means I'll likely be stuck here forever.

Inside, the Illiana fairy is licking Sentry's eyelids. I blink hard to make sure I'm seeing it correctly.

I walk over to get a better look. She's actually licking his eyelids. And he just stays still on his knees like a stone soldier, letting her do whatever she pleases.

"What is she doing?" I hiss. "Stop her."

The witch bows to the queen. Normally, a woman would curtsy, but she's apparently not bound by the normal etiquette rules of the court.

"I see that her transformational madness is taking a gentler form than your first child," says the witch.

"Yes, I suppose so." The queen does not sound pleased.

She watches Sentry and the other woman with a distasteful look on her face. If I didn't know better, I'd say she looked almost jealous. But jealous of what, I couldn't guess.

"It's still weird and inappropriate," I say sullenly. Certainly, I have to admit that it's better than her ripping out his throat, but I don't have to admit it out loud.

"Does she think she's a lizard and he her child?" asks the queen.

The witch glances at the Illiana girl and Sentry. "More likely, she probably thinks of him as her mate. Perhaps we should consider ourselves fortunate that her actions haven't progressed beyond licking his eyelids."

The queen raises her noble chin and looks down her

perfect nose at the girl. "I command you to stop licking my guard. He's my property, and I have not given you permission."

I raise my ghostly brows at that. She didn't seem to have any problems with her first "child" tearing the throat out of that other guard.

The Illiana girl continues to lick the rest of Sentry's face as though she hasn't heard Malyn. She does it in a loving, methodical way, making sure to cover every inch of his face with her tongue.

"Sentry, how can you stand that? That's disgusting." I pucker my face in the same way I used to when I ate an especially sour lemon.

Sentry doesn't answer.

"Are you there, Sentry? Has she put a spell on you?" I lean over to get a better look at his face to see if he died or something while I was gone. His chest moves rhythmically up and down with his breath, so I know he's alive.

"We have bigger things to discuss, Your Majesty." The witch moves further into the chamber.

"What is that?" asks Malyn.

She turns to look at the witch. Malyn stops and stares, her body freezing with tension.

I look too, trying to see what she's staring at. What I see chills my bones.

Malyn is staring at my reflection in the cracked mirror.

CHAPTER 56

I stop breathing as I meet Malyn's eyes through the mirror. Her look is intense. She recognizes me.

I can't tear my eyes away from her. The cracks in the glass run jaggedly across her face, splitting her image into pieces as she stares at my reflection.

"What is *she* doing in my chambers?" asks Malyn through her teeth.

Her beautiful face is hard and cold. I stand frozen, unable to breathe.

"That's what I needed to talk to you about, Your Majesty," says the witch. "We have an unexpected guest."

"She is no guest." Malyn doesn't take her eyes off me.

She takes a deep breath and raises her chin, looking even more regal than she already did. "Since this little imp wants to participate in the ritual badly enough to come uninvited, we'll have to give her a proper welcoming." Her harsh tone belies her words. "Bring her to me."

"Come, spirit," says the witch. She turns toward me. Is she guessing by my reflection in the mirror or can she truly see me?

"What should I do?" I'm not sure who I'm asking—the witch, Sentry or me.

"Come to me," says the witch.

Sentry stays silent. My instincts scream for me to run and take Sentry with me.

But my head tells me to stay calm. Didn't the witch say that she was going to improvise as she went along? She sounded sincere. This is her chance to make a difference—to help the people of the kingdom.

I made my decision in the hallway when I followed her in. So I hesitantly walk over to the witch and the queen. Remembering that the looking glass shows my face, I do my best to look confident and unafraid.

"Good." I can't see the witch's face, but she sounds encouraging.

Malyn's face might as well be shrouded too, because I can't read a thing in her expression. She steps over and casually picks up her broken mirror.

A part of me expects her to hold it in front of her the way Nightmare Malyn did, but of course, this Malyn can see for herself. She still holds it at an angle to see me, though. That makes sense since she can't see me directly.

As I near, I get a moment of warning as the hairs on the back of my neck stand. But before I can react, Malyn swipes the mirror at me like a sword.

I jump as the mirror comes at me.

There's a pull from it. It grabs me, and I feel heavy, unable to skitter away.

Malyn turns the mirror and swipes at me from the other way. This time, the gilded frame clips the edge of my shoulder.

Instead of simply grazing me, it catches me. It's not a hand, exactly—more like a force. It pulls me sideways into the glass.

As I fall back, the faces of the queen and the witch distort. The beautiful face of Malyn and the gaping darkness of the witch's cowl elongate and warble.

I can even see Sentry behind them, still kneeling on the floor. He's embracing the Illiana girl, who looks back at me with a sly smile.

And then I'm caught in a whirling darkness.

CHAPTER 57

I wake to the steady throbbing of my finger. It reminds me that I pricked it with a glass shard. The next thing I notice is the background ogre noise of frustrated cursing and grunts from a distance.

The bed beneath me is firm and the body that I cling to is warm and soft. It's a girl, and she's breathing to my exact rhythm.

My eyes fly open. I'm lying in bed hugging my own body. My finger throbs even though the mirror shard that pricked me was tiny and long gone.

How long have I been lying here? How long since I left the castle?

I have no idea. It could have been a heartbeat or a fortnight. Did the mirror claim power over me when it drank my blood? How long did it keep me in its whirling darkness?

It's strange to think of the mirror as though it's a living thing, but I can't help it. That looking glass is more alive than my body. I admit that isn't saying a lot. But I swear that cracked mirror has an agenda that's as evil as Malyn's or the Dark King's.

If the only thing it did to me by drinking my blood is to send me to the Waking and suck me back here again, then I'm all right with that.

I'm safe.

Or as safe as I can get.

So why do I feel so threatened?

I try to make sense of what just happened. My best guess is that I went to the Waking because I was pricked by the mirror shard. It tasted my blood and called me to the Waking.

It could have trapped me there forever—a ghost in a material world. But it didn't.

Why?

My mind dances around the one answer that keeps coming back to me. I don't want to think about it.

I come up with other reasons as to why the looking glass toyed with me like that. But I can't escape the fact that the most likely reason was to send me to the Waking so that the real mirror could follow me back to my tower.

I glance around my chamber. I see nothing but stone walls and the four posters of my bed. I don't see the cracked mirror, but I still feel threatened.

I worry over Sentry too. Is he enslaved? There's nothing more frightening than the thought of being enslaved, not just of body, but of mind. And possibly in his case, of his soul.

My curse is terrible, but at least my soul and mind are still mine. The thought of anyone being trapped like that—especially brave, loyal Sentry—makes me sick.

I roll away from the warmth of my body and get out of bed. I usually don't stay longer than I have to here, but right now, I feel so rough that I need the security of my tower.

No matter how boring and old it is, it's the only home I have. I suppose the same goes for my sleeping body. No matter how much I resent it just lying there, motionless and out of my control, it's the only body I have. And there's comfort in being here—my only haven, such as it is.

I pace. Around and around the small tower I go. My mind races through all kinds of scenarios. Plans form and get discarded, only to be supplanted by new plans. Time passes, but I have no idea how much.

Nothing I think of will help me, Sentry or any of the people in Midnight. One thing keeps coming back to me, though. I managed to affect the guard in the Waking.

It wasn't much, but it was something. It was enough for the guard to react. Who knows how much he would have reacted if he was normal instead of a sleepwalking, cursed slave of the evil queen?

The noise outside my window gets louder, interrupting my thoughts. It's coming from the courtyard below just like the last time I was here, but it sounds closer now.

Closer? Maybe not, or at least not much closer. Bronson sounds alarmed, though, nearly frantic.

Usually, when a "rescuer" finally realizes that *he's* the one who needs rescuing, his yells get more frantic. The difference is that by that time, they're so injured and mired in the thorns that they can barely shout.

Bronson doesn't sound like someone who needs rescuing. He sounds angry. Territorial.

I rush to the window.

Bronson is looking back at the wall and yelling up a storm. He calls out words I don't understand. Ogre cursing, I assume. I turn to where he's looking.

The wall is moving.

Or more accurately, the thorn bush over the wall is moving. It jerks and shifts in a way that's obviously not from the wind.

Now that I'm paying attention, I can hear something

unnatural from the other side of the wall. No voices, but it sounds like wheels rolling over dried branches.

A loud boom shatters the air. I start in surprise and grip the windowsill.

The outer wall trembles from impact.

Bronson lets out a war cry, showing his broken teeth and thick tongue. His muscles bulge and his neck strains as he yells into the air.

Another thunderous boom that shakes the wall.

I back away from the window, overwhelmed by what's happening. This tower is my only sanctuary. It may be a prison, but it's a prison lovingly designed by my father and mother to hide me safely until someone can rescue me.

I'm not naive enough to think that whoever is outside my courtyard is here to rescue me. I can feel the evil intent in the wind as another world-shattering boom resounds.

I'm panting. My body is breathing so fast that I worry... what? That I'll be knocked out?

I try to slow my breathing anyway. I could run. But that won't help me. Besides, what kind of coward am I to abandon my own body in a time of need?

I slam my ghost fist into the stone wall. I always knew there would come a time when I'd have to either go away to let the world do what it will to my body, or stand by and watch helplessly.

Another slam.

This time, something breaks.

I can't help but go back to the window. The wall below is broken. It's not crumbling as I expected. Instead, it's opening like a gate.

I realize that it *is* a gate. The brambles were so thick that I didn't even see that there was a gate there.

One part of the gate falls, smashing through the cushion of brambles. It lies there at an angle, as helpless as my body.

It's thick. I assume it's made of metal or heavy wood, but it's so covered in vines that I can't tell. It's not heavy enough to completely crush the brambles in the courtyard, but it shoves them aside and puts a serious dent in them.

The other part of the gate swings brokenly into the mass of thorns inside the courtyard. In the opening, I see a huge war machine made of thick wood and metal. It swings an enormous tree trunk that must have smashed through the gate.

The battering ram is on a platform with wheels. There are soldiers pushing the machine forward as it shoves against the brambles.

Standing on the platform is their leader, yelling orders to the men. Like the other soldiers, he wears a helmet so I can't see his face. But I recognize his voice.

It's Sentry.

CHAPTER 58

*I*t can't be Sentry. I must be mistaken.

But the commander calls out again for his men to push the battering ram, and I know that it's him.

Sentry walks back to the rear of the contraption and hops off. He mounts a horse behind the men pushing the war machine and waits.

I suppose most people would call their progress slow. But my life has crawled at a glacial pace, and I'm having trouble wrapping my mind around how fast life is changing.

The battering ram shoves through the brambles in the courtyard at an alarming speed. At this rate, they'll be through the courtyard in less than an hour.

I reel at the thought. In less than an hour, they'll be at my tower.

Out of instinct, I try to turn into a large bird so I can fly and get a better look at what the soldiers are doing. But nothing happens. I'm not in the Dreaming.

Sentry and the soldiers are a real part of the Waking, and that's what I'll have to deal with.

I run over to the sleeping girl on the bed. She looks dead in every way except for the shallow rise and fall of her chest. Helpless. Alone.

I shake her, hoping she feels something. But my hands flow through as usual, and the sleeping form doesn't even flutter a lash.

I hesitate. I don't want to go inside my body. I always have this fear that once I go in, I won't be able to come back out. And this is not the time to be stuck in my body.

But I have to try. I can't just abandon myself to the queen's army. Malyn is going to take me and bury me some-place where no one will ever find me. She can't risk someone taking away her greatest source of power.

I let out a long breath and slip inside my body.

As soon as I'm inside, I feel like I'm wrapped in a blanket that's too tight and too thick. I take deep breaths to try to calm myself. It doesn't work.

I use all my willpower to raise my arm, to kick my leg, to roll over.

Nothing. Not even a twitch.

I try again.

Then again.

I try until I'm drenched in sweat.

Apparently, I have an effect on my body even though I can't move a single muscle. It's really uncomfortable and hot now. I feel smothered in my burial dress and the bedding.

I'm convinced the bed canopy will fall on me and suffo-cate me. I have to get out.

In my panic, I can't do anything. That just makes me thrash all the more. I try to scream, but my mouth won't open.

I'm stuck. I can't get out.

My breathing is so fast and shallow that I feel lightheaded. I thrash inside my meat trap, screaming in my head. I can't...I can't...

You can.

It's my own voice in my head, yet it has the calm overtones of Silver. It has the determination of Bronson when he told me how certain he was of his goal.

I take a breath and let it out slowly. I breathe in and out at a pace that I control. Then I slip out of my body. Before I know it, I'm standing beside the bed, staring down at my still form.

Closing my eyes, I move away until my back is against the stone wall. There, I slide down until I'm sitting curled on the floor with my head on my knees.

Silver.

Can I find her? Can she help me?

But the only way I can reach her is in the Dreaming. Seeing her faceless there is more disturbing than I care to admit.

In my head, I immediately hear her telling me that I can help myself. That there's more to me than I realize.

Confidence is hard to embrace while curled on the floor, waiting for soldiers to drag me away and lock me up forever. But I force myself to go through the motions anyway.

I think through my resources—people or things that could help. I might be able to reach the wolfkin if any of them are dreaming in their wolf form. But based on Ketter's nightmare, they have their own problems to deal with. Silver is unreachable now in the Dreaming. Sentry is lost to his eye-licking fairy.

There's just me.

I take a deep breath and accept myself as an asset to my situation.

There must be something I can do to affect the soldiers, even if they're in the Waking part of my courtyard. If I'm a ghost here, I should be able to do what ghosts do, just like when I visited the Waking.

I get up, determined to do *something*. I run at the window. I close my eyes and try not to worry.

I jump out of the window.

CHAPTER 59

I can be melodramatic at times. But I didn't think I'd really jump out of a window until I did it.

Jumping from the top of a tower is ill-advised for most occasions. But doing it in the Waking—which my tower exists in—is definitely not wise.

But stubborn me, I do it anyway. Well, it might be more about desperation than stubbornness, but it's hard to tell the two apart sometimes.

As soon as I leap out of the window, I know I'm in trouble. I fall like a rock.

But I don't just fall through the air unencumbered. My leap didn't clear the brambles climbing up my tower.

I fall through the brambles, getting torn to shreds on the way down. I cry out in rage and pain. Aren't I just a ghost? How unfair is it that even in ghost form, I'm—

That's it. I should be like the wind. There is no form to shred.

Just before I land face-first into the thicket of knife-sized thorns, I curve in my trajectory.

I'm flying. Well, at least I'm no longer falling.

I'm in the Waking. And I'm floating on air.

I try not to think about it too much. I'm afraid that realizing that I shouldn't be able to fly might make me fall. I feel heavy just thinking about it.

Light. Light as air, light as mist.

I keep that image in mind, convincing myself that I'm like a cloud in every part of my being.

Sure enough, I float higher.

Up close, I can see why even enormous ogres have died on these thorns. Now that I see what the brambles truly look like, I'm surprised that anyone ever tries it.

Some are sword-sized, while others are needle-sized. The combination of the two is the deadliest thing I've ever seen.

I float above Bronson. Up close, he looks worse than I imagined. He smells worse than I imagined too. Broad-faced with nostrils big enough for a horse and carriage to ride through, he won't be winning any beauty contests.

He's strong, though. I didn't realize how big and muscular he is. He's stabbed on every side by thorns. Blood trickles down so profusely that he looks red under the moonlight.

"Sorry," I say to him as I fly by.

I don't know if he hears or sees me. He roars his outrage as he twists to confront the new invaders.

I land lightly on the battering ram. I wish I weighed more to make it harder for the soldiers to push the contraption into my courtyard. Then it occurs to me that maybe I *can* weigh more.

I imagine myself to be a giant boulder. I don't actually turn into a boulder, but I can feel myself feeling heavier. My feet feel like they're indenting the wood. When I look down, I see that they are.

It'll be interesting to see what the soldiers think of the

indentations of my feet on their battering ram. The contraption slows down. The men pushing it grunt and heave, but it moves slower and slower into the courtyard.

I'm giddy with the fact that I seem to be able to affect things in the Waking in the same way that I can in the Dreaming. Well, maybe not quite in the same way, but in *some* way.

A part of me worries that my growing abilities are just making Malyn stronger, but I'll worry about that later if I survive. Right now, I need those abilities.

I step along the battering ram to the back where I can see the men better. There are half a dozen soldiers pushing the contraption. There are far more men behind them, but there's only room for six. Any more and the thorns would get them.

Bronson shoves and hacks his way to those six men. When the soldiers see the bloody ogre coming for them, they shuffle back into each other with wide eyes. They're trapped, though, as the soldiers behind them won't budge.

I have to admit, Bronson does look frightening.

"Go get 'em, Bronson!" I say. "Don't let these skinny soldiers invade your territory."

I leave him to wade his way to the soldiers.

Behind the soldiers is Sentry. He looks handsome and stately on his steed. If I didn't know better, I'd say he was the one who was meant to rescue me.

But there's something odd about him. It takes me a moment to identify what that is.

He sits ramrod straight on his horse. His shoulders are even and wide, his legs exactly where they should be on a horse.

He looks like a perfectly formed statue. Or perhaps it's more accurate to say that he looks like a painting done by a talented apprentice who hasn't yet mastered the art of breathing life into his pictures.

There's something odd about Sentry's eyes too. They seem shinier than they should be. They're not flashing or anything, but the more I look, the more I can see a reflection of myself.

No, not me. A female face, though, looking out through his eyes. It doesn't make sense. I have to get closer to get a better look.

His irises are shiny and mirrored. There's someone there, peering out. It reminds me of someone peering into a mirror and seeing me on the other side.

I suddenly fly away just as Sentry grabs for me. My heart is racing as I swerve to look back at him. His eyes track me.

He can see me. Or more likely, whoever is looking through the mirrors of his eyes is watching me.

Queen Malyn. Who else could it be? She must have wrestled him away from that eye-licking fairy and taken control.

My heart aches knowing just how deep Sentry is under Malyn's control. Sentry points to me.

"There!" he calls. "She's in the air."

The soldiers beside him throw nets into the air where he's pointing. The meshed weave comes right at me.

I don't even have to concentrate to make the nets flow through me. It's what's been happening to me for years.

I fly up anyway to get out of their reach. I perch on a sword-sized thorn on the wall and watch the soldiers below.

Sentry doesn't seem to care much that I've escaped. It breaks my heart to see him like this. He's not faceless, but I'm not sure that what's happened to him is much better.

I want to call out to him from this safe distance. To ask him if he's all right. To see if I can wake him out of his spell.

But I've seen the power I'm up against. Between Malyn,

her mirror and the witch, my little plea for Sentry to wake up won't do anything but bring attention to myself.

Sentry calls for the men to keep pushing the battering ram through the courtyard. They push with all their might. The strain shows in their corded muscles all along their bodies.

Step by step, they make steady progress toward my tower.

CHAPTER 60

I'm sitting on the sword-sized thorns on the wall of my courtyard, watching the soldiers progress toward my tower. The soldiers keep trying to steer the battering ram clear of the raging ogre, but Sentry won't let them. He forces them to take the shortest route to the tower, bringing them directly to Bronson.

Bronson defends his territory—or maybe he's defending his princess. He sounds like he believes that, but I can't help but feel like a prize being fought over.

If they can fight to win me as a prize, then so can I. I have the most to gain or lose in this battle. And I have more powers than I realize. How else could I sit on this deadly bush of thorns and watch the fight in the first place?

Of course, any new tricks I learn will only expand Malyn's power, but I have to try to save myself.

I wish I had someone to teach me, but no one in history has been in the Dreaming for as long as I have. It's up to me to figure out what I'm capable of.

I fly down, careful to stay behind Sentry so that he won't

see me. I hover beside a soldier in the back of the procession and whisper in his ear.

"Sleep. You're so sleepy. Wouldn't you rather be with your girl at home? You can do that right now. All you have to do is lie down and dream of her."

The soldier yawns.

Excited, I continue whispering. The man falls behind the others as his steps get smaller and slower.

"Think of a nice cushion for your head. The sunshine on your face. How about a full belly after your mother's excellent meals?"

His head begins to droop, and he uses his pike as a support rather than a weapon.

It's working. But at this rate, it'll take me a year to get all the soldiers to fall asleep.

I know the mirror can see me through Sentry's eyes. But can it hear me as well?

Fear pierces through me as surely as one of these thorns. I can't help but be afraid of that looking glass. There's something beyond sinister about it.

But it doesn't look like there's a prince on his steed galloping to rescue me. I must rescue myself. And in order to do that, I need to take some risks.

I yawn, loud enough for everyone to hear. I keep an eye on Sentry, but he doesn't turn to look at me. It doesn't mean that he doesn't hear me, though. I don't think he's deaf. But the mirror looks out through his eyes. What he hears may not go back to the mirror the way his vision does.

I yawn again—loud and slow.

A couple of the soldiers yawn. A few more soldiers near them yawn. Then it spreads.

I've always been fascinated by how people catch yawns the way they might catch the flu.

"Sleepy," I say in a lullaby voice. I yawn loudly again.

"Dreamtime. Let's all go into the Dreaming, shall we? No more work, no more fear. The sun shines there and people laugh. There's food aplenty and girls, oh so many girls."

Is the battering ram slowing?

At that moment, Bronson reaches the side of the procession. He hacks and slashes at the soldiers with his sturdy stick as though they are the thorn bush.

Bronson is both strong and fierce. He's driven to fight for his territory and his princess, while the soldiers simply want to stay out of trouble.

The soldiers scatter and back off as much as they can without attracting the ire of their commander. Bronson would have chased them all away, I'm sure, except that they seem to be more afraid of their commander than the angry ogre.

As fierce as Bronson is, he's just one ogre. The queen's soldiers outnumber him, and they bring him down by sheer force. I feel bad for Bronson as he goes down like a giant swarming with ants.

"Ignore all that," I whisper to my own group of soldiers. "It's just someone else's dream. It has nothing to do with you. You're safe and sleepy."

I keep talking in a soothing voice, doing my best to be sleep-inducing.

One of the soldiers nods, then jerks his head back up. Another stumbles over his dragging feet.

Then one after the other, they droop to the ground like rag dolls and fall asleep.

CHAPTER 61

I'm stunned.

I had no idea this was even possible. I look at all the soldiers around me who are on the ground, gently snoring.

Bronson is at the bottom of the pile of sleeping soldiers, snoring loudly.

I look up with what must be a delighted expression and see Sentry. He's the last one standing.

He doesn't look remotely sleepy.

If anything, his eyes are shinier than ever. Queen Malyn stares furiously at me through them. Her normally beautiful face is so marred with rage that she looks hideous.

"I know you're in there, Sentry. Fight it. Please."

Sentry blinks twice. Then he gets off his horse. Alone, he climbs onto the battering ram. When he reaches the front end, he rips the thorns ahead of him and steps into the thicket.

"Sentry, no!"

He begins to bleed almost immediately. The thorns are so high that he almost drowns in them.

"No! Come back." My voice breaks. "Sentry, please."

A particularly large thorn stabs him in his shoulder. He keeps moving forward, shoving it aside.

Malyn has full control of him. She doesn't care if she kills Sentry so long as he follows her will.

Expanding my capabilities has only made her control over Sentry stronger. She'll push him until he's dead.

And then what?

The soldiers will wake eventually. I might have newfound powers to put them to sleep and send them to the Dreaming, but I can't keep them there forever.

And even if they all run away, Malyn knows where I am now. She'll send more soldiers. And more. And more. Until she has me in her clutches.

This is not a war I can win.

I want to savor my victory for a while longer. I want the queen to know that I am not powerless.

But my moment of pride will surely cost Sentry his life. And what about my friends? Will the queen somehow take her fury out on them?

I make my decision and rush back to the sleeping men.

"Wake up!" I kick the soldiers. "Get up! You have work to do."

The soldiers rouse slowly, groggily. I interrupted them in the middle of their dreams. As soon as they get to their feet, though, they see Sentry tearing himself up to pieces on his way to the tower.

The soldiers rush to get back to pushing their war machine.

The battering ram rolls up to Sentry and the soldiers urge him to get on before they roll him over. For a heart-stopping moment, I worry that he won't listen. What if Malyn and the mirror force him to continue just to punish me?

But Sentry does get onto the battering ram. He's torn and

bloody—cut and stabbed in a thousand places. He doesn't seem to notice, though.

Sobs rack my ghostly body. I don't know if I'm crying for Sentry or for me. I suppose both.

I watch as the soldiers push steadily through the thorns that have protected me for decades, getting ever closer to my tower.

CHAPTER 62

$\mathcal{I}$ sit on the edge of the bed beside the sleeping girl. As always, she lies there, looking serene. Even in the worst of times—which this certainly is—she just lies there, being what she is. An empty body that refuses to wake.

"All this time, I blamed you. As if you had anything to do with it."

Even now, though, I want to yell at her to get up, to fight, to do *something*, anything. But in the end, it's my job to protect my own body, isn't it?

Sentry's dark helmet shows up at my window. I've never seen anyone climb up the tower before, so this is new. Not unexpected, but it's still a shock.

He's streaming in blood. His helmet protected him from the worst of it. And despite his eyes being vulnerable and open to attack, they seem unharmed but for the unnatural mirrored reflections where his irises should be.

Sentry is hurt, but he was protected by Malyn's power. After all, the thorns themselves are from Malyn. She must have made sure that they wouldn't kill her own servants.

Sentry's hands are a mess, and he's bleeding everywhere.

The thorns were sharp enough and strong enough to pierce his leather armor, but they didn't stick to him. Unlike Bronson, Sentry doesn't have a single thorn in him.

He heaves himself up onto my windowsill. There he rests, breathing heavily. Queen Malyn stares through his eyes with open triumph at the sleeping girl.

If he was a stranger and I was corporeal, I could shove him. Then I would stay safe for a little longer while he fell to his death.

Sentry sighs with exhaustion. Hearing it reminds me that he is a person, not just a puppet.

"Are you there, Sentry? Can you hear me?"

He doesn't look up at me. Queen Malyn is laughing in triumph as she looks out through his eyes at the sleeping maiden.

For the first time, I see my body the way a stranger might see me. A fresh young woman, lying on a white canopy bed. A breeze blows through the window, ruffling the light curtains gathered around the four posters.

The crescent moons of her lashes accent her smooth cheeks and red lips. Her hands lie on top of each other in the center of her chest. It's been so long that I never even see my dress anymore, but now, I see that it's the kind of dress my mother would have put me in if I was to meet my prince for the first time.

Young and fragile, feminine and regal.

Sentry looks at the girl in the bed, mesmerized. Maybe in another life, another place, it could have been a different kind of meeting between us. But now, I feel like he's the man who was sent to carry me to my funeral.

He steps over to the bed and gently pulls me to him. For a moment, I think he's going to kiss me.

But of course, he doesn't.

He pulls my body into an embrace, then lifts her over his

shoulder. With all his blood dripping, I'm surprised she doesn't slip right off him.

He manages to steady himself and walk back to the window. By the time he begins climbing through, he's carrying the body like it's a part of himself.

I stand hovering by him as he climbs to the outside of the tower. I'm convinced that he'll drop me. His hands are bloody and must be slippery. But he manages to hold on to both my sleeping body and to the twisted trunks of the vines.

That's when I realize that the thicket of brambles that's always protected my tower has lost its thorns. It's just a criss-cross of bare trunks the size of thin trees. They may be the size of saplings, but the trunks look ancient, with cracks running through the rough bark.

Sentry uses the strong lattice like a ladder. Despite his burden, he has no trouble climbing down.

When he reaches the ground, his men try to take the girl from him. But Sentry will have none of it. He holds my body in his arms and leads the way back through the path they cut.

The tower feels empty with the bed holding nothing but rumpled sheets. There's something essential missing now that there's just me without my shell.

I fly down to follow. Wherever my body goes, I must as well. It occurs to me that all those times when I thought of the tower as my sanctuary, it was actually my body that gave me comfort all along.

My body is my home, not some stone room. It seems obvious now, but it hasn't been for so long. I have harbored a resentment for my body for so long now that I almost didn't know how to be with it. I've spent so much time demanding my flesh to follow my will. I was cruel in the way I thought of it as being stupid and willful for not moving, not listening to my commands, not being like everyone else's body.

But now that I see the helpless, limp girl being carried

258

away, all I want to do is protect her. This body is the only one I have, and it's no use blaming her for my troubles.

I follow Sentry as he walks out of the courtyard through the ruins of the gates. I intend to follow all the way to whatever dank hole Queen Malyn decides to throw me into. I have this fear that if I don't know where my body is, I might be lost forever.

But as soon as I reach the gate, I hit an invisible wall.

I can't move past it.

A soldier walks right through me as he follows Sentry. The slimy feeling of someone passing through me is shocking under normal circumstances, but it's especially bad this time since I'm not prepared for it.

I shimmy over a few steps and try to get past the barrier. No luck.

The soldiers walk through me as I move side to side, exploring every inch of the gateway. I try to ignore the icky feeling of the soldiers. What I care about is that I can't move beyond my courtyard walls.

I can only stand here, watching my body being taken away.

CHAPTER 63

*T*he last of the soldiers hitched their horses to the battering ram and rolled away some time ago.

I stand at the border between my courtyard and the rest of the world, unable to move forward and unable to go back.

The moon shines down on the forest outside my courtyard. In the center, it's a mass so thick that even the moonlight has trouble penetrating. But it practically glows along the treetops and edges where the moonbeams seem to spear it.

Behind me, the silence is only broken by a loud snoring. Bronson lies in the middle of the path, facedown. He looks like a pile of coal under the moon. His breathing is steady and slow as he snores.

Apparently, he didn't wake with the rest of them. Looking closer, I can see why.

He has a bump on his head. It's swelling enough to look like another head that's trying to work itself out. The soldiers did not go easy on him, despite greatly outnumbering him. Cowards.

"Well, that's just great. You and me, Bronson. Looks like we're all that's left."

I walk over to him and sit in the dirt. The battering ram must have had some kind of metal nose that went all the way to the ground, because it tore up the bramble from the roots.

The ground is cold and lumpy, but there's an odd comfort in sitting beside the sleeping ogre the way I always sat beside my sleeping body. I can feel the subtle warmth coming from him. I suppose that was always the case when I sat beside myself too, but I wasn't aware of it until now.

"I'm sorry."

I don't even know what I'm sorry about. For hating my poor body and blaming it for all the things it couldn't do. For hating Bronson for being an ogre instead of a prince. For not being able to help Sentry or any of my friends.

Mostly, I think I'm sorry for failing to protect myself. My body is lost, completely out of my control, and I don't even know how to find it.

There's nowhere for me to go. No one for me to turn to.

Bronson twitches in his sleep. He's dreaming. I can see it in his eyes as they move rapidly back and forth beneath his lids. I can feel it too.

There's a subtle pull that lets me know there's a window into his dream. All I have to do is step into it to escape my current reality.

An ogre's dream is bound to be utterly disgusting, but the temptation is undeniable. Apparently, I'm in the mood to punish myself.

I flow into Bronson's dream.

For a moment, I'm disoriented.

I'm back in my tower, standing beside my bed. My body is there, sleeping peacefully as usual.

Beside the bed is a prince. He's dressed in fine armor that was obviously crafted by a master. It's etched with a crest on his chest. It looks familiar, yet I don't recall where I've seen that crest before.

He takes off his helmet to reveal a very handsome face with dark hair and hazel eyes. His hair is damp and disheveled from his helmet.

I'm so mesmerized by this man that I forget I'm in a dream. Then I notice that my body isn't really mine. If I described her, it would sound like me, but her jaw is too heart-shaped, her lashes too long. She's taller and thinner than me as well.

That snaps me into remembering that I'm in a dream. I look around. Where is Bronson?

There's no place to hide in the small tower room. Odd. I don't think I've experienced a dream where the dreamer isn't in it. Occasionally, a dream has nothing to do with the dreamer, but they're usually lurking somewhere nearby, watching.

I notice something even stranger. The handsome prince is glowing a little while my body is not.

"Oh, you can't be serious." I put my hands on my hips and glare at the prince.

The prince looks at me. He is so handsome that it's hard to remember anything else.

"No, I don't believe it." I look under the bed. "Bronson, where are you?"

"I'm right here," says the prince.

I bark a laugh. "Thank you. I needed this right now. I didn't think I could find anything funny after what just happened in the Waking."

I scrutinize him, looking for any hint of piglet ears and beady eyes. All I see is a man so handsome that he could only exist in a dream.

"This is how you see yourself?" I ask. "Really?"

The difference between this beautiful prince and the ogre

who's been sweating and grunting outside my tower for days is so extreme that I have to bark another laugh.

"And how should I see myself?" he asks.

It seems rude to describe what he really looks like. I can't think of a kind description of any part of him. "Why are you in this ridiculous guise, Bronson?"

"What's so ridiculous about it?" He looks down at himself as if to see if he has an egg stain on his armor.

"Why would an ogre like you want to look like a man?"

He frowns. "An ogre? What have I done to deserve such an insult?"

It's my turn to frown. "Don't sound so offended."

"Most people would sound offended when called an ogre."

"An ogre wouldn't." I jerk my chin at my sleeping body on the bed. "What are you planning to do with her?"

He looks a bit sheepish. "I'm going to kiss her."

"That's awfully rude of you, kissing maidens like that without an invitation." I tense, thinking much worse could happen. After all, it is *his* dream.

"I have an invitation."

"What invitation?"

"Well, it's a rather old one, but the invitation stands so long as this princess remains asleep."

"Enlighten me. What invitation?"

"When the princess fell under an evil fairy's spell, the old king of Midnight hid her in this tower. The location was a deep secret, but a letter was sent to all the neighboring kingdoms. Nowadays, that would never happen, of course. The Kingdom of Midnight is isolated and no one dares to come in or out without the Dark King's permission. But back then, it was possible."

I don't bother to tell him that the Dark King is dead.

"What did this letter say?" I'm interested in his story

despite the ridiculousness of this ogre who pretends to be a man. My father would never have sent one of those letters to an ogre.

"It told of his daughter's curse and invited—no, pleaded for a prince to set her free. The old king offered his daughter's hand in marriage to the one who kissed her awake. The problem was that it didn't give the location of the tower."

"And it took you this long to find her?"

He grins. "Hardly anyone in my generation even knows about her. My uncle tried to rescue her. We thought we'd lost him, but eventually, he came back. He was permanently injured and forever haunted. He wouldn't speak of it until I told him that I was going to try to rescue a princess. Then he only talked to me about it to convince me to give up the quest."

"Why would you try it if your kin came back broken by the quest? And by that time, surely the Dark King had taken over, so you wouldn't even get a kingdom as a reward."

"Have you no sense of adventure?" He gestures to his sleeping princess. "She needs to be rescued. Who doesn't want to be a hero?"

I had no idea that ogres wanted to be heroes. Or that they had uncles. If he was telling me this in the Waking, I wouldn't believe him. But dreamers fully believe their dream reality, so they rarely lie.

"What are you going to do with her once you wake her?"

"Marry her, of course."

I flinch. I look at the perfectly handsome prince and wonder—why couldn't he be real? And why couldn't he have come sooner?

I sigh, slumping my shoulders and bowing my head in defeat.

CHAPTER 64

*B*ronson looks perplexed and a little offended at my reaction. "Among my people, it would be a great honor to marry me."

"I'm sure it would be. For *them*. But I'm just getting a little tired of people using the poor little sleeping maiden as an excuse to further their own agendas."

"What agenda? All I'm going to do is wake her and free her from her curse."

"You're not going to show her off? Prove to your uncle and the world that you are such an amazing hero that you conquered the quest that no other could accomplish?"

"I'm allowed to take some pride in rescuing my princess, but I don't need to be crass about it. If she doesn't like it, she can go back to sleep." He says this with such confidence that it's clear he doesn't believe that anyone would ever reject him.

"And if she wants to be awake and live her own life?"

"Why would she want that?" He arches his brow in a regal fashion. Bronson must have seen a highborn sometime in his life, because he's mimicking the mannerism of an arrogant prince perfectly.

"Perhaps she wants to pick up her own life from where she left off."

"But that's not possible. The kingdom is no longer hers."

"And you don't care? All you'd get out of the marriage would be this tower."

"And her claim to the Midnight throne."

"Ah. I see. As her husband, you would have a claim to the throne, thus putting you on equal or better footing with anyone who might challenge you. I wouldn't have guessed that you'd care much for political weddings."

"She's comely enough and of royal blood. I could do worse."

"You sound like you don't care much, but anyone who came this far would have to care quite a bit. You risked your life daily to get here."

"I did, and I would do it again."

"Why? Are the women in your kingdom so terrible?" I imagine female ogres are probably as hideous as the males. Perhaps they might have fewer warts and smell a bit better.

"They're all the same."

"Unlike the one who is asleep and mysterious." And human.

"Make fun of me all you like, little wraith. The princess will be beyond grateful when I wake her."

"She'll see your true form and probably run screaming from you."

He frowns deeply. "If she's not happy with me, she's free to choose another."

"Truly? Your kiss is obligation-free, despite the king's promises?"

"Truly. I do not sell my kisses, regardless of what the merchant class says."

"You have a merchant class in the kingdom of ogres?"

Bronson sighs heavily. "Do you mind?" He motions toward the sleeping girl. "I've come a long way to wake the Sleeping Beauty."

I nod and step aside. No need to needle him further. He must have heard that my father sent letters to the noble houses and neighboring kingdoms. Certainly, Father did not send any missives to the ogres, but stories get around.

I have to admit that, in his dream form, he's everything I could hope for—except for that overconfidence. But handsome or not, there's still the chance that he'll eat her the moment she wakes. Dreams can only disguise one's nature for so long.

"All right then," I say. "Let's see."

Will he devour her? Or kiss her? Not that it matters. But if I don't distract myself, all I'll have to think about is the soldiers carrying off my body to some place I'll never find.

For the first time, Bronson looks nervous. Maybe he's not so sure of himself after all.

He bends over and plants a chaste kiss on the sleeping girl's cheek. He stands tall again and looks down at the girl.

"What is it that you expect to happen?" I let sarcasm drip even though I know what he expects.

"That she wakes."

"Well, she's not waking. You must not be a wonderful kisser."

"I'm a fine kisser. I just don't want to take liberties, even though her father has already given permission to kiss her awake."

"How long did it take you to find her?"

"Don't know. It was either three months or three years."

I'm not surprised. I wouldn't expect an ogre to have much of a sense of time.

"Time is strange in the forest." His voice is hushed, letting me know that even ogres are afraid of the forest. "For all I know, it could have been thirty years."

Bronson bends over again to kiss the princess. He looks like the perfect prince kissing his perfect bride. It's all too pretty for it to be anything but a dream.

This time, he plants a gentle kiss on the lips. I'm surprised at how gentle he can be despite his true nature.

The sleeping girl does not stir.

Interesting that even in his own dream, he seems to know on some level that he is not suitable for a princess. He looks crestfallen. Then he looks at me as though it's my fault.

"I didn't do anything." I throw my hands in the air. "It's *your* dream."

"How do I wake her? Her father's letter said a kiss would break the curse."

"I—" My words dry up as the girl stirs in the bed.

At first, it's the smallest change in her breath. Then there's definitely a shift in her shoulders.

I can hardly breathe. Even in dreams, I haven't seen my body move a single strand of hair or a twitch of a finger.

The girl coughs—a small, delicate cough. I have to remind myself that my body is not actually waking up. It's an ogre's dream, and he can do what he will. That girl is clearly just a specter.

The princess gets up gracefully. Her dress looks nothing like mine. The style is more current with sleek, floating sleeves that show a layer of inner lace rather than the old-fashioned puffy short sleeves that mine has. This princess looks modern and fashionable.

Bronson looks enchanted. His eyes are full of wonder and…dare I say love?

She leans right into his arms. He enfolds her in his embrace. And the two kiss.

CHAPTER 65

*B*ronson and his dream princess kiss.
And kiss.

And kiss.

"All right, enough." I can't help the disgust. I don't care if he looks handsome in his dream. An ogre is an ogre, and no amount of dream-wishing is going to change that.

I wave my arms to clear the dream. Nothing happens. I'm still in the tower and the ogre still looks like a prince, and he's still kissing his dream princess.

I wave my arms again, willing the dream to merge with another dream, any dream. No change.

"What have you done with my abilities?" I demand as I shove my face uncomfortably close to his kissing face.

He waves a hand at me to go away, not bothering to stop kissing his dream specter.

"How come I can't make you stop dreaming this?" I ask.

"Maybe your powers don't work on the prince who is meant to wake the princess," he says from the side of his mouth as he continues to kiss the girl.

"Impossible." Is it? "You're using some kind of ogre dream power or something."

He doesn't answer. I see their tongues slipping back and forth and I want to vomit.

"Stop it."

They keep going.

I turn away from them and pace. I probably should just leave his dream, but I have nowhere better to go, do I?

"How did you know to find me?" the girl specter asks.

Bronson cups her delicate face in his hands. "Your father did everything he could to save you, even if it meant begging his enemies for help."

I swallow at the thought of my proud father begging for help.

"He was a good king and a good father." Bronson strokes the girl's cheek.

"And you were moved by his plea?" she asks, adoration in her eyes.

"I was in search of a quest all my life, and didn't even know it." Bronson's voice is intimate and hushed. "All my life, I felt restless and empty, looking for something that I couldn't even describe. When I read the letter your father wrote, pleading for someone to find and wake his daughter, I knew that was what I was meant to do."

"How did you know?" asks the dream girl. She has a kind and wise smile, and I wonder if he expects me to be like that.

"Your father described you in his letter. How much spirit you had, how you were capable of anything once you set your mind to it. He included a drawing of you, and didn't even have to say how beautiful you were. I longed to meet you even before I finished the letter. I knew immediately that this was the quest I'd been looking for. That you were the one I was meant for."

The girl takes a deep breath and sighs. She makes it clear by her gaze that he is her entire world.

He touches his forehead to hers and whispers, "I've been so achingly lonely my whole life. I'm the third son of a wealthy king, which gives me no destiny other than waiting for my brothers to die. But they are well loved and will be great kings. I can do naught but wish them well."

"So you chose your own destiny," she says breathlessly.

He nods. "Going on a quest to rescue my bride was the first thing I wanted to do."

"Why?" asks the girl.

The adoration in her eyes is hard to watch, but I can't tear my eyes from the couple. She may not be me, but she looks similar enough. Bronson must have memorized the drawing of me.

"Because unlike most nobles at court," says Bronson, "I wanted to know what it felt like to have adventure…and I wanted to know what it felt like to truly fall in love."

The way he whispers the words sends a shiver through me.

Love isn't a word I like to use. There are a lot of things that need to come together to make my awakening a reality. A million things could go wrong. And by the look of things, they have. To add love as one of the criteria would make the whole thing laughably improbable.

But there it is, right in front of me.

CHAPTER 66

"Whose dream is this?" I spread my hands out, frustrated by being sucked into something I don't want to feel.

I don't want to know that my father was brought to his knees trying to save me. I don't want to be taunted by a vision of what I can never have.

"Ogres don't dream of love," I say. I know I sound belligerent, but I don't care.

"And that's why you should know that I'm not an ogre," Bronson growls. "But perhaps *you* are. Will you please leave me to my dream? It's a good one, and I want to enjoy every bit of it."

The girl doesn't seem to know I exist. Nor does she respond to her prince talking to me. It's as though he never speaks to me in her world. She simply stands in his arms, looking adoringly at him.

"If you're not an ogre, then what are you?" I ask.

"A prince. How many times do I have to say it?"

"From what kingdom?"

"Everness."

"No one believes in Everness anymore," I say.

I know it's our neighboring kingdom, but those who grew up during the Dark King's reign think it's a child's tale.

"Well, I'm trying not to believe in you, but that doesn't change the fact that you're still here, does it?" he asks.

"You'd be killed or kidnapped for ransom if anyone knew that you were royalty from Everness."

"Certainly. If the fairies or wolfkin or ogres or witches didn't get to me first. This land is full of deadly enemies." He looks down at the dream girl in front of him. "But it was worth every moment."

"Stop looking at me like that. It's creeping me out."

He turns to assess me. "You? What are you talking about?"

"Never mind. What if I told you that this little princess of yours is gone?"

He frowns. "Gone where? Someone else woke her?"

"Not exactly. They've taken her."

He nods, looking strained as though reaching at vague memories. "I remember… Where did they take her?"

"I don't know. Out into the woods. Can you follow their tracks?"

He nods. "Shouldn't be hard with that colossal battering ram they're rolling through the underbrush."

"You remember?"

He nods again. "I think so."

"Can you take me with you?" My words come out hushed and rushed.

"Why would I do that?"

"I can help you."

"How?"

I shrug. "I'm useful in many ways. I have no doubt that I can help."

"Why would you want to? What does a wraith care about whether I find my princess?" He glances at his dream girl.

She's frozen in her adoring smile, her whole body beginning to look misty.

"Oh, you'd be surprised at what I care about," I say. "If you take me with you, I promise to help."

He crosses his arms and stands with his feet apart. He looks rather skeptical and unmovable.

"Explain to me what you get out of this deal," he says. "I don't want any surprises if I agree to work with you."

I consider telling him the whole truth. It would be a relief to have someone know what I'm going through. But that someone should be Silver or one of the wolfkin—someone I trust and have a history with. Seeing how easily Queen Malyn can turn people into her dedicated slaves makes me cautious.

"I'm a ghost who is stuck here. I can't get out on my own. If you take me with you outside of this courtyard, then I promise to help you on your quest to find your princess."

"You're imprisoned here?"

I nod.

He thinks about it. "How do I know that you won't tear me to pieces when I get you out of your prison?"

"Why would I bother? I have no aggression toward you."

He gives me a sidelong look.

"Well, only a little. And not anymore. Not if we're partners. Look, the longer we dawdle, the farther away they'll take your princess. If we don't catch up to them soon, they'll take her to the queen. Trying to get her out of Midnight Castle will be impossible. We need to reach them while they're still in the forest. It's the only chance we have."

He sighs. He knows I'm right.

"All right," he says. "How do I take you with me?"

That's a great question. I have to think about that before I come up with an answer.

"Let me ride in your dream as you walk out of the courtyard."

"How do I do that?"

I chew on my lip and frown. "I don't know. Can you walk and dream at the same time?"

"Of course not. If I'm dreaming, I'm asleep."

"Maybe you could try to be in the twilight of waking and move at the same time? Some people do sleepwalk."

"Not me."

"How do you know? Have you tried it?"

"Nobody ever *tries* to sleepwalk. It's a thing they do."

"Maybe they would if they had good reason to try it. Now, you have a good reason."

He sighs. "All right. I'll try it."

I beam. Then a thought occurs to me. "What do I look like to you?"

He cocks an eyebrow. "Like a squat little troll. What else would you look like?"

"A troll? You look like a prince, and I look like a troll?"

"I *am* a prince, and you *are* a troll."

I take a deep breath. "We are going to finish this conversation another time. I don't want to wake you with my screeching."

"The last thing I want to hear is troll screeching."

"I'm not—" I curl my lip at him.

"Don't distract me. I'm going to try to move toward the gates."

I walk out of his dream to direct him. I get some satisfaction in seeing his rolls of flesh and bald ogre head with pointed ears.

Somehow, though, there's also a bit of disappointment too. I suppose I got used to seeing him as a handsome prince.

CHAPTER 67

"This way, ogre." I keep my voice hushed. I want to sound like the wind, gently guiding him.

In the Waking, Bronson the ogre staggers and stumbles over the crushed brambles. I walk back into his dream to keep him dreaming.

"Stay with me," I say.

In the Dreaming, Bronson the handsome prince has his eyes closed and is drifting around in the tower with his hands out in front of him. He's ghostly and barely visible in the Dreaming.

He's drifting in the twilight between realms—half dreaming, half-awake—walking in a sleepy, dreamy state.

His princess sits on the edge of the bed, looking sullen now that her dreamer is occupied. I'm sure I don't look like that at all when I'm sullen, but just in case, I'll have to practice that pout. I can see why men would be attracted to her.

I shake my head. This is getting too strange even for me.

I walk back out of his dream and guide the sleepwalking ogre. It shouldn't be hard, since he fell asleep on the pathway carved by the soldiers. It's a straight shot to the gates. But the ogre isn't very good at sleepwalking, and he keeps wandering off the path.

"Almost there. Just keep walking."

When he nears the gates, and it's a sure thing that he'll cross, I rush back into his dream. I sit down next to the dream princess.

If I squint, I could believe that she's my body come to life. I didn't know that ogres have such great imaginations that they can dream such an accurate depiction of a drawing they once saw.

We both wait anxiously. If this doesn't work, this dream princess is as close as I'll ever get to my body again.

A deep sense of protectiveness washes over me. I suppose it's true what they say—you never know how precious something is until it's taken away from you.

"I'm sorry for being so mad at you," I say.

Being a specter, the girl doesn't reply. But I like to think that she appreciated my apology on behalf of my body.

I don't know the exact moment when Bronson crosses the threshold of the gates. I only know that his dream ends abruptly.

Like a bubble popping, I'm booted out of his dream and tossed out into the forest.

In front of me is the ogre, flat on his face and groaning. He must have tripped. Behind him are the overgrown walls of my courtyard.

I get chills looking at my keep from this side of the walls.

The tower beyond it is tall and intimidatingly high. The walls and broken gates are covered in dry brambles. There are no leaves, only thorns.

The thorns of the tower fell off but the ones on the wall

are still there. They look dry and brittle, though, as if ready to fall off any moment.

I've never seen my tower from this angle. I've looked down from the window so often, but never saw below the treetops.

I'm out. I'm in the Waking.

I look at my hands to be sure. I can see the ground right through them. I'm a ghost. But a ghost in the Waking.

The underbrush beneath the ogre is crushed and torn with wheel marks. They've been trampled beneath horse hooves and soldier boots.

The ogre rolls off his belly and sits up groggily. He puts his head in his hands and groans. Bronson is still bleeding little streams all over him. The leather bits he wears to hold his tattered clothes together are scratched everywhere.

"They went that way." I point to the wide swath of crushed underbrush leading away from my tower.

"My feet are full of thorns," says Bronson. "I can't get far until I pull them out."

"That'll take too long."

"Then you go and find her while I pull these infernal thorns out of me."

I kick the ground in frustration. A couple of dry leaves fly up in the air.

I stare at the leaves as they settle back down. I kick again, this time at a pebble.

The pebble jumps a little, then rolls.

I grab a thin branch and shake it. It shivers, dropping leaves over me.

"Ahh!" I laugh. "I'm a ghost!"

"Of course you are. I could have told you that. Who ever heard of a ghost who haunts you in your dreams and then follows you when you wake?" The ogre pulls thorns out of the bottom of his foot.

"I can move things," I say. "I can affect things." I go around pulling and kicking leaves, marveling at being able to interact with the world.

Did leaving the tower through the Waking free me in some way that opened up stronger abilities? Not that I'm anything more than a ghost, but I exist here now in a stronger way than before.

"That's great. Perhaps you can use your marvelous skills to move these thorns out of my feet?"

"Right." I make a face as I near his feet. They're swollen and full of hairy warts. And the smell...

"What?" asks Bronson. "Feeling sorry for the pain the thorns are causing me? Is that empathy I see on your face?"

"That's exactly right." I don't bother to hide my disgust as I reach for a thorn.

The thorns come out with a pop. As soon as a thorn comes out, the ogre's skin scabs over.

"At least the bleeding stops when you pull out the thorns," I say. "Hey, concentrate on your feet."

Bronson pulls a thorn out of the side of his neck with a little pop. "That one's been bothering me since I first came over that wall."

"I'm sure there are plenty that bother you just as much that are on your feet."

He's covered in thorns. He looks tempted to take out the ones on his face, as his hands hover around his cheeks.

"Concentrate," I say, pulling another thorn out of his sole. "We need to move."

He goes back to taking out the thorns on the bottom of his feet.

When we finally get the last thorn off his feet, he sighs with relief.

"Now if you could only help me get the ones off my bottom, I could sit more comfortably."

"Don't hold your breath, ogre. Besides, you need to be running, not sitting."

He chuckles as he gets up. I have to admit that I'm a little impressed despite myself. I doubt if I could think that anything was funny if I was covered in thorns.

He begins to jog through the woods. I flow just behind him. I have no trouble keeping up. Silver was right. Thinking by the rules of the Waking will only hold me back.

For the first time, I feel hope bubbling up.

CHAPTER 68

The ogre has impressive stamina. I suppose I knew that, since no one could make it as far into my courtyard as he did without amazing stamina and strength. Still, he's keeping up a good pace through the woods even after days of suffering.

I'm sure he hasn't slept a wink since he found my tower. No one could possibly sleep wrapped in a thorn bush.

He's even agile enough to take out thorns as he jogs. I do my best to help him. We're both better off with him recovered as much as possible.

The path is just wide enough for the battering ram. The soldiers must be following the same path they razed when they came to my keep.

"Can you move ahead and find them?" he asks. "Come back and tell me what to expect. How far ahead, how many, what weapons."

"I'll try."

I'm in new territory. I don't know what I can do here. This isn't the Dreaming, but I'm more a part of the Waking than I have been since before the curse was triggered.

I fly ahead, following the path. It doesn't take long before I see the slow-moving group of troops.

The first things I see are the foot soldiers behind the battering ram. A few men walk in front of it, but the bulk of the group walks behind. A team of horses pulls the battering ram along.

Ahead, there's another group on horses. The foot soldiers are some distance behind the lead group and falling farther back.

Even from here, I can tell that Sentry leads the riders. Behind him is an open wagon where my body lies. I move ahead to get a better look.

They took care to lay down my body. She lies on a makeshift bed of layers of blankets. There's one covering her as well. Her head is cushioned with an embroidered pillow nice enough to be from the queen's chamber.

Even though they move faster than the rear group, there's a gentleness to the way they start and stop the wagon. And the wagon driver does his best to avoid the biggest ruts and bumps.

They don't want to wake me.

If my heart could sink any further, it would. I knew that Malyn wanted to keep me asleep forever, but seeing it in action is harder than I thought.

I avoid getting in Sentry's line of sight. I don't want him to see me. I have to assume that those mirror chips in his eyes will be able to see me. Besides, I can't bear to look at him.

It's time to be useful. I count the soldiers on horseback and the ones on foot. I burn every detail into my head so that I can report it to Bronson.

I rush back to the ogre before I forget any of it. He's not that far behind. When I see him, he looks different.

"Did you wash up while I was gone?" I cock my head.

"Why would I do that? To impress you?" He plucks a thorn out of his hairy armpit.

"Maybe you want to impress the princess when you wake her."

The thought of kissing this ogre makes me grimace. But I suppose it might be the lesser evil compared to being asleep forever and used by Malyn.

"Maybe you should tell me what you saw instead of insulting me," he says.

"That wasn't an insult. I implied that you looked washed." I blink innocently. "For a change."

"I'm flattered. That's almost a compliment, and the nicest thing you've ever said."

He plucks another thorn out of his leg. I'm relieved to see there are fewer warts on his leg than on his feet. He's making progress, but since he's covered in thorns, it could take days at this rate to get them all out.

"Six soldiers on horses with the wagon holding the princess," I say. "Fourteen men on foot. All are carrying weapons—pikes and swords, from what I could see. One battering ram pulled by four horses."

"How far apart are the foot soldiers from the horse riders? Are they in sight of each other?"

"For now. But they were getting farther apart even as I watched."

"Do you think the foot soldiers will stop if the battering ram stops?" Bronson pulls another thorn out of his hip.

"Stop how?"

"Say, a broken spoke?"

"Hmm. They're not going to leave a valuable war machine behind, so they'll need to fix it if something's broken," I say. "A soldier will be afraid to leave the safety of the group to walk alone into the forest while the rest are fixing the battering ram. They're not fearless ogres like you.

So, yes, I think the foot soldiers will stop and stick together."

"Can you do it?" he asks.

"Break a spoke?"

"Doesn't matter how you do it. Just stop their progress. Slow them down so they're separated from the riders."

"I can try. What are you going to do?"

"Go get my woman."

A lopsided grin splits his face, showing a peek of his broken teeth. There's probably moss growing on his gums too.

I try not to wrinkle my nose.

Bronson resumes his jog toward the soldiers. I fly ahead to see what ghostly trouble I can cause.

CHAPTER 69

*S*lowing a group of foot soldiers is not as easy as it sounds. I watch them to see if I can spot a weakness.

I think about breaking an axle, but that would take tools I don't have. I could try to put them to sleep again, but that would take too much time.

I'm about to give up when I see an interesting portion of the path that might be of use. It cuts along the side of a hill. On one side is a grove of trees that loom precariously over the path.

Erosion has taken the dirt that used to support the trees, causing bare roots to hang in midair above the path. A couple of the trees look like they should have tipped already.

Those trees must have roots that reach into the hill to allow them to stubbornly cling to the hillside. Still, the erosion is extreme, and I'm sure those trees won't last through the next rain. It's remarkable that they're still standing.

I float over to them, looking down on the foot soldiers

coming down the path with their battering ram. I pick a tree that's already dead.

Concentrating on feeling heavy, I shove against the tree with all my might. For good measure, I imagine it letting go of its tenuous hold on the hill and falling onto the path.

I push and push until, finally, the tree tips.

The loose soil crumbles, giving off a rich scent of loam. The tree's remaining roots snap as the trunk falls.

It tilts and lands directly across the path. The fall isn't far enough to break the tree, but it does make a resounding boom through the forest. Its branches spread across the path, making it impossible for ordinary wheels to roll through.

The battering ram is obviously not an ordinary cart. It has proven that it can roll through thick brambles full of thorns. I'm sure it can get past a tree that was light enough for a ghost to push. But it'll slow the group down.

The foot soldiers stop, cursing. They grumble about whether to unhitch the horses and push the battering ram through in the same way they got through the brambles. But the soldiers are tired and don't want to push the heavy machinery over a tree.

They argue over which is more work—pushing the battering ram over the fallen tree or moving the tree out of the way.

In the meantime, the riders ahead disappear out of sight with their open wagon holding the sleeping girl. Mission accomplished.

Moving closer to the soldiers, I listen to them argue. I feel a deep satisfaction at having affected my environment so profoundly. I exist, and here is proof.

Beside me, the horses hitched to the battering ram snort and stamp their feet restlessly. As I near, they try to rear from me, pulling against their harness. I back away as soon as I notice their skittishness.

Can horses sense me? There are stories of animals being aware of ghosts. Perhaps there's something to those old stories.

I leave the grumpy soldiers and the skittish horses to see what's happening with the lead group. Bronson didn't tell me what I should do after I stopped the foot soldiers, but I have to assume he's planning on attacking the riders.

I find him skulking around in the bushes, watching the riders. He got here surprisingly fast. He must have had to run around the foot soldiers to catch up with the horsemen. Luckily, the riders only move as fast as the wagon carrying my body.

"What's your plan?" I whisper into his ear.

He startles then glares at me.

"They can't hear me." I lower my whisper in case they can. "All right, the one in front might be able to. Maybe. He can see me but probably doesn't hear me."

Bronson glares at me some more as if to accuse me of keeping information from him. I shrug.

"I'll ambush them." His voice is barely a whisper.

"There are six of them. One of you. That's five more than you, in case you can't count that high."

"I can count just fine when my life depends on it."

"Do you have a plan?"

He shushes me.

"I should have known better than to let an ogre plan."

He shushes me again. He's stalking the riders who've slowed down. They're grumbling impatiently about the foot soldiers, debating whether to wait for them.

"I'll go see what's holding them up." One of the horsemen turns around and trots back to the foot soldiers.

I hold up five fingers to Bronson, then point to him and show one finger. He rolls his eyes and waves me away.

He continues to stalk the riders, and I continue to be

convinced that he has no feasible plan. I'll have to take things into my own hands.

Ignoring Bronson's frantic gestures for me to stay out of sight, I go over to the wagon. I'm careful not to cross Sentry's line of sight. I'm no fool.

I'm not sure what I intend to do. I just have a vague notion of distracting them somehow so that Bronson can get my body out of here.

I admit, it's not much better than no plan, but since no one can see me, I can improvise. It turns out, though, that I don't have to do much of anything.

As soon as I near the path, the horses begin to snort and paw the ground. I almost want to slap my forehead for not coming up with this plan before.

I spread my arms and try to look scary. The horses become skittish, sidestepping and snorting. The riders try to control the horses but only manage to dance their horses in circles.

"What's wrong with them?" asks a rider.

I want to yell and roar to scare the horses, but I'm deathly afraid that Sentry will hear me. He doesn't seem to realize that there's anything wrong until one of the horses bolts past him. The rider loses all control and jounces on top of his horse like a child.

I duck behind the wagon as he turns. I shut my eyes like a little girl riding on the hope that if I don't look at him, he won't see me. I don't know what would happen if he did. I'm pretty sure that it wouldn't help our cause.

With me out of sight, the horses settle. They're still nervous but no longer seem ready to bolt. I can hear the riders soothing their horses and can tell by their murmuring that they're regaining control.

When I open my eyes, Sentry is back to leading the group

with his unnaturally mirrored eyes looking forward. I sneak out from behind the wagon and jump out at the horses.

I savagely growl, hoping that whatever Sentry hears, he'll ignore. I wave my arms around and leap beside the horses.

The nearest horse rears on his hind legs.

His rider clings on, not even bothering to try to control his horse until all four legs are back on the ground. Another horse takes off at a gallop.

The other horses whinny and sidestep as their riders try to regain control. The wagon bucks and jerks as the horses try to break free. The driver loses his grip and falls off with a scream.

After that, the wagon takes off down the path without a driver.

Sentry moves out of the way of the runaway wagon, just in time. The other horses gallop down the path as well.

I can only watch as the wagon holding my body shakes and rattles as the horses drag it away from me.

CHAPTER 70

I watch forlornly as the last horse and rider disappear into the forest.

This wasn't exactly what I had in mind when I decided to take things into my own hands. I pick myself up and float as quickly as I can to catch up to the riders.

I don't even want to think about what Bronson is saying right now. I'm sure his cursing has gone even beyond when he was trapped in the brambles.

The horses race ahead, ignoring the wagon still hitched to them. My body jostles back and forth in the back of the open cart. If it was anyone else, she'd be awake already.

The wagon jounces more and more out of control. My head and limbs are being tossed around, hitting the sides of the cart. I feel the cold certainty that the wagon is going to tip any minute.

Not knowing what I can do to help, I race to the wagon. It's agonizing to be so helpless. There's nothing I can do if the wagon tips. The spell keeps me asleep and keeps me from aging. It does nothing to save me should I crash out of a careening cart.

Ahead, a lone rider manages to regain control of his horse and slows down. He turns his horse, forcing the wide-eyed mare to his will, even though she obviously doesn't want to turn back to the thing that frightened her in the first place.

The rider's eyes flash, catching what little light there is filtering in through the canopy. It's Sentry.

He rides the horse while Queen Malyn rides him. Like the horse, I hope Sentry is fighting against her, but I see no sign of that.

Jerking his reins this way and that, he holds his frightened horse in place and waits for the wagon to catch up to him.

A streak of brown leaps off the hillside and lands in the wagon. For a moment I think it's a wolfkin. But as soon as he lands, he resolves into a large shape resembling a boulder-like ogre.

In a flash, Bronson gathers up my body. There's a moment when he steadies himself on the rocking wagon. It bucks so violently that I'm sure he'll fall backward and break his neck.

"Come on, Bronson," I whisper, desperately rooting him on.

Somehow, Bronson manages to hold his balance even with my body in his arms.

The wagon heaves again. For a heartbeat, it rolls on two wheels as the other side gets thrown in the air.

Bronson leaps out of the wagon just as it tilts completely.

One entire side of the wagon explodes into shards as it hits then drags along the path. The frightened horses don't even slow as they drag the wreckage behind them.

Bronson hits the ground, curled into a tuck. He rolls down the hill, crashing through the underbrush, protectively hugging my body.

A scream tears from my mouth as I watch Bronson disappear into the underbrush. Before I can chase after him, I hear galloping hooves racing toward me.

I look up, sure that Sentry heard me and is coming for me. It's Sentry, but I'm not the one he's after.

He swerves off the path and forces his terrified horse down the hillside. His horse resists as she whinnies. Her eyes roll with fear and her legs lift as she tries to rear up.

Sentry yanks his reins as the horse fights him. The two of them tumble down into the underbrush. The mare screams and snorts as she slides.

I rush over to see if Sentry has been caught beneath the horse. The mare rolls and manages to get to her feet.

Me coming close to her doesn't help. The horse whinnies so loudly that I'd swear someone was eating her alive. I try to back away in hopes of calming her. I don't get far before she bolts.

I'm left in the dust.

My emotions are a jumble of jagged, contradictory feelings. I'm both worried about Sentry and hoping he's down for good. I'm terrified about what injuries my body may have. For all I know, I could be a ghost for real by now.

I'm even worried about Bronson. Really worried. That shows how confused I am.

I see Sentry moving down the hill. He's partially running and partially sliding. Ahead of him is the lumbering form of Bronson.

The ogre is strong, but he has my body in his arms to slow him down. Even worse, he seems to be running at less than full speed. He's being careful not to drop his princess. One more tumble and who knows if that fragile neck of the girl in his arms will be able to withstand it.

Sentry, on the other hand, has no such burden. He races ahead and is fast closing the distance to the ogre.

"Look out, Bronson!" I yell.
Sentry leaps and tackles the ogre.

CHAPTER 71

*B*ronson stumbles as Sentry tackles him. He tips over and drops my body. But even in the midst of being attacked, he's careful not to smash her into the ground. He rolls at the last moment to try to cushion her fall.

My body slams into the dirt and rocks.

I gasp, wondering if I'll feel it if my bones break. Will I know if my body dies?

Sentry and the ogre grapple on the ground. They're hitting each other, grabbing and slamming, kicking and thrashing.

Bronson is strong but has no weapons. Sentry, on the other hand, already has his knife out. He's doing his best to slash Bronson.

This fight won't last long. Maybe Bronson would have the upper hand if he wasn't dehydrated and exhausted from days of being trapped in the brambles. And I swear he's somehow lost some of his bulk since the last time I saw him.

I shake my head. I suppose I just thought of all ogres as being huge and bulky, this one in particular. But seeing him grapple with Sentry, I realize he's not that large after all. The two are close to the same size.

I rush over to see if my body is still alive. My head is bleeding and my arms landed in an extremely awkward position. She looks like a rag doll tossed to the ground, but she's still breathing.

Bronson rolls as Sentry tries to slash his throat. He shoves the knife away, trying to jostle it out of Sentry's grasp. But Sentry pulls it back and lifts it to stab Bronson.

I kick it out of his hand.

The knife flies and lands in the dirt nearby. Sentry reaches for it, but Bronson wrestles him back.

This is going to go on until one of them tires. Sentry will surely be the last one standing. I'm amazed that Bronson has made it this long without collapsing. Even ogres must have their limits.

"Forget him," I tell Bronson. "Kiss her."

I point to my body lying awkwardly nearby, half draped over a rock and bush like a piece of laundry laid out to dry. I have no idea if a kiss from him will work, but we're out of options. Both my nannies and Malyn said that I would wake with a kiss. This is as close to the requirements as we're going to get.

Bronson has blood in his eyes. He's so fiercely in the throes of the fight that I'm not sure he hears me. Even if he did, the thought of kissing must seem ridiculous compared to the imperative of kill-or-be-killed.

He leaps at Sentry as he tries for the knife again. Bronson grabs Sentry's leg, pulling him back from the knife with brute strength.

"Listen!" I yell in Bronson's ear. "If you wake her, he'll have no reason to fight you. His mission is to bring her back asleep. *Asleep.*"

"So what?"

Bronson grunts as he drags Sentry's leg toward him. Sentry twists and kicks with all his might. Bronson takes a kick to the face but keeps his hold on Sentry's leg.

"So if you wake her, he might walk away from us."

Bronson snorts. "You know nothing about men. He's got the bloodlust in him now. Neither of us can walk away until one of us is dead."

"You mean *you* won't. *He* doesn't want to be here in the first place. He's being controlled by the queen. And she only cares about keeping the girl asleep."

I'm not as confident as I sound. I don't know if Malyn only cares about getting her prize. She could get angry and command Sentry to kill us even if I'm awake.

"It's our best shot," I say. "Kiss her and hope you wake her."

I don't need to tell him that he's exhausted and won't last much longer. He knows that better than anyone.

With a giant heave, he flings Sentry aside. In a heart-stopping moment, Bronson has one shot at either kissing the sleeping princess or trying to grab the knife.

Bronson leaps toward my body.

I can barely stand to look. If I'm wrong, Sentry will kill him.

"I'm sorry for everything I ever said to you," I blurt out to Bronson.

I rush toward Sentry, trying to be as heavy as I can. In the mirrors of his eyes, Malyn glares at me with fury. She knows what's about to happen.

Now that Sentry is no longer grappling with Bronson, he manages to pull out his sword.

I crash into him, letting my fear and anger toward Malyn blot out my sympathy for Sentry. This is not the time to pull my punches.

Sentry staggers but doesn't fall. I try to grab his wrist, but that's not as easy as grabbing a rock. A rock doesn't resist.

Sentry walks right through me on his way to Bronson. His eyes reflect Malyn's determined face.

I like to think her expression is contorted with evil fury, but it's probably mine that looks like that. I scream my frustration and anger.

Just then, Bronson kisses the limp girl.

His back is to us, exposed. He's an easy target.

Sentry raises his sword to strike.

I tense to leap at him, but I feel dizzy and weak suddenly. It feels like a whirlwind is thrashing in my head.

I stumble and crash onto my knees. I waver there for a moment with the edges of my vision going dark.

I can't breathe.

Can't think.

Can't...

And then I black out.

CHAPTER 72

The world is nothing but painfully bright colors. I can't see much of it since my lids are mostly closed, but even the dim light filtering through my lashes feels too bright.

Then I realize that it's not the colors that are painful. I feel bruised and aching all over. And why do I feel so awkward and drained, like I tumbled in a waterfall and was spat out along shore?

As if from far away, I hear panting. The breathing gets louder and the world slowly comes into focus.

There are two sets of breathing. One from the person who is very close to me and the other from the man who stands behind him with a raised sword.

Shock wakes me into clarity. My eyes fly wide open and I gasp.

A roaring builds in my ears, and I have to raise my hands to cover them. But that only makes the roaring louder. I realize that it's the sound of blood rushing through my veins.

I blink hard, trying to make the double vision go away.

The fuzziness fades, and so does the roaring in my ears. My cheeks feel hot, even though my back is freezing.

A realization dawns on me. One that I have trouble grasping.

I'm in my body.

And I'm moving.

Well, sort of moving. My body is not working or behaving the way I remember, but it's a dramatic improvement from lying prone and frozen.

I move my hands again. They jerk a little, trembling, but move in the general direction I want.

Bronson stares at me in awe. Despite having risked his life and going through so much pain to reach me, his expression makes it clear that he can hardly believe that a kiss really would wake the sleeping princess.

Awake.

And with a body.

It's a good thing I'm already lying down. I'd probably collapse from the shock otherwise.

Sentry stands over Bronson with his sword raised. He's frozen in his stance, staring at me. His eyes flash with mirrored light.

There's a muscle in his jaw that's twitching. Is he fighting Malyn? Arguing with her? Or is that just an involuntary thing that has nothing to do with the real Sentry trying to fight Malyn's control?

"It's over." My voice is rusty and dry. It's like I haven't drunk anything for a hundred years. "I'm awake. I'm free."

Malyn stares intently at me through Sentry's eyes. She looks like she's having trouble believing what she's seeing. Like someone whose life plans are crumbling before her eyes.

Sentry maintains his strike stance with his sword in the air, but his knuckles are white and his sword is trembling.

Malyn is certainly spiteful enough to kill me now that she's lost the battle. It'd be just my luck to wait decades to wake up just to be killed in the first moments in the Waking.

In the mirror of Sentry's eyes, the intensity drains out of Malyn. She blinks heavily. She seems to be having trouble keeping her head up. She looks exhausted, like someone who has been sleep-deprived for years.

My nannies were right. They were telling me the truth of what happened on the day of my curse. Malyn told me nothing but lies to confuse and scare me.

Now that I'm awake, she can't draw on my sleep to renew herself anymore. I feel immense satisfaction over her exhaustion. She won't be able to draw on my Dreaming powers to reshape the Waking in whatever nightmarish way she planned.

Malyn blinks heavily again.

Then her head falls back against a chair. She slowly lolls to the side and her jaw goes slack as she slumbers.

CHAPTER 73

*S*entry blinks hard. Hope strikes through me with the possibility of him breaking free of Malyn's control.

His eyes still reflect Malyn sleeping, so I know that she's still riding him, but his posture relaxes. He lowers his sword.

"Sentry?" *Please let me reach him.* "Is that you?"

Sentry sheathes his sword but doesn't answer me.

I'm still lying on the ground, although a little less awkwardly now that I've taken my arm down from curling over my head like a rag doll.

Sentry's expression doesn't change. It's neither angry nor disappointed. This was his expression the entire time he fought with Bronson. His face may still be there, but his expression is so blank that it might as well have been wiped clean.

Bronson watches Sentry warily. Little by little, Bronson crouches in expectation, his muscles tense, ready to leap.

I try to move away from Sentry in case he changes his mind about using that sword.

My legs feel like pudding, and my arms have the strength

of wilted flowers. Even the muscles in my torso don't behave the way I expect them to. I have trouble rolling.

It's not that my body won't move when I will it. It moves, but it seems to have forgotten the art of it. After a couple of tries, I manage to roll clumsily off the uncomfortable rock and bush.

I feel so heavy and lethargic. There's a throbbing, angry feeling concentrated on my head and back. It takes me a moment to realize that it's pain.

This is what I dreamt of all these years?

It takes me three tries to sit up.

"I'm awake." My throat is dry enough to hurt. "The spell is broken. I'm useless to your queen now. Sentry, please wake up."

Sentry is looking at me but doesn't seem to see or hear me. All I see when I look at him is Malyn's slumbering face.

Motion on the edge of my vision catches my eye. On the path above us, his riders are gathering.

They must have managed to gain control over their horses and found each other. They look down the hillside at us, tall and forbidding on their horses. Shadows stretch long and thin across the hillside, making them look inhuman.

Their horses nervously step sideways. It can't be me. I'm no longer a ghost.

I could swear the faces of the riders shift. Their smooth, blank faces begin to take shape. Cheekbones become more prominent and mustaches and beards darken on most of them.

In the center of their facial hair, color blooms. Their lips were pale and now they're blood-red. I didn't notice until now that the riders seemed particularly pale.

They had their faces, but Malyn must have been testing her new powers on the riders as she had on some of the low castle servants. She must have drained some of their personal power and taken pieces of their souls.

Now, they're returning to themselves as I watch. I'm immensely relieved to see that waking me means cutting Malyn off from the source of her new powers. I don't have to find out how far she would have gone once she got used to them.

"The queen's spell is broken," I whisper.

I look at Sentry with hope beginning to blossom. It dries up when I see him.

I suppose I expected to see Sentry transforming back to himself the way his riders are. I assumed that if the queen's spell was broken, then Sentry would be free too.

I'm finally free. How can anyone else still be trapped?

There's an ache in my chest that won't go away. I don't know Sentry very well, but I could have gotten used to having him in my life. To having him as my friend. Maybe more.

But seeing Malyn's reflection still in his eyes, I know that's not ever going to happen. The queen owns him the way she used to own me. Worse. She never owned my inner self, just my outer shell.

Malyn seems to own Sentry through and through. Even though she's asleep, he doesn't seem free to be himself.

The Sentry I met is gone.

Whatever spell he's under, it's unrelated to the one that shattered when I woke. My heart feels so heavy to see him this way. I wish there was something I could do for him, but I think that's beyond me right now.

I look at Bronson. I didn't just wake, did I? Bronson woke me.

And by my father's own proclamation, I'm promised to whoever manages to wake me.

Father meant well, of course. Better to be promised to a

prince—or anyone, really—than to be asleep for eternity. He never said it, but I think he thought that would be worse than being dead. At least with death, my spirit would be free. Perhaps my father was right.

At any rate, I was—am—of royal blood. I will not shame my line by reneging on my father's promise of my hand in marriage.

I glance at Bronson again. He's sweating and blubbery, and I can't help but wish he had fewer warts on his face. Of course, right now, I'm not sure which is less attractive—the warts or the thorns that are still sticking out all over him.

I look back at Sentry. Handsome, perfectly formed Sentry. A part of me wishes he'd pick up that sword and do us all in with it. That would solve the whole distasteful situation.

Instead, Sentry's unnatural eyes slide right past me. He sheathes his sword and climbs up the hill mechanically. He moves stiffly like a puppet, showing no trace of the animal grace he had when I first met him. When a rock rolls and hits his leg, he doesn't even flinch.

Above him, the riders look around bewildered. I wonder if they have any idea where they are or what they're doing here. They murmur in hushed tones. I can't quite hear their conversation, but I catch one word: *sleepwalking*.

They seem to have come upon an explanation that suits them. Without looking back, they turn their horses.

Sentry makes it to the pathway and climbs on his horse. His eyes flash from the moonlight as he glances down at us one last time. Then he kicks his horse into a gallop.

I watch him ride into the darkness of the woods.

"Goodbye, Sentry." The words crack my throat and hurt as they come out.

CHAPTER 74

*O*nce the queen's riders are gone, it's just me and Bronson. My newly regained body is as clumsy as can be. But it's awake, and that's all that matters.

Bronson watches me with curious eyes while he absentmindedly plucks thorns out of his bulbous nose. Neither of us say anything for a while.

After several tries, I manage to stand on my feet. I sway, feeling wobbly. He puts out his hands and hovers near me, ready to catch me should I fall.

But I don't fall. I take a hesitant step.

Like most people, I was a baby when I took my first steps as a child. I don't remember it, although my mother once told me what a breathless moment that was for her. I feel like that now. I'm both the mother and the child as I take my first steps.

It's an amazing feat to balance a corporeal body on one leg while the other moves forward. Every muscle needs to adjust and do its part. It's like stacking rocks on top of each other and expecting them to all cooperate in order not to fall. How does anyone ever accomplish this?

My other foot manages to land and steady the rest of me before I topple. My first step.

I'm breathing like I just ran across the forest. My heart is pounding in my chest.

Bronson smiles. His teeth are broken and rotting, but his eyes are bright.

I can't help but smile back.

"Good job, Briar," I say to my body. "You can do this."

I take a deep breath and take another step. Then another, then another.

It gets easier each time. My muscles are beginning to remember what it's like to move. I can't go very far, though, without having to sit on a rock and rest.

"This is going to be a long journey," I say, still smiling.

Then my smile dries up as I realize that I am completely at the ogre's mercy. I can't even walk ten steps, much less run.

"What, I suppose you'll want to toss me over your shoulder or drag me by my hair to your lair?" I stick my nose in the air and take on my most royal stance.

He snorts. "Why would I do that? You're the most ungrateful creature I've ever known."

"What do you mean?"

"Don't think I haven't figured out that you're the wraith that's been bothering me all this time."

"Oh, that."

"Yes, that. So much for my dream princess. You're not even worth dragging to my lair. You probably wouldn't have a clue as to how to sweep a cave or cook a meal."

"I didn't know that ogres ate cooked meat. I thought they simply tore the body-temperature meat off the bones as their meal is screaming and thrashing."

"That is a favorite dish. But occasionally, we like to put on a show of civility, especially when there's a princess to impress."

"You're going to impress her by having her sweep your floors and cook for you? Why would an ogre want his floors swept anyway? I wouldn't think you'd care about such things."

"I care. The pesky bones get in the way when they pile up at the cave entrance."

All I can do is stare at him in horror.

He bursts out laughing.

Despite the snorts, I swear that he sounds more human. Or maybe that's the effect of hearing him laugh.

"You're so easily fooled," he says. "I don't know how you ever managed to survive for so long." He pulls out another thorn.

"What you mean is that I'm so optimistic and capable."

"Right. That's exactly what I meant when I said that you're easily fooled."

"I'm beginning to think that you are, perhaps, not the right match for me," I say with all the grace I can muster.

I draw myself up to my full height. I only go up to his shoulder, but I'm not in a physical duel so it doesn't matter.

"Your father's promise—"

"Everyone knows that a promise to marry a princess is simply a promise to be the king of her kingdom. Well, you can have it. Just let me go."

"I can have your entire kingdom? You mean the one that's being ruled by an evil, all-powerful queen?"

"Yes, that one. You can have it. And if you can ever muster up the people's loyalty, I'm willing to announce to them that you are their rightful king."

"And then the all-powerful evil queen will just hand over the kingdom?"

"You'll have to go to war with her, of course. But you'll have righteousness on your side. And with all your charm and personality, how could the people possibly not follow you?"

"And where would you go while I'm conquering the kingdom?" He calmly plucks more thorns, giving me a look that tells me that he knows I have nowhere to go.

"I'll stay with friends."

"What friends? Who do you know who is still alive?"

"I have friends."

He raises his brows, looking unconvinced. "Have you met these friends?"

"Of course I've met my friends."

"Did you do that while you were sleeping? Or were they infants when you met them?"

I *was* asleep when I met them. His question highlights the fact, though, that I've never actually met my friends in the Waking.

"It's very rude of you to ask such a question." I try to sound as dignified and offended as I can. "You're implying that I am destitute and friendless."

"The world has changed much since you fell asleep, little princess. Life would be far better with a friend, even if you think him an ogre."

"I don't *think* you're an ogre. You *are* an ogre."

He shrugs. "Perhaps I'll grow fond of you thinking of me that way."

"You're not going to deny it anymore?"

He shakes his head. "Why should I care what you think of me? You're just reminding me to not feel any pressure to marry some girl I don't even know. No need to feel responsible in taking care of some spoiled child with ancient sensibilities of marriage and duty."

There's an odd sense of abandonment that settles over me.

He's right. I don't know if I'll be welcome at either Silver's or at the wolfkin mansion. The wolfkin were only my friends because I was useful to them. Now that I'm back in the Waking and in a weak body, I'm not sure that I am useful to anyone.

I glance at Bronson who is taking out one thorn after another. I wonder if he has anywhere to go now that he's accomplished his quest to wake the legendary Sleeping Beauty of Midnight.

I suppose we have that in common, Bronson and me. We're now both wondering what comes next for us.

My quest was to wake from the curse. And now that I'm finally in the Waking, it's time for me to figure out what's next. According to the stories, I should happily spend the rest of my life with the prince who woke me.

It turns out that forging a new life in what is essentially a new body is harder than I thought.

But whatever happens, I want to be awake and alive, ready to navigate it, rather than passive and asleep. I get back up on my feet.

"I'm ready. Let's go."

ronson plucks out another thorn before walking with me. He flicks the thorn away.

We walk up the hill in silence. I wobble and drag my feet but manage to keep up a steady, slow pace. Bronson doesn't seem to mind. It gives him plenty of time to dawdle and pluck out more thorns.

"Are you losing weight?" I ask.

"What? Since yesterday?"

He looks down at himself. His filthy rags are tattered and covered in thorns. He's been concentrating on taking out the thorns from his body and not bothering with the ones stuck in his rags.

Now that I know him a little better—and now that we've kissed—I have a hard time looking at him. He's the dirtiest creature I've ever seen. His rags are bloodied and caked with so much dirt that he's practically dressed in mud. It's hanging on him like he's been shrinking.

I hope he's not getting too hungry. He may have been joking when he talked about the bones in his cave, but I can't get the image out of my head.

"Thank you," I say stiffly.

He doesn't say anything for a moment. I'm tempted to glance over at him, but I keep going.

"You're welcome. You don't have to betroth yourself to me."

Now, I look at him to see if he's serious.

"What kind of an ogre are you?"

"Apparently, not a very good one. I mean, not a bad one?" He makes an exaggerated expression of puzzlement.

"Were you really looking for me? Or did you just come across my tower hidden in the forest?"

"I searched everywhere I could before I finally admitted to myself that you must have been in the forest."

"Why? Don't ogres live in the forest?"

He ignores my question, even though I'm genuinely curious as to his reasons.

"I don't think your family meant for you to be in the forest," he says. "I think they build your fortress near the woods, but the forest has spread over the years."

"You know, you're awfully logical and well spoken."

"Is that a compliment? First a heartfelt thank you and now a compliment? What will people think?"

"I suppose we'll find out."

My stomach flutters at the thought of others seeing him —the prince who woke me. My prince, I suppose.

I imagine how people will react. The shock and horror on their faces. Will Silver look at him that way too? And what about the wolfkin? Will they all reject me as their friend?

It dawns on me that I'm neither the odd girl in the Dreaming nor a ghost in the Waking. I could have other friends if I'm lucky enough to make new ones. But not if I'm the girl with the ogre.

I reach over and pluck a particularly offensive thorn.

How diabolical could Malyn be to create such a nasty patch of thorns?

"People might be mean to you when we reach the village," I say.

"Really? Why so?" He looks genuinely curious.

"Because they've never seen an ogre before. You might frighten them."

"I suppose I am a bit filthy." He sounds like he doesn't really care. Or maybe he doesn't understand how scared people might be.

That worries me. Frightened villagers can become dangerous.

"Don't you worry," I say. "We managed to beat the evil queen. We can certainly manage a few gawking villagers."

"Have you never been gawked at before? Surely, with all your noble upbringing, you must have been gawked at all your life."

"And that's why you should follow my lead. I'll handle things when we get to the village."

"Are you worried about me?" There's amusement in his voice.

Sure, his brawn could handle most battles, but he's no match for the cruelty of the world.

"Of course not. You'll be fine. I'll make sure of it. Just stick with me."

He smiles. This time, the grime on his teeth doesn't bother me. I suppose I'm getting used to him. He bows in a laughably gentlemanly manner.

"As you wish, my lady."

We walk in companionable quiet the rest of the way. We stop regularly so I can rest. When we do, I help him take out his thorns.

CHAPTER 76

The Forest of Midnight can be a frightening place. There were all kinds of nightmares about it in the Dreaming.

"Do you know where you're going?" I ask.

"Why would I know where we're going?" asks Bronson.

"Wait. You're not following me, are you?"

"Of course not." He looks around at the woods. The trees all look the same to me. "Let's go that way." He points in a random direction.

"You have no idea where we are."

"We're in the forest."

"And how do we get out?"

"By walking."

"How long?" I ask.

"Well, I think I wandered around for three...days? Months? Hopefully not years. And then I found you. Don't *you* know how to get out?"

I have no idea what to say. Is it possible that I finally managed to wake my body only to die wandering in the forest?

"Aren't you a creature of the forest?" I ask.

"As much as anyone. But I don't know this part of the woods."

"You mean the spooky part?"

"Yes, that part."

Ogres almost never leave the woods. Bronson must be used to every creature, every sound in the forest.

Yet he freezes as soon as he hears the growling.

The sound is low and menacing. It's coming from the shadows above us on the hill.

I try to see through the dim light. It's twilight and hard to see. But in my tower, it's almost always twilight, so I'm used to it.

I take a step toward the sound. Bronson immediately puts an arm out in front of me.

He's tense and crouched for battle. He has no weapon and is probably more exhausted than I am. Yet he steps in front of me.

Protecting me. Sheltering me.

"What do you think it is?" I whisper.

Bronson shushes me urgently.

A wolfkin steps out of the shadows. His coat is thick and white. His growl is low and threatening.

"Ketter? Is that you? It's me, Briar."

His snarl grows louder. Bronson steps squarely between me and the wolfkin.

"Ketter, if you hurt my friend, I'm going to choke you with a spiked collar with the spikes on the inside. You understand me? I mean it."

Ketter stalks in a semicircle in front of us. Bronson turns to continue to face him. He has his arm out to make sure I stay behind him.

It's sweet. I can't remember the last time someone looked out for me like this.

"Behave for once, Ketter," I say. "Don't embarrass me. This is my friend."

There's a moment when I wonder if being awake means I'm no longer an ally to the wolfkin.

Ketter has never liked me. But then again, Lanson once told me that Ketter just acts that way to everyone and that the only way to tell if he likes anyone is to wait and see if he attacks that person. I suppose the time has finally come to see if I'm one of those people Ketter might attack.

Bronson roars, puffing up to his full size. I must say that he sounds intimidating. But of course, no beast is as intimidating as a wolfkin.

Ketter, always up for a fight, crouches and looks ready to leap at Bronson. His sleek muscles shift in the moonlight.

I step in front of Bronson. "Knock it off right now! I said he was my friend. Back off or I will complain bitterly to Lanson and Silver."

I can only complain if Ketter lets me live. I'm not in the Dreaming anymore, which means I can be killed as easily as any village girl. Easier, since I'm weak as a newborn.

But there's power in confidence. Even if I can't complain to his pack mates, I've always been able to use nightmares as a threat. He doesn't have to know that I don't have my Dreaming powers anymore.

To my relief, Ketter finally stops growling.

He sighs loudly, making it clear he feels put-upon. He sits quietly like a well-behaved pack soldier.

"Good dog," I say.

Ketter growls.

"Just kidding. Thank you, Ketter. Good to know we're still friends."

Ketter grumbles.

"As you can see, I'm awake. I'm also incredibly...tired."

I almost said "weak," but that's never a good idea around a

wolfkin. It doesn't matter how good of a friend you might be. An admission of weakness is an invitation for a wolfkin to maul you.

"Can you find us shelter?" I ask. "Maybe get us to the wolfkin den or Silver's cottage?"

The white wolfkin gets up and slips into the shadows.

"I think he wants us to follow," I say.

I look at Bronson and see that he's staring at me in awe. I smile.

"And you thought I was just a pretty face. Come on. Ketter isn't exactly patient."

I lead the way into the shadows, following Ketter.

CHAPTER 77

*I*t feels like it takes forever to finally reach shelter. By the time we get there, I'm almost delirious with exhaustion.

For a girl who slept for decades, I sure do get tired fast. You'd think that I could go for at least a month without needing to rest. Instead, it turns out that my body needs rest the way a wolfkin needs fresh meat.

Despite my new appreciation for my body and all the requirements to keep it healthy, I have no choice but to keep pushing. Sleeping on the forest floor is not a good option for someone who can't even run for her life if she needs to.

We trudge on forever. I fear that having my body will be useless, because I'll be an old woman by the time we make it out of the forest.

Bronson nudges me here and there by offering a hand. I'm pretty sure there's a smirk hiding in the shadows of his face when he does it. Whether the smarminess is actually there or not doesn't matter. I'm glad for it, because I'm too proud to take his help. And that just keeps me going for a little while longer.

Finally, we break out into open moonlight. A sprinkling of cottages sit in the clearing. I recognize the scene.

"We're on the outskirts of the village," I tell Bronson. "That's Silver's cottage."

The flowers in her garden are in full bloom under the moonlight. Colors flood the yard around the little cottage, making it stand out amongst the drab brown of the other houses.

My exhaustion lifts as we head toward Silver's home. I'm surprised to feel anxiety growing in me as we near it.

Questions nag at me. Will she be the same person she was in the Dreaming? Will she still be my friend now that I'm awake and in a clumsy body?

And most important of all—what will she think of Bronson? Strange that should be the question that makes me the most anxious.

The usual response to an ogre breaching the edge of the forest is to gather a crowd and kill him. I can't let that happen, even if it means I have to go back into the woods with him.

"Let me take the lead," I tell Bronson. "No matter what Silver says, just know that she's a good person and she's my friend. You are not to try to harm or threaten her in any way."

Bronson slides a sidelong glance at me. "Why are you so worried about her safety? Haven't I proven myself to be a perfect gentleman?"

"It's not her I'm worried about. If there's one person who can take on an ogre, it's her."

Ketter growls, his white fur flashing under the moonlight.

"Aside from the wolfkin, obviously," I say.

"Don't you think this ogre farce has gone on long enough?" asks Bronson. "It was never funny to begin with."

The door to the cottage opens. Light spills out and a trim

figure steps onto the porch. Her face is in shadow, and I worry that Silver will be a stranger to me.

There's a tense moment as she watches us. I inch closer to Bronson, needing to show Silver that he's all right.

If she attacks him, can I stop her? If I wasn't so exhausted and worried, I'd laugh at the thought of winning a fight against Silver.

Then Silver steps into the moonlight. Her face lights up with a smile as she opens her arms to me.

We've never met in the flesh. She looks different in the Waking, as I'm sure do I. But none of that matters. I recognize her instantly, and it seems she recognizes me as quickly.

I race up to the porch and run into her arms. Her hug feels warmer and more welcoming than it's ever felt before. A sensation of security and happiness radiates from my chest and all along my body.

"I always knew you'd come to me in the flesh one day, Briar." Silver rocks me gently back and forth. "Welcome to the Waking, my dear girl."

I want to stay in her arms all night the way I used to with my mother when she was still alive. But I'm no longer that little girl. So I pull back before Silver feels awkward about having to push me away.

She has lighter hair than what I'm used to seeing. There are fine lines around her eyes, and her skin isn't as tight and perfect as I'm used to. But she's still Silver through and through.

There's not an ounce of fat on her. Her muscles in the Dreaming match her muscles in the Waking—hard and uncompromising. I'm a bit surprised at that.

I suppose I always assumed that her muscles and skills were exaggerated in the Dreaming, just as her youth was exaggerated. But it turns out that Silver sees herself clearly. Maybe it's the people in the Waking that don't understand her true youthful nature and the people in the Dreaming who do.

Her eyes are brighter here than in the Dreaming, though. Jewel eyes that sparkle in the moonlight. Only, those eyes aren't watching me. They're watching Bronson.

"He's all right," I say anxiously. "He's my friend."

Am I embarrassed to say that he woke me? That he kissed me? That he's the one who rescued me?

Bronson went through a lot to rescue me. Risked his life, maybe even his soul. Suffered through constant pain and fear as he trudged through the forest and then through the thorny courtyard to find me. All for the honor of rescuing the fabled Sleeping Beauty.

I can't take that away from him. Certainly, I can't steal that honor away from him merely because I'm embarrassed to have people know that I've been kissed by an ogre—that I'm promised to marry an ogre.

I flinch at that second thought, but I stiffen my resolve. Bronson deserves his rewards. At the very least, he deserves recognition.

"He rescued me. Woke me with a kiss. I'd be the queen's eternal prisoner if it wasn't for him. He's...my hero."

As I say the words, I realize how true they are. I look over at him, and my expression melts into a grateful smile.

"And what is your hero's name?" asks Silver.

"Bronson," I say.

"Where do you hail from, Bronson?"

I open my mouth but nothing comes out. I probably should have introduced him as Bronson the ogre. Or perhaps Sir Bronson? They both sound ridiculous, given that he's the dirtiest creature ever to come out of the forest, although I'm sure I come in as a close second.

"I am Prince Bronson of Everness." He bows formally to

Silver, even though a real prince would never bow to a flower peddler.

"It's an honor to meet you, Your Highness." Silver doesn't sound condescending, but she does sound casual enough to make it clear she doesn't believe him. She executes a perfect curtsy.

"Are you, perchance, the crown prince of Everness?" asks Silver. "If so, you take great risks coming to Midnight."

"No," he says. "The crown prince would never be allowed to leave Everness. I, on the other hand, am free to go wherever I please. I am the third son. Should the line of succession ever come down to me, I fear Everness would be in deep enough trouble that it likely wouldn't be worth inheriting at that point."

"So you figured you might as well try your luck at rescuing a princess in peril," says Silver.

"Quite right. I intended to rescue one from a dragon, but I'm afraid the dragon got impatient with her. She was nothing but princess-shaped charcoal by the time I found her."

"I was your second choice?" I put my hands on my hips.

"Third, actually. No offense. You had a rather prickly reputation, and no one had managed to rescue you in more than a generation, so who was I to assume that I would be better than the others?"

He has a quirk to his lips, and I can't tell if he's serious or not.

"Ah, but you were, Prince Bronson. Clearly, you were." Silver sounds as though speaking to a real prince. The only telltale sign is that she stands tall and meets his eyes like an equal.

I have to admit, though, that I wouldn't be surprised if she would do that even in the presence of true royalty. Bronson has the grace to bow his head in acknowledgement of Silver's gracious comment.

"Well, this is lovely," I say. "But would it be possible to let us stay here for the night? *Both* of us?"

I know Silver is my friend. Her hug was as warm as I could have dreamt. But I still feel a moment of uncertainty.

What if she welcomes me but not Bronson? I wouldn't blame her, but I feel duty-bound to him. Besides, I realize that with all we've been through together, I feel an undeniable tug of loyalty.

Silver raises her brows a fraction. She's surprised at my insistence on including an ogre. In a way, so am I.

"Of course." Silver steps aside to show the doorway. "Please come in."

CHAPTER 78

Silver makes tea while we tell her what happened. Bronson corrects me when he catches me embell- ishing, but I notice that he takes a couple of dramatic liber- ties with the telling as well.

I help Bronson take the thorns out while we talk. We place them on a cloth so as to not leave them all over the floor.

The pile of jagged thorns grows as I pull them out of Bronson's back and shoulders. He concentrates on places he can reach. He has a hard time doubling over to reach his feet and lower legs, since that pushes his thorns into his belly.

I kneel beside him to work on his lower legs. Silver pauses to watch us.

The surprised look on her face tells me how strange this must look. I am a princess who is kneeling before an ogre to help take thorns out of his legs. It's an intimate act, and I become aware that these kinds of things aren't done in the Waking.

There are rules here. Etiquette to follow. Expectations to live by. But I haven't lived by any of those in a very long time.

I go back to my work. I've been asleep long enough that I don't care how I look in the Waking. When you have nothing, not even control over the tiniest aspect of your body, your values and priorities become very clear.

Now that I'm finally awake, all I want is to live a life in harmony with my body and spend my time with true friends. The trappings of status and expectations mean very little to me anymore.

Bronson woke me and rescued me from Queen Malyn. If that's not a friend, I don't know what is.

Silver continues with her tea preparation without commenting on my strange behavior.

"This will help you sleep." Silver sets down two steaming mugs.

I stare at her, feeling a jolt of fear. "I'm not sleeping." I shake my head. "I've spent far too much time sleeping. It's time for me to live a life."

"You must be exhausted. You need to sleep." Silver's voice is gentle yet firm.

I am exhausted. Even though I haven't been awake for a full day yet, my body is so tired that I'm quivering inside. I ignore it.

"I'm not ever going to sleep again. I've had enough of that." The mere thought makes me want to run out screaming.

Silver kneels beside me. "It'll be all right, Briar. We'll be right here to wake you in the morning."

"How do you know I'll wake?" The panic threatens to overflow. I do my best not to show it, but Silver can see it.

"The curse is broken," says Silver. "And if you have any trouble waking, we have your...friend. He can wake you just like he did before."

I look over at Bronson. He nods reassuringly. By the fire-light, he looks more human than before.

"Well, in any case, Bronson can't sleep with all these thorns on him." I pluck one out of his thick calf.

"The thorns are almost all out, I think." Bronson squirms to reach behind him to pluck out a thorn that I missed from his back. "It's hard to tell, though. I'm tingling and prickly everywhere. But I think that was the last one."

I pluck a small thorn that's camouflaged by his leg hair. "*This* is the last one."

I hold it between my forefinger and thumb. There's a drop of blood on the end of the thorn. I toss it on top of the pile with my face wrinkling in distaste.

The pile of thorns is alarmingly large. I give a grateful look to Bronson and nod my thanks again. He went through unimaginable hardship to reach me, and I feel pretty bad about insulting him so many times.

Bronson sighs. His eyes are drooping and he looks like he could sleep for a week.

That nervous tingle rises again at the thought of sleep.

"I'll take first watch while you two get some sleep." I get up, trying to look alert. "You never know what the queen might try while we're sleeping."

It's just the three of us in Silver's cottage. Ketter trotted back into the forest as soon as it was clear that Silver would take us in. Without even a grumble of goodbye, he disappeared into the wooded shadows.

"If the queen shows up here with her army, you being awake isn't going to make a difference," says Silver. "So you might as well get some rest."

"She's worse than the Dark King," I say.

Silver nods. "We weren't expecting peace and prosperity when she took over. We needed to delay the king's plans against Everness."

"What plans?" asks Bronson, looking fully alert. "He's planning to attack Everness?"

"Not anymore," says Silver. "Our war remains here in Midnight. We made sure of it. We cannot allow the Wild Wars to affect the rest of humanity."

"At what cost?" I ask.

"That remains to be seen," she says.

I should have known that Silver wouldn't help Malyn without a compelling reason. As a leader of the Order, she is involved at a much higher level of court intrigue than I am, and sees a broader picture.

Silver brings out a thick quilt and lays it by the fire. "Whatever it is that's about to befall the kingdom, it's unlikely to happen tonight. You've won your battle for the day, Briar. Now it's time to sleep." She must see the fear in my face. "You'll have to do this sooner or later, my girl. Might as well do it now."

"Will you wake me in a few minutes?"

"A full night's sleep is better."

"Not if I'm plagued with nightmares about being trapped forever in the Dreaming."

"The curse is broken," says Bronson.

"Please." The word doesn't come easily to my lips. Both Bronson and Silver seem to understand that.

"All right," says Bronson. "You fall asleep. We'll wake you. Then you'll know for sure."

He doesn't sound as certain as his words. I glance at Silver. Her lips are tight in a thin line of tension. Despite their reassurances, I'm not the only one who's worried.

I take a deep breath and let it out slowly, just as Silver taught me to do to manage the jitters before a fight.

"Not every battle is physical," she says as she smooths out the quilt on the floor. "And not every battle has an outside enemy. Sometimes, the one you must make peace with is yourself."

I nod. She's said something like this several times, especially when I was angry with my body.

The curse is gone. I'm free. So why don't I feel like it? Why do I still feel like I'm walking into a steel trap by going back into the Dreaming?

Maybe this time, I'm not trapped in my tower, or the Dreaming, or even my sleeping body. Maybe I'm trapping myself with my own fears.

I sigh, too exhausted to untangle my thoughts. I lie down on the quilt, but I'm terrified to sleep. I fidget and flex my hands and tense my leg muscles, simply to remind myself that I can.

"I won't be able to fall asleep." But even as I say the words, I realize that it comes out as a mumble.

I am more exhausted than I can remember ever being. But it's the natural exhaustion of a weak body needing to rest, not the unnatural sleepiness of a spell.

The warmth of the fire washes over me. The quilt is thick and comfortable even on the hardwood floor. I reach out to either side of me and put my hands out.

Bronson clasps my right hand. Warm and strong. Silver clasps my left hand. Small but firm.

I hold them as tightly as I would if I was drowning. A spike of terror engulfs me as I feel myself falling asleep.

And then I'm drifting. Drifting into the Dreaming.

CHAPTER 79

There's a storm gathering outside my tower window. The twilight is darkening and the clouds threaten to pour a torrent of rain into my courtyard. The wind blows dried thorns through my window as though they were leaves.

The window is framed in brambles, growing on every side, threatening to cover my window completely. The thorns are covering half the opening, and I can see them growing thicker.

Anxiety stabs into my stomach. What will I do when I can't see the clock tower anymore?

My tower room feels as tight and claustrophobic as a coffin. I won't even be able to see if there are any rescuers trying to climb over the wall.

I remember something. It's important, but I can't quite recall what it is. I turn to look into the chamber.

My bed is empty. The drapes along the four posts flap and dance in the wind. There's a profound emptiness to the tower now that it's missing my body.

The covers are tossed to one side of the bed and my slippers are gone. Those slippers have been waiting for me to get up for so many years that they should be dust by now.

Terrified, I look down at my feet.

I'm wearing those slippers.

I start to breathe so fast that my head feels dizzy. I lean into the window, tearing at the brambles with my bare hands.

"Let me out. Let me *out!*" I scream through the window.

Thunder drowns out my scream. It doesn't matter. No one would hear me anyway.

My hands bleed from the thorns. I swear I can feel the room behind me getting smaller and tighter, trapping me within its walls forever.

CHAPTER 80

I gasp and bolt upright.

The fire in the hearth crackles and warms my shoulder. I'm gripping hands in both of mine.

"It's all right," says a masculine voice. "You're all right."

It takes a moment for me to realize that I'm awake. In Silver's cottage. And the ogre beside me is Bronson, my rescuer.

"I'm awake." The whisper barely makes it out of my stiff lips.

My heart pounds in my chest. My hands sweat as I clench Silver and Bronson's hands so tight that I must be hurting them. I feel the cold seeping through the blanket from the floor even as my shoulder feels hot from the fire.

This is my body. Feeling real sensations in the Waking.

"I'm awake."

A strange half laugh, half sob escapes me. It turns mostly into laughter with a bit of sobbing.

Silver squeezes my hand and lets go.

I fling myself at Bronson, giving him a hug. "I'm awake." My voice breaks.

"Yes, you are." He hugs me back. "And you didn't need any help in waking."

He's bulging with muscles, but they're leaner than I would have guessed. Warmer, too.

I laugh and declare myself awake again. I almost can't believe it.

My finger catches on something sharp as I hug Bronson. It's a tiny thorn.

"Hold still." I manage to grab it and pull it out.

When I pull back from Bronson, his huge head and shoulders deflate.

"What's happening?" I watch with wide eyes as Bronson changes.

The ogre begins melting.

"Bronson!" I reach for him, trying to hold him together.

His head deflates and sprouts thick hair. His piglet ears curve and begin to look like human ears. His warts and rolls of flesh melt away into hard, sleek muscles.

What's left is a man.

The same handsome man I saw in Bronson's dream. He's wearing tattered, blood-soaked clothes that look like they were once of high quality. He wears a scratched and empty scabbard that looks custom-made for an ornate sword.

I stare, slack-jawed.

"What?" asks Bronson as he scratches the spot where I pulled out the thorn.

"You're...you're a man." I can't take my eyes off him.

"Yes, thank you for finally acknowledging that. And all I had to do was risk my life, crawl through a courtyard full of cursed thorns, and—"

"Cursed," says Silver. "That evil..." She mumbles a string of creative swearing so intense that it makes me blush. Silver must have spent a lot of time in rowdy taverns to learn those swears.

"Cursed?" asks Bronson. "Who's cursed?"

"Nobody now," says Silver. "Be careful of those thorns. There's more to them than they look."

I look at the thorn between my fingers. "You mean the thorns changed him?"

"Or just made him look changed," says Silver.

"So he was never an ogre?" I stare at Bronson's strong jawline and perfectly human eyes.

Bronson frowns. "I told you I wasn't." He looks at the thorn in my hand. "You weren't just insulting me, were you?"

"When the thorns stuck into you, you transformed into an ogre," says Silver. "Or they cast a glamour that made you look like an ogre."

"Why?" I ask.

"Because anyone who climbed through the brambles was defying Malyn," says Silver. "If anyone got stuck in the brambles, no one would bother to try to rescue an ogre. And if he actually managed to rescue you, you would reject him."

"But I didn't look like an ogre. I checked myself several times because she kept calling me one. My hands were human. My body was human the entire time."

"That must have been part of the curse," says Silver. "If you weren't aware that you looked like an ogre, you would naturally walk into a village or meet people before you managed to get all your thorns out."

"And they would have killed you." My head reels with the realization of how close we were to walking into a trap.

"Our new queen seems to believe in punishing anyone who dares to defy her," says Silver.

"You could have died." I stare at the new man who has taken the place of my ogre. It's not that I want him to be an ogre, but it feels a little like a betrayal to be glad that he's gone.

"But I didn't die," he says. "Thanks to you." He rubs the back of his neck.

It's strange to see him with hair and a normal-sized head. Even his nails look more refined, even though there's still dirt beneath them.

"Without you," he says, "I would have spent days trying to get the thorns out. Assuming I lived that long."

"You would have gotten them out sooner," I say.

"I couldn't reach half the ones you took out. And who is brave enough to approach an ogre, much less help one?"

"That evil, horrible..." I repeat some of my newly learned curse words.

"Swearing doesn't become you, Briar," says Silver. She smiles, though.

"I rather like it," I say.

"Me too," says Bronson.

He really is quite handsome. His dark hair glows with the firelight that also illuminates his wide shoulders. His very human eyes have a deep glow of interest and humor.

He has the kind of spark that dreamers never have, and I'm mesmerized.

"Are you truly a prince of Everness?" I ask. It doesn't matter at all to me if he's royalty or not. But I am curious.

"Finally, you're beginning to fawn over me. It's about time." He shakes his head.

"I'm not fawning. It's a simple question."

Bronson smiles brilliantly. "Yes, I'm truly a prince of Everness."

I think this through with wonder.

"I can hardly believe that anyone could be so evil as to do this to us," I say. "Are there any good fairies out there?"

"Sure," says Silver. "Good fairies, bad fairies, and fairies who don't care to be one or the other. We may be at each other's throats, but we're not that different. They probably think we humans are all as bad as the Dark King."

"We have all kinds in Everness," says Bronson. "But Midnight is infamous for their bad ones."

Silver yawns. "It's long past my bedtime. You two can get to know each other in the morning when you're not keeping me awake."

She gathers two more quilts and lays them on the floor beside me. "I apologize for the crude accommodations, Your Highnesses, but it's the best I can do."

She doesn't sound at all reverent or apologetic. Nor does her body language convey anything but casual exhaustion.

"I'll have to sleep here with you two for decorum's sake," she says. "Wouldn't want you sleeping in the same room without a proper chaperone."

She lies down on her quilt, turns her back to the fire and settles in. "Good night."

Instead of being offended, Bronson looks amused. "This is the best accommodation I've had in a very long time. Thank you for your hospitality."

He lies down on his quilt and gives me a smile. It's a beautiful smile with not a single wart to be seen anywhere.

I settle back on my own blanket and bask in the warmth of the fire. I'm still nervous about going to sleep, but this time, I feel more secure. I remind myself that I did wake up. That sends a thrill through me.

My body is exhausted. And no matter how excited my mind is, my body is my partner again, and I'm committed to taking care of it. I close my eyes and drift off to sleep.

CHAPTER 81

I'm back in my tower.

Lightning strikes and thunder rumbles through the twilight. The storm clouds churn as though ready to boil. I have trouble seeing much of it, though, because the window is mostly blocked.

The bramble is growing into the window, closing it on all sides. There's only a small hole where I can see the clock tower and the courtyard below.

I start to spiral into panic, worried that I'll be buried in my tower. I pant, feeling like the walls are closing in on me.

I'll never get out. I'll rot here forever.

A wind blows into my tower chamber and billows the drapes on my four-poster bed. The bed is empty with the covers pushed aside.

Wait.

This is all familiar.

Am I...dreaming?

I look at my hands. They're glowing. I'm a dreamer.

Lightning flashes and thunder booms. I can almost see the sharp thorns growing into my window.

My first impulse is to wake myself up. Maybe I could shout into the ceiling to wake up.

I'm convinced that it won't do anything. I can't wake up, remember? I'm...I'm...

I remember Bronson, the prince of Everness who woke me with a kiss.

I remember Silver, my friend.

I slow my breathing. Remind myself how completely immersed dreamers are in their dreams. I watched them all the time, lost in their own realities, never realizing that it could be their playground.

Facing the window, I sweep the air with my hands with forceful intent. Some thorns wither and fall off. It's not dramatic, but it's enough to tell me that I'm in the Dreaming.

The fear melts away, replaced by curiosity. I bring my arms together, this time with full conviction and confidence.

The thorns shrink back and shrivel until the window is clear. I sweep the air again. This time, the storm clouds fade, and the sound of thunder becomes distant and soft.

I laugh with delight. I'm back in my element. And now that I know I can wake, I feel a surge of joy and comfort to be here.

I run at the window and leap out with my arms and legs stretched.

Confidence and conviction keep me from falling.

I'm flying.

The wind blows in my face and my hair flows behind me like a banner. I fly around my tower and over the bramble-filled courtyard. Then I head out into the twilight sky of the Dreaming.

I consider changing the sky to daylight but decide against it. I'll see it in the morning when I go back to the Waking. Back to Bronson, back to Silver, and back to my body.

Another delighted laugh bubbles through me as I fly to explore my twilight domain.

Midnight Tales novels

Cinder & the Prince of Midnight

Ruby & the Huntsman of Midnight

Briar & the Dreamers of Midnight

Hansel & the Witch of Midnight

Don't miss a new story from Susan EE!

Sign up to hear about them at:

www. S u s a n E E .com

Aim your phone camera at this image to see the Midnight Tales novels